MW01143962

HOT TICKETS !!

A WEEK ON MAUI

a novel by

KAREN JEFFERY

RESOURCE UNLIMITED ◊ ASHLAND, OREGON

Copyright

Editing, Layout, Design, Photography, Cover Art by Publisher,
RESOURCE UNLIMITED
574 E Main Street, Suite 2
Ashland, OR 97520 USA

Visit our website at:
www.mauiwriter.com/resource.html
First Printing: May, 2011
ISBN-13: 978-1461115991
ISBN-10: 146111599X

This book is also available in all major ebook formats.
Visit: www.mauiwriter.com/HotTickets.html

Also by the author:
Neosomaniac ~ Mad about Islands
1 photographer, 20 years, 80 islands

Acknowledgements
&
Mahalos

With gratitude and love for my three children, Julie, Peter, and Jeremy. For my birth family, my created family, and my global family.

For all my Maui friends...and the island of Maui – my own personal heartthrob.

Thanks to the nanowrimo team, who challenged me to fast track something...and I did, picking the shortest month of the year to go on this fun adventure.

And to the online communities for assistance and guidance through new learning curves.

Deep Mahalos and respect to all the writers I've read and enjoyed.

Mahalo to teachers and professors who supported me from Irma Erickson to Bill Gholson.

And friends and family over the years who always encouraged my writing.

Bless you all.

TABLE of CONTENTS

Title Page
Copyright Page
Acknowledgements & Mahalos
Dedication

For my three precious ones:

Julie, Peter, and Jeremy

~

my dearest loves and greatest teachers

with deep Aloha

one

SIGNS

"Fore!" she shouted, watching her shot slice off towards a foursome on the second green. She fumbled in her pocket for her vibrating Iphone and found the button through her glove, turning her back to the wind and answering, "Chloe Beech".

"I've got them! Meet me at Jake's at eight." Mattie sounded more upbeat than she'd been in weeks. Like she hadn't cried in hours.

"I'm across the bay with mom," Chloe said. "Golf day." Chloe didn't really care about the game, but it got her out of the office every other Thursday afternoon, which to a workaholic was both a relief and a terror. She persisted for her mom, having always been a 'good daughter'. "It'll probably be closer to nine. Save a table and don't steal my bartender."

Chloe and Mattie had a running joke about bartenders, having slept with a few and fantasized about many more. Okay, most were gay, which made the selection process even more interesting and may have accounted for the number of gay friends they acquired over the years. Either way, bartenders were fun and ripe for fantasies. But with Mattie out of commission for nearly two years with stockbroker-boyfriend Tom, Chloe had them all to herself. If she wanted them.

Mattie was calling from the travel agency, closing up for her boss – who happened to be her aunt and who always left by three. It wasn't the job she intended to keep when she first hired on during her second summer at University, but it was then the perfect accoutrement to college life and came with all the glamour of hot tickets to exciting places. Mattie had been to Paris, Spain, northern Italy and Southern France, Thailand and Peru, Costa Rica, Australia.

Still she was stuck. She felt it in her bones – her fine petite bones, especially now that she and Tom had split. She sensed finally that he was never that into her, but it took three months after the break up for Chloe and Jill to fully convinced her how selfish and childish he was. He wasn't really, but that's why it took such convincing. Besides they had already tried retail therapy.

"Wanna catch a bite?" Mattie asked.

"Don't wait for me. I'll grab something at the clubhouse with mom, try to avoid rush hour traffic."

Chloe and Mattie shared space together in an old Victorian on Nob Hill. The house had been in Chloe's family since her father, a San Francisco real estate player, acquired it when one could actually afford city real estate. Chloe had grown up there until she left for Berkeley and a dorm room just off campus. When her dad died suddenly Chloe's mom, Tilly, decided as part of her grief therapy to remodel the family home and enlisted Chloe's help – which got the good daughter back across the Bay. Within weeks, Tilly relocated to a senior retirement village in Walnut Creek, encouraged by a few transplanted friends, where she hoped to escape a lifetime of memories for more sun and regular golf.

When Tilly moved, Chloe got stuck with the decision about selling the 'old vic' versus splitting it into two townhouse apartments. Mother simply wouldn't have the former, and then Chloe met Mattie, making the second option moot. Chloe had called The Trip Agency initially from the yellow pages, looking for first class tickets, limousine pick-up, and a suite at the Four Seasons for a well-heeled European investor coming to inspect some luxury condos in a project at the Marina. She and Mattie became fast friends, and she scrapped the townhouse idea altogether, Mattie moving in as a roommate and paying near market rent – which was enough to cover the taxes, insurance and utilities, including high speed cable, routed wirelessly throughout all three stories.

"Did you reach Jill?" Chloe asked Mattie, watching her mother take a beautiful swing off the tee. Tilly was still a knock out, even after three children and a working life. Her red hair was bobbed to just above her shoulders, and she wore a fabulous new golf outfit. More to the point she enjoyed a ten handicap. "Nice shot, mom." *Awesome*, Chloe thought. *I must be missing the golf gene.*

Mattie could tell Chloe was multi-tasking and fragmented as usual. "Yep. She took her bike to work, so she'll be a bit late too. Wants to drop it off first and taxi to the bar."

Jill was the third musketeer – or stooge. They switched triumvirates at will, depending on whether they were swashbuckling heroines or bumbling idiots. Just turned thirty, she had a trendy apartment in Pacific Heights and would never dream of sharing living space, having had her fill with dorm life – which included Chloe when they were classmates at Berkeley – and a childhood with four brothers, also of Dutch ancestry. Jill was five foot five with killer genes. A natural athlete, she was also brilliant in a summa cum laude/mensa way. Even with great DNA and a first class University education, she always said she got her Masters from the School of Hard Knocks. Paid handsomely working in IT for a brokerage firm in the financial district, Jill made her 'real' money through an online business, selling search engine optimization services for small businesses and building web sites for good friends…like Chloe. After just two years with the side gig, Jill needed to diversify her investments, which was the first time she called Chloe for property and how she acquired her great condo with stunning bay views.

"Okay then. We'll catch up at nine," Chloe signed off. Her mom was sighing and rolling her eyes, signaling her displeasure with her daughter's near addiction to her iPhone. Tilly didn't even own a cell phone and was resolute about avoiding 'all those geeky gadgets'. "That contraption's worse than your

3

crackberry," she said, nodding disapproval.

"Get over it, mom. It's Mattie my friend, remember? We're leaving in two days, and we need to coordinate things."

It would only be the second time Chloe had flown across any sea, and she was a bit nervous. Nervous mostly about leaving her work...and really wanting to bring some sort of solace to her dearest friend. Despite the weeks of convincing about Tom, Mattie still wore an unremitting sadness around her eyes, which – when they weren't red – were the color of a Tahitian lagoon on a clear day. And Chloe, a couple of years older, a mother figure to Mattie, simply had to come up with an Rx. She saw it as her calling.

It was all she thought about for weeks until one day she had dropped by the travel agency to take Mattie to lunch. There it was on the front window:

A WEEK ON MAUI!

A two by four foot poster covered with images of paradise seared into Chloe's brain and clutched at her heart. In that instant she decided to take Mattie to Hawaii. Maybe Jill could come too.

Neither of them needed convincing.

two

JAKE'S

Chloe was an inadvertent entrance queen. She entered the North Beach bar with her usual flair, quite oblivious to it all. But at nearly five foot ten with huge hair (a highlighted Bonnie Raitt red), sapphire eyes, and skin the color of apricots in summer, she always drew stares. Whenever rushed or stumped for outfits she wore her signature necklace – a strand of jewel quality black pearls in every unique shade of peacock, mauve, silver and mercury, navy, eggplant, and aubergine. It was a gift from a Tahitian client who owned a pearl farm in Manihi, a thank you for Chloe's assistance over the year if took to bring his family to the states and get his two pre-teen boys into private school. She wore it with boot cut jeans and a crisp white shirt so one couldn't decide whether to stare at the girl or the treasure grasping her sleek neck. Probably both.

Guys were already circling Mattie. Petite and blonde, she was a natural man magnet. Forget that she occasionally had split ends and dark circles, and her high-pitched little girl voice drove them mad. It even squeaked sometimes when she got excited or teary, but she also had great bones and luminous skin like fine Thai silk. And long blonde California-girl hair. Beyond her looks (usually the main attraction), it was her fragility that seduced.

"Over here," Mattie called to Chloe, already making her way to their favorite corner of the bar. Jake's was a happening place, and one of the perks of working their way through generations of bartenders was that the trio could always find

5

seats. "Jill just called. I couldn't hear her, but I think she's on her way."

Chloe hugged her friend then smiled at Fred, Thursday bar guy. "I'll have my regular." Not that she had a regular, but she always ordered one, waiting to see what they surprised her with. She took one sip. "Gin and tonic. Not what I guessed."

"Want a cosmo?" asked Fred.

"No, what I want is a life. I'd settle for a good night's sleep, but this is great. Thanks." She turned to Mattie. "So where are they?"

"Hang on, Hang on. There's such a thing as protocol. I'm waiting for Jill."

"Okay, but can you tell I'm excited?" Chloe focused briefly above Mattie's head at a guy, reaching across the bar for his Corona. *Cute,* she thought, *for someone else.*

"This week I pulled out all the stops to my anticipation," Mattie said, giving Chloe a little squeeze. "Thanks for this, but do me a favor. If I'm not cured by a week in paradise, throw me off the bridge!"

Notwithstanding wanting to get over Tom, Mattie had had found it remarkably difficult. Despite friends and a fifty-hour work week, and a couple of okay rebound dates, she spent too long obsessing about Tom and wondering what was wrong with her. In reality Tom had met someone else on a business trip to Phoenix and for nearly two months had been seeing her secretly, so Mattie had every reason to be pissed off, to want to put it all behind her. Still she couldn't. He had been 'the one', her rock and future, and shaking her good feelings towards Tom was much harder than utilizing her bad ones.

Chloe, always the cheerleader, gave her another big squeeze exuding genuine concern. "We always get over them. Just give yourself time."

"Aloooooha!" Jill's familiar husky voice came from the crowd. She threaded her way through, wearing tight, low-slung jeans and a red leather jacket, perky as usual with her short, sassy, nearly black hair and indigo eyes. It wasn't the color of

Jill's eyes people noticed first but the luminous whites, which advertised high intelligence and great health. "Whoa. I am sooooo ready for this trip! Where's my ticket?" Jill was high-fiving each friend and wagging a finger at the bartender. "Red wine," she ordered. *For my health*, she thought.

Bartenders weren't Jill's type, even though both hetero males and lesbian females always came on to her. Jill liked athletes, especially competitors. The sport itself didn't much matter; she was into everything physical – hiking and biking, climbing and running, working out at sports clubs. That's who she met, and that's who she liked – macho guys with great buns. Still she was a veteran flirt.

"You got it, Jill. How you been?" Fred kept his primary attention on the three babes, refilling the bowl of pistachios and putting a little plate of garnish, fruit and olives, in front of Jill as volumes of orders came across his bar.

"Here they are," said Mattie, handing Chloe and Jill each a ticket, wrapped in a tropical Hawaiian shirt jacket. "It's really eight days, sort of like a baker's dozen – a Maui week. The package includes a rental car and a suite at the Fairmont Kea Lani, somewhere in Wailea." Mattie stumbled over the pronunciation like a first week in language class.

"Gawd," said Jill. "Could it sound more foreign? I thought Hawaii was in the USA."

"Oh, come on, you could use another language," said Chloe, knowing full well that her friend spoke several. "Besides we're on a mission: to get Mattie over Tom. Over him for good."

"No need to worry," said Jill. "I've put out a fatwa against him."

"Come on, guys. It's not like I'm such a case anymore. I mean I appreciate your concern, and it probably is cheaper than therapy, but I'm going to Hawaii to have fun, just like you. And who said you were both perfect anyway?" Mattie knew better.

"I'm going to get away from double shifts," Jill chimed in, swilling her glass. I'll have to check in daily with my online biz, but I'm covered at the office. They got some temp who may or may not know what he's doing. Whatever. I can fix it all when I get back."

Not to be out workaholicked, Chloe spoke up. "I'm making sacrifices too. I've prepped my clients, escrows and assistant. I'd love a job where I could really get away. I was a journalism major after all – thought it was the road to freedom back then. Tell me how I ended up in real estate brokerage, chained to my desk like a prisoner of some dark world?" Though beautiful she looked exhausted, with little wrinkles hovering around her eyes and puffy little circles beginning to emerge from lack of sleep. She wasn't sure if the fatigue was from slogging away long, hard hours or from a career that was really her dad's, not hers.

"That's easy, Chloe. It's in your blood. And what you trained for most of your life. When you were ten you were planting realty signs all over the avenues. I mean, aren't you fourth generation or something? If you want a change, make it. At least you have a security blanket."

"Like you don't?" Mattie questioned Jill. "None of my friends makes as much as you."

"Yeah, and I plan to spend it all in Hawaii." Chloe and Mattie chuckled together, knowing they'd have to pry every dollar from Jill's tight little fingers, and ordered another round.

"Let's dance," Chloe suggested, getting up and handing her purse across to Fred. A local band called 'Jammin' was in the middle of a blues set, picking up steam. The three girls crowded their way onto a small dance floor, Jill flirting with everyone along the way.

"I hope the Maui guys are hunks," said Jill, slowly shaking her slim hips as Mattie and Chloe twirled around her. "I checked it all out on the net, and word has it the guys are Hawaiian gods – large bronze boys who love foreign babes."

"New hunting grounds then?" said Mattie. "Another manhunt? Gawd, the last thing I need is another man. I'm going tropo just to be with you guys."

"Sure you are," Chloe and Jill said in unison.

Shortly after midnight they split, sharing a cab and dropping Jill off along the way.

"Meet us at our place Saturday at eight am, and we'll share an airport shuttle," said Chloe, opening the taxi door for Jill. "Bring an extra bikini and enough sexy sandals for all of us." Jill had a reputation for her hot shoes. "I'll pack one in each color. And bring my passport in case we decide to go on to Bali. Bye, loves."

"See ya, Jill. Fat chance on the Bali extension. I have to get back to my job."

"You never know. What will be will be." Jill had a habit of always tagging conversations with old clichés.

"It's just a week on Maui," said Chloe. "Get used to it."

"All for one and one for all," said Jill, skipping up the steps two at a time.

"I can't wait," said Mattie, turning to Chloe, her dimples hiding in a grateful grin.

three

THE OLD VIC

Chloe had managed to schedule Friday off, clearing a long weekend plus the week away. This was the day to start her novel. Or do laundry. But as a cold orange sky wove its way through the Golden Gate she realized she had not written a word all day. Instead she had called her computer techie in a panic.

It began when she unpacked her laptop for the trip. It was hiding in a corner of her home office, behind an easel that had taken precedence at some point during the past year or two. Chloe juggled a full time real estate career with leftover yet persistent callings to paint and write and live an artist's life.

Nearly two years ago she had finally indulged her bohemian urges, going to Paris to flirt with the muses, convinced that places have power and that all she really needed was a change of scenery to launch her life's dream. She had always thought it was her calling to create something beautiful and haunting and unique in the world, so while Tilly ran the family empire and funded Chloe's experiment to show her motherly support, Chloe took an apartment on the Left Bank then moved to Montmartre and hung out with a theatre troupe she met at her own private writing café – the one she hung out at, Mont Blanc in hand, downing croissants and petit cafés, hoping the muses would find her there, well caffeinated and ready. Instead she joined a cooking class offered by the lead actor, worked her way through every market in central Paris, gained eleven pounds and fell in love. Madly.

In four months the bloom was off the rose; she had seventeen pages and a couple of partially covered canvasses, jiggling hips and a bruised ego. It was time to go home. Her laptop had not seen the light of day since – she lived on her iPhone now – and it needed updating. Norton anti-virus, Windows upgrades and patches, defrags, backups. She thought it happened when she upgraded her Zone Alarm program. All of a sudden when she rebooted and tried to log on with a new wireless card (she couldn't be bothered to buy a new laptop), a weird page of html coding came up. Zap! She was frozen out.

Eli, Jill's tech partner, was a few blocks away and heard the panic in her voice, so he moved some clients around to work on her Toshiba, cleaning up the registry and uninstalling a myriad of useless programs, which had grown and morphed since the last time she called. He re-installed some anti-spyware software and fussed for hours over the zonelabs error that was freezing her Internet.

"I HAVE to have access," she pleaded, leaving it to Eli while she caught up on phone calls and finished marketing plans and detailing a spreadsheet for the new Bay View project.

When he left she re-booted the laptop and carefully composed an e-mail, copying to both Jill and Mattie: "Tomorrow!" was all it said, with a little smiley face □. Not much for a writer, but sometimes one word can say volumes. Besides she was out of practice – except for contracts and marketing plans and endless business letters and proposals. She hit 'send' and a radiant smile grew from her warm core, spreading slowly like the grey-orange sky moving east now over the rooftops of her city home.

Chloe was up early. She was always up early, so she dialed Jill. "Good morning. This is your wake up call. Are you up, sweetie?"

(Groan) "Yea, Chloe. I'm here," Jill said in a deep, gravelly voice. "Sleepy but here. I packed last night, so I just have to slip into my Sketchers and I'm there. Did you call me a taxi?"

"Pick up at seven. I have coffee on and chocolate croissants. See you soon."

Jill hung up, rolled over and thought momentarily about diving back under the covers, just for a minute. She had been out late last night with a pair of biceps she met at the club. She was always meeting guys while working out, some of whom she flogged off to Chloe – who never met anyone. Or did, but they were usually clients and very married. *Why are investors always married?* had become Chloe's dating mantra. She had a thing about avoiding married men that Jill didn't quite share. Still Jill only fixed Chloe up with single, non-gay guys, and she met tons of them. One just yesterday.

Mattie groped through her closet, weary and anxious at the same time. With all the traveling she'd done, you'd think she'd have it down, but she stood in the middle of a mess, calling down to Chloe. "Help! Do I wear shorts to arrive comfortably and use the blanket on the flight, or jeans and hope my thighs don't sweat between the arrival gate and the taxi?"

"You always ask the tough ones," said Chloe, walking in and handing Mattie her new jeans. "Wear flip flops. Take socks for the plane. As if you have thighs."

You'd have guessed that Chloe was the veteran traveler. In fact she was more the den mom or scout leader. The three had been friends for so long, people thought them sisters – except for their looks, each being quirkily individual.

Chloe went around, shutting drapes and closing blinds, stopping to appreciate the magic of daylight. "*Here comes the sun,*" she sang in a low, slightly off-key alto. The house was lovely in the morning when sunlight refracted through beveled stained glass windows and Austrian chandeliers, bounced off high white ceilings with their crown moldings, settling on ancient hardwood floors with patterns of shadows and prisms and crystal magic.

Chloe lived on the first floor with its master suite, two guest rooms, home office, library – stuffed floor to ceiling with a three-generation book collection, a main salon and anteroom off the foyer, with a hallway nearly wallpapered with family photos, framed in silver. A formal dining room sat twelve comfortably, expanding to sixteen if necessary, but it was the enormous tiled kitchen and breakfast nook that gave Chloe the most pleasure. Everyone knew that Chloe did her best work in the kitchen.

There was a fabulous herb garden in the small yard at the back. Just steps down from the kitchen, Chloe grew lemons and limes, hardy bushes of rosemary, swiss chard and lavender, three varieties of basil, chives, dill and fennel, garlic and parsley, savory and thyme. She preferred the lemon thyme but grew both…just in case. She tossed them in salads and coaxed flavors from curries and stir frys. Romaine and arugula fought for space amongst the hearty hydrangeas and gardenias that hated winter in the city even more than Chloe. In spring daffodils, jonquils, and lilies rose like brightly colored elves, and in summer every flower that grew sprouted in her garden and brightened tables and windowsills throughout her home and office.

Mostly the garden brightened Chloe – who found it a solace, an escape, and a source of endless nourishment. The southern boundary along the fence line was filled with pines and firs the family had planted from numerous live Christmas trees. All fully grown now. A hand-laid pebble pathway labyrinthed around organic plants – mostly herbs and salad greens, and near the center sat a faded teak bench where, sitting for five minutes here and twenty there, Chloe could change the world. In the corner furthest from the house, an old, faded tarp covered a compost heap, and seeing it, Chloe thought for a moment, *I haven't been in the garden all month.*

Mattie enjoyed a suite of rooms upstairs. She had the ancient clawed bathtub, the rec room with ping-pong table, large screen TV, an old jukebox and player piano. The upstairs commanded a sweeping view over the Bay – from the Bay Bridge, across Alcatraz, beyond Tiburon and the North Bay burbs, clear around to the Golden Gate, a shimmery symbol of this magnificent city.

The top floor was like a turret, a large circular room with windows and panoramic views all around. Chloe's dad had reserved it as his private getaway, his retreat, filling it with hand-woven silk carpets from Kashmir and huge pillows. And a small writing desk on the east side of the room for those times when he actually got away from work and found moments to pen poems. Since his passing, Chloe took refuge there from time to time, adding a shrine and candles, yoga mat and Tibetan bells, coming up whenever she needed shelter from the storm. Usually she was just too busy, and weeks would go by without a visit.

Her bags already by the front door, Chloe rustled around the kitchen, pouring another cup and bagging the croissants for the shuttle. For just a moment she smiled, thinking about the trip and what she hoped it would mean for Mattie. Chloe had taken the brunt of Mattie's sadness, holding her through rivers of tears, bucking her up through truckloads of self-doubt, taking her shopping, foreign filming, barhopping...anything for distraction. She'd even taken her on an overnight to a little inn in the redwoods, but of course that had backfired. Tom had taken Mattie there on the night they first slept together when it was all so romantic and hopeful.

"Oh gawd, Chloe, I look horrible." It was Mattie, stumbling down the stairs. "I hope I just need some caffeine."

"And chocolate," Chloe chimed in, nodding to the croissant bag as she locked the kitchen door and emptied the dish rack."And you're missing an earring." She handed it to Mattie, her little lost girl.

"Where's Jill?" Mattie always worried about time schedules. Her parents and Catholic school drilled it into her for years: be on time. Somehow promptness, like cleanliness, was next to godliness. Mattie missed out on the cleanliness part and just fretted whenever anyone was late.

Jill on the other hand was raised in a large family, and if

you were always on time you wasted your entire life waiting for everybody else.

"Maybe she slept through the taxi," Mattie fretted.

"Not a chance!" said Jill, striding through the front door. "So where's my java?"

Chloe managed the luggage to the foyer as Mattie and Jill poured mugs of steaming French roast and fumbled through the croissant bag.

"I can't believe we're three thirty-somethings, well two actually (Mattie was a year younger) and have never been to Hawaii. Where have we been hiding? And why?"

"We just needed a good excuse," said Chloe, putting her arm around Mattie.

"I know I've been your project for a couple months now, Chloe, but everything's going to change. You'll see. I'm on the lookout for peace of mind...and a new love. He'll be cute and smart and rich enough to take me away from all this."

"Gawd, you're such a romantic," said Jill. "Mine's a hunky brown Hawaiian surfer dude, built enough for a week of keeping up with me."

"Whoa, ladies." Chloe jumped in. "I thought we were going to be *together*. If you're both going to leave me, I'll hide out in little cafés or on the beach, writing my memoirs. Not that you noticed, but I may not want to be in real estate forever."

"I thought you got over all that in Paris," said Mattie.

"Writing, schmiting. You could use a little action, girl," said Jill, licking the chocolate off the croissant with a suggestive flair.

The doorbell chimed, and Chloe jumped up.

"Jim's here!" She had called her friend, a published writer by day and cab driver by night. He made exceptions for friends, and being an old high school buddy, Chloe counted. "Are we all packin'?" asked Chloe, grabbing three laptops and struggling with her shoulder bag. "I thought we were going on vacation."

"Your chariot awaits," Jim said, hugging Chloe and

grabbing a few suitcases.

"Just the romance you wanted, m' lady," Jill nodded to Mattie.

"May all our dreams come true," said Chloe, turning on the hall light and locking the front door behind her.

Mattie hesitated, fumbling in her bag, then turned.

"Wait, I forgot my ticket."

four

FLIGHT

The five-hour flight was uneventful. Chloe started working a spreadsheet on her laptop but within an hour buried into a book. Her carry-on was stuffed with books she hoped to read during the week. She loved to read, but rarely found the time any more.

Jill finished her third mai tai, tipping the glass back to catch the last drop, downed the small bag of airline macadamia nuts, and crushed the package in her hand. As the flight attendants in the back of the plane prepared the 'meal', she walked back and winked at the tall one, then jogged her way around the plane, bumping seats and passengers along the way, oblivious to the glares. She ended up back at the rear, chatting up a couple of male flight attendants. It was sort of like the bartender game and kept her guessing, but it also kept her jogging round and round. Any excuse for some exercise, she thought, inhaling the stale air.

Mattie stared out the window, conjuring up day-by-day, night-by-night romantic fantasies for her well-anticipated Maui experience. She closed the book she had brought along and drifted into her favorite fantasy about a tall, dark and handsome lover. Sometimes she told Chloe about her fantasies, and Chloe often said, "why don't you write a screenplay?!" But Mattie knew she didn't have the discipline. Still she loved the movies she made in her head, and she smiled as she drifted off.

By lunchtime, they had settled back in together, three across on the right window, row twenty-eight. As Jill buckled back up and lowered her tray she turned to Chloe and Mattie.

"OMG!!! Did you see the hunk two rows behind us?"

"I thought you were in the back hanging out with the gay stews," said Chloe.

"Yeah, and he was back there, coming on to me. Says he's an environmentalist on his way to a job with the State of Hawaii. Something about invasive species, whatever that is."

For all Jill's brilliance and savvy, she played down her natural intelligence and was attracted only to body builder/jock types, so the fact that this new guy seemed to have attraction and a brain took Chloe and Mattie aback.

"I just don't get it, Jill. Never have. You work in the financial district, have yummy, rich, cute guys, not to mention the Silicon Valley tech dudes, all around. What's your thing for brainless pants with great abs?"

"Well, Chloe, if you must know. I prefer a body fuck to a mind fuck, and all the guys I work with just want to work women over. Seriously. Oh, they'll pretend to come on. They're attracted to chicks, especially babes (brainless or not), but in the end they want to mess with your head to get control. Jocks just want to fuck you. It's that simple."

"Yeah, but then it's over. Don't you want a relationship?" It was Mattie, ever hopeful, putting her normal spin on the complex dating world, after having been dumped unceremoniously by the love of her life. It turns out he had been seeing other women, but neither Chloe nor Jill had the heart to inform her. Instead Mattie let Tom convince her he just wanted other things. Like a family. Naturally Mattie agreed. Woops, wrong ploy. At one point he even said he was relocating to the East Coast, but when she said she'd move with him, he changed that story too. In fact he had already decided he didn't want a girlfriend. He wanted to screw…everybody.

"I grew up with four brothers, doll. I know guys. Besides, who in their right mind asks for a world of hurt?" Jill defended herself, nodding to Mattie.

"I'm with Mattie on this one; it just seems so cynical. Can't you give them a chance? They are after all, individuals just like we are," said Chloe.

"Not," Jill protested. "They're invasive species." The troika burst out in hearty laughter.

"Oh, my gawd," Jill said, inspecting her meal tray. "It's full of invasive species too...headed non-stop to Maui. And what's with the pink surprise dessert? Good thing I'm fortified."

"Mine looks fine," said Mattie, poking around the vegetarian plate she'd special-ordered.

"It's airplane food. What did you expect?" said Chloe, picking through what looked a bit like chicken and dead peas, smothered in pale gravy, pushing it to the back of her tray. "Have another drink, Jill." Chloe reached into her bag, bringing out a small Tupperware container with grilled chicken and avocado sandwich on rosemary-foccia with roasted pepper mayonnaise, watercress and clover sprouts. A bosc pear.

While Jill and Mattie had coffee, Chloe read to them from her book. "It's Mark Twain's, *Letters from Hawaii*:

The loveliest fleet of islands that lies anchored in any ocean...the peacefullest, sunniest, balmiest, dreamiest haven of refuge for a worn and weary spirit the surface of the earth can offer."

"Are we worn and weary?" Jill asked, peeking around to the tall, dark and handsome two rows behind.

Chloe continued, undeterred. *"Away out there in the mid-solitudes of the vast Pacific, and far down to the edge of the tropics, they lie asleep on the waves, perpetually green and beautiful, remote from the work-day world and its frets and worries, a bloomy, fragrant paradise, where the troubled may go and find peace, and the sick and tired find strength and rest. There they lie, the divine islands, forever shining in the sun, forever smiling out on the shining sea, with its soft mottlings of drifting cloud-shadows and vagrant cat's paws of wind; forever inviting you, never repulsing you; and whosoever looks upon them once will never more get the picture out of his memory til he die."*

They quieted, reflecting on their trip and the lovely fleet. About fifteen minutes before landing, a short pictorial came on about Maui, which got everyone's juices flowing.

"Just look," said Chloe, taking off her earphones. It's paradise! I'm inspired already. I'll write the great American novel. What could be a better setting?"

"Check out the hunks," said Jill, watching as very defined Hawaiian dancers got down into their quads.

"Fleet Week!!"

"It's all soooo romantic," swooned Mattie, applying another coat of lip-gloss.

five

LANDING

"Let the games begin!" Jill slapped Chloe across the shoulders and nudged her forward into the terminal.

"It smells just like Bali," Mattie said, breathing in the moist tropical air and mixing it with memories of gardenia and frangipani.

"Mmmm," said Chloe, captivated by the natural perfume. Like a lover's initial attraction high on pheromones, it took her breath away, She was having an experience she'd never had before. She had learned early on to notice those moments, lean into them, celebrate them even. Once she was hit by a wall of Phoenix heat that nearly knocked her out, by the panicked suffocation of a Milwaukee winter when ice crystals formed instantly in her nostrils, by air so polluted in Newark she was reluctant to breathe, but the bouquet of sweet-scented extravagance that infused her now caught her totally by surprise. "We're not in Kansas anymore. Seriously, I didn't know a place could smell like heaven."

"Okay, it smells great. But where are the boys in the loincloths?" said Jill, scanning the crowd for the famed Hawaiian greeters.

It took nearly thirty minutes for Mattie to find her way back through various scanners and screening stations to the arrival gate – where she re-entered the plane, escorted, to look for the purse she was certain she had stashed in the seat pocket.

Meanwhile Chloe had picked up numerous visitor guides – the Best of Maui, 101 Things to Do on Maui, Maui Weekly, etc.

– and gathered their suitcases off the carousel while Jill walked over to the rental car kiosk to chase down their vehicle. Some haggling and a free upgrade later, Jill circled the airport, pulling in when she saw the Hawaiian Air sign. She waited there, putting the top down and setting all the buttons to radio stations until a portly security guard in a neon orange shirt and black polyester pants flagged her on. As she circled again she saw another Hawaiian sign and realized the first one had been for departures.

Chloe was waiting curbside with the six bags and a trio of laptops. "Where's Mattie?" she asked as Jill opened the trunk and helped her load it.

"I thought she was with you."

"She was, but she left her wallet on the plane."

"Oh great, we've lost Mattie. That girl would forget her head if..."

"No I wouldn't." Mattie suddenly appeared, running up, breathless and waving her billfold. "Found it...right where I left it." She grinned her petulant yet adorable little grin, and they peeled off, reveling in sun on skin, wind in hair, the balmy warmth of a tropical February day. Soon enough they were headed south, across the isthmus, Chloe deciphering the map while Jill managed the traffic.

"They have everything here – Costco, the marts, traffic," Mattie said, clearly disappointed. "I thought this place was supposed to be a step back in time. You know, the paradise of my imagination."

"Honey, we're still in America," Jill said. "Any place we can go without passports is gonna be pretty much like home except for weather and accents."

"I think we turn left up here," said Chloe, pointing to a crossroad. "Turn left. Go to the end of this road then turn left again." Jill flicked her turn signal, glad to have a co-pilot.

Mattie was reading signs and commenting on all the sights. "Sugar Museum. Okay, maybe we are back in time. Can either of you imagine advertising the glories of sugar back on the mainland? Seriously, we're all low-carb now. Or wanna bees."

"Or guilt-ridden when we're not," Chloe joined in.

"I think it's cause they make sugar here. Er, or, grow it…something like that. See the belching smokestacks. Looks worse than a nicotine addiction."

Jill flicked the left turn signal. "It's like everything else. Follow the money. At one time sugar was king here. In fact they dethroned a monarch for it."

"Can we come back someday?" asked Mattie, an admitted sugar freak. "Maybe they have a tasting tour."

In twenty minutes, thanks to the co-pilot's expertise with her iPhone's GPS, they pulled into the hotel's porte cochère.

"Well, well," said Jill. "Here they all are, just waiting for us." She eyed several well-built local bellmen, dressed in bermuda shorts and aloha shirts, hustling around, meeting and greeting, flashing smiles, parking cars. Jill sparkled at the one who came around to the driver's side.

"Now we're talking Hawaii," she said, grinning and slipping him a fiver. "Aloha yourself. Does it really mean you love me?"

Whitewashed Moorish architecture ascended from the sand, as if rising from the beaches of northern Africa or Spain in a time very far away. Columns and ribbed and tunnel vaults reached skyward towards horseshoe arches and a barrel ceiling, curving over koi ponds, fan and parlor palms and opening out to a sea so sparkling it reminded Chloe of snow, all frosty and diamond like. The airy courtyard, sweet with the breath of flowers, was a garden oasis. Hallway arcades marched away from the center with mosaic tile ornamentation and carved surfaces, creating illusions that left them speechless. *Fortresses and mosques. Persia. Turkey, Morocco. A crusade to Mecca. Casablanca, Marrakesh.*

Chloe watched thoughts drift as she stood by a reflecting pool. It was intriguing and foreign and not at all like the thatched look she had expected here in the islands.

"A princess lives here," Mattie finally said in her sweet diminutive voice.

"Yea, three of them," said Jill. "And a world of princes."

There were a few glitches at the front desk, for which Mattie took the blame while Jill asked to speak with the manager. In no time the tough brunette negotiated a room upgrade and a complimentary bottle of champagne, and they were in an elevator surrounded by walls of square beveled mirrors, framed in rosewood bead molding. Exiting on the top floor they landed not in a hallway but in another world – a circular open space with Persian carpets, soft camel sofas, piled with plump embroidered pillows in a rainbow of colors. Bougainvillea spilled out of terra cotta pots in the tiled archways, open to the beach below and a horizon of eye-searing blue, and for a moment they were in a minaret, transported to the harem of some Middle Eastern Emir in the Ottoman Empire.

Then they were bouncing on a king sized bed and hanging off the railing of the deck giggling like schoolgirls at a Lady Gaga concert.

"Can you believe it?" asked Mattie. "Smell that air. Check out the ocean...it's sooooo blue! Turquoise actually."

"What are those circus tents down by the pool?" asked Jill, putting the champagne in the mini bar fridge.

"They're cabañas around our oasis. We're in the Arabian-Hawaiian nights," said Mattie, thrilled with the romantic architecture, the size of the suite, and the glorious bathroom.

"Whoa, check it out," Jill said. "Hunks all around the pool. Beach boys!!" She got into a flutter orienting her suitcases and getting to a bikini. "Anyone else for the pool?"

Chloe was unpacking her things into the left third of the closet and the bottom drawer of an antique dresser while calling housekeeping for an iron and more hangars.

"Sure, I'll go," said Mattie, finding her swimsuit. "Come on Chloe, we can fuss later. Surf's up and so's the sun. Let's go."

"Save me a chaise. I'll change while I wait for the maid."

"Not 'maid'. It's 'housekeeping personnel' or 'guest attendant'," Mattie corrected her.

"Well, don't linger. We're ordering you a mai tai." Jill said, rounding the door and bounding down the hallway.

Chloe closed the door behind them, and for a few moments she sat on the edge of the bed, looking over their new world, happy and inspired. Then she took out her journal and wrote until 'guest attendant - Maile', knocked at the door. By the time Chloe got poolside and found her friends, they had finished her mai tai and theirs and ordered another round.

Mattie spied her first. "I was thinking the drinks here were expensive, but that's the best nine dollar high I've had in awhile. I'm gone already. Gone with the place where sky meets sea, gone with how warm it is for winter..."

"Yea, yea, you're a goner," Jill said. "Only it was one and a half drinks...or thirteen fifty's worth, plus a tip, which we'll have to leave if we want service tomorrow."

"I'm amazed you can still add, given your state," Chloe flicked Jill with a towel then arranged her beach chair just so, catching full sun on her winter-white body, tucking the plumeria blossom behind her ear and taking a long draught off the end of Jill's mai tai. "I've only got a week to go from white to brown. Better get busy."

"Without passing red...puh-leeze," said Jill, remembering a summer in the high country. It was their sophomore year. "Remember, Chloe? We hiked up to Rim Rock Lake and lay out lizard-like all afternoon, talking shit about some guy who just broke your heart. By the time we got back we couldn't move for our burned, swollen faces and tits."

"All week I couldn't wear a bra, but then I couldn't stand the feel of my blouse against my nipples either. Gawd we fried ourselves, blisters and all."

"Ugh. That sounds awful. I sunburned on my first trip to Spain, but I've been into sunscreen ever since. Here," Mattie offered a huge bottle of goo to Jill and Chloe. "I've got another in my bag. Slather it on, girls!"

25

"Have you met the bartender yet?" asked Chloe, orienting to familiar territory.

Mattie replied, a little glum. "It's a girl, so that makes it easy. We'll just order poolside. Have you seen the beach boys?"

Jill had positioned herself right under the lifeguard stand, rolled over, winking up at him. Another with movie star looks – okay, maybe an action figure star, all biceps and quads, stopped by with their drinks which were all dressed up with fruit and baby umbrellas, and a dish of macadamia nuts.

"Oh, my gawd! Look at those nuts," exclaimed Mattie, grabbing a handful.

"Indeed," said Jill, staring right into the server's crotch.

"Can you help me out, darlin'?" she looked up, catching his eye. "What do y'all call yourselves here? We know the maids are housekeeping personnel, but what exactly are you?"

"Aloha. I'm da server, Kimo." He was a caricature of an island beach boy – huge, about six foot four, thickly muscled and cocoa brown with jet black eyes and hair. A whale tattoo leapt up his forearm, and a tapa pattern circled his bicep.

"An dey not housekeeping personnel. Fo real, we all guest attendants, but we beach boys too. Mostly we just da kine folk who own dis land – who had it stolen by da US soldiers, doing dirty work fo da big corporations."

"Oh, just like today."

"Now don't interrupt, Chloe," Jill nodded back to Kimo.

"We all stay working two-tree jobs just fo feed our keikis an live in little hot boxes uddah side town."

"When god gives you lemons…" Mattie was into her second mai tai, so Jill saved her with a towel whap.

"If you wan go fishing sometime, my bruddah and I can take you out. Cheap. Well, cheaper than the guys with the brochures."

"Oh, fun!" shouted Mattie. "We'll pack a picnic…"

"No worries. We bring everyting, even sunscreen," Kimo went on, selling now.

"I stopped at the concierge desk to check out what's

happening." Chloe pulled open her bag and spread brochures on the chaise lounge. "Are any of these good?" she asked, deflecting Kimo's attention from Jill who was googly-eyed by now, checking out his bulging pecs, thighs like tree trunks.

"I can't really socialize now wid da house so full en orders pileen up all over da place, but I can meet you later en help you make one plan. I'm stay off four 'clock."

Jill slipped him her room card and winked as he took it and walked away. "You had me at hello," she whispered in her deep Kate Hepburn voice.

"Could you be more obvious, Jill?" Mattie was always a little shocked at Jill's aggressive flirting, preferring a more demure role, especially on first meetings.

"More drunk is the word," Chloe sipped her drink and chewed on the pineapple. "Are you sure you'll make it to four?"

"Sure, honey. Just need a little nap. Jetlag and all that."

"I'll read you to sleep then." Chloe began, "this is Mark Twain, heading for Hawaii:

Leaving all care and trouble and business behind in the city, now swinging gently around the hills and passing house by house and street by street out of view, we swept down through the Golden Gate and stretched away toward the shoreless horizon. It was a pleasant, breezy afternoon, and the strange new sense of entire and perfect emancipation from labor and responsibility coming strong upon me, I went up on the hurricane deck so that I could have room to enjoy it"

"We've done it," said Mattie, rolling over and re-applying. "Like Twain, we all got away."

Jill rolled onto her stomach, untying her top. "*To be born is to be shipwrecked upon an island.* Paul Theroux. Mosquito Coast."

"You're such a cynic, Jill. Listen to this. Twain wrote this, years after he left the islands:

"No alien land in all the world has any deep, strong charm for me but that one; no other land could so longingly and so beseechingly haunt me, sleeping and waking, through half a lifetime, as that one has done. Other things leave me, but it abides; other things change, but it remains the same. For me its balmy airs are always blowing, its summer seas flashing in the

27

sun; the pulsing of its surf-beat is in my ears; I can see its garland crags, its leaping cascades, its plumy palms drowsing by the shore, its remote summits floating like islands above the cloud rack; I can feel the spirit of its woodland solitudes; I can hear the splash of its brooks; in my nostrils still lives the breath of flowers that perished twenty years ago."

"I saw the mountain poking through the lei of clouds, but I never thought to put it that way. Besides a rack is for lamb, not clouds." She went on reading to Mattie, "and from the back cover:"

"I went to Maui to stay a week and stayed five. I had a jolly time. I would not have fooled away any of it writing letters under any consideration whatever."

"I can so relate right now. Time to get out of my book and out of my head. How about a swim, Mattie?" Chloe jumped up then noticed that Jill and Mattie were both sound asleep. She ran down to the beach, leaping in. *Heaven, just like I hoped.*

The water was a sensual delight, mercury on skin, beading and flowing. She started slowly, gliding, then swam a great distance, nearly down to the Marriott and back, at home in the liquid aqua paradise. She took long, languid strokes, remembering the summer cabin on the lake where her dad first taught her to swim. Her lungs expanded and heart pounded as she became acutely aware of both her vulnerability and her strength, her human present and her dolphin past. Ancient and timeless memories flooded over her with the rush of muscles and breath. Chloe was home in the soundless peace of an ocean world.

six

ITINERARY

At four fifteen they heard a knock at the door. Jill had been up in the room for an hour or so, freshening up and putting away her things. Mattie and Chloe arrived just minutes before, and the three had been pouring over brochures, trying to decide which of the shows would be too touristy, and wondering why in the world someone would take a Lavender Tour or visit Maui's Surfing Goat Dairy.

"Maybe there's a good surf break there, which means surfers." Jill of course caught that wave.

"Or maybe they have wine and goat cheese tasting." Mattie was stretching here, but by now they were all planted firmly in Maui soil and watered with mai tais.

"Just halve the price of our room and we can afford our bar bill," said Chloe, not quite slurring, having caught up with the other two after her swim. "Maybe we should each pay cash for our drinks."

"Sure," said Jill. "Like you don't drink as much as I do." She didn't, but it wasn't worth an argument, and besides one never won an argument with Jill. Probably a defense mechanism she honed to brilliance growing up with all those brothers.

Jill crossed the room, checked herself in the entrance mirror. Her tits spilled out of her black bikini top just so, and she nodded appreciatively and opened the door.

"Why Kimo, darlin', what kept you so long?" she drawled, imitating some sort of southern belle.

"Hey, we all stay Maui time seestah, 'specially when we pau hana, uh, finished work," Kimo grinned, clearly checking Jill out better now and locking into the fabulous dark pools that were her eyes.

"Come on through," Chloe invited him to the lanai, where she had a notepad and brochures spread on a blue-tiled table. There was a lovely lilting cadence to Chloe's voice. She shared the tonality of her mother, and over the phone few could tell them apart. "As nice as it is, we don't just want to sit around the pool all week. We're here for Mattie." She gave Jill a look from the corner of her eye. "A break-up thing, and it's time she's over it. Jill's always cruisin' so guy hangouts work for her, and I'm gathering information and experiences for my writing."

"What's the best fun?" Jill chimed in. "And do we really have to see that funny sounding mountain by sunrise?"

"Haleakala," said Kimo. "Holly (like the Christmas stuff) - auk, as in Auckland - à – là, like da French. Sunset mo bettah, er, even better, but any time day stay ok. Just take cameras en warm da kine clothes. It freezin' up dere."

"Haleakala (*pronounced a little off*). What's with all the native words? I thought this was America?" said Jill.

"Stay da Hawaiian nation, but opinions stay diff'rent. Kimo broke into a few sentences of pidgin, which to their untrained ears sounded like a foreign language.

"Whoa, is that Hawaiian?" asked Mattie.

"Naw, stay pidgin'. Da kine talk what most locals speak he'ah. You gotta study Hawaiian in school or fine one ole timah to he'ah da language. But da words stay simple. Fo real. Wid only twelve lettahs, five vowels and seven constants, it mo simple kine den engleesh. You get em down, da names en places, by da time you stay go. Well, maybe not dat soon, but haoles who move here no tongue tie so much after 'bout six months."

"So tell us about the boat," said Jill, bringing the conversation back.

"We get one trimaran, fully loaded. Some braddahs built er

30

for us at dere shop over Haiku-side. Dat's on d'uddah side d'island. Really nice country. Cool en green. But we keep er ovah Ma'alaea Harbor. We most times charge ninety-five per person, but we let you have a private trip with lunch and be'ah for only two fifty."

"Two even and you're on," said Jill, "but you have to bring a few guys for my suitemates so it feels like a party."

"Do you have snorkels?" asked Chloe.

"And fishing gear?" Jill continued.

"Get everyting. For two hundred you get a few guy friends, bait, lines, en snorkel gear. Lunch too. Good kine lunch. My auntie en make em. You bring cash and two beach towels each. Get 'em at da pool. Tomorrow ok? Dat my only day off dis week. Gotta check wid my uncle, den I call you wid da pick-up time. Uncle Kaika meet you he'ah at da hotel while we stay prep da boat."

"Sounds good. I'm in," said Chloe.

"Sounds romantic – a sail out to other islands with a boatload of friends," said Mattie.

"Can you help us with our itinerary too?" Chloe insisted.

"Well, Hana's a must! I get one uncle who stay take you on one farm tour Kipahulu side, work da lohi – dat's taro – and swim da Seven Pools. He en Auntie Emma get one small B&B on da coast. Hana Ranch stay way s'pensive kine, en Keoki can show you da botanical gardens, da bes beaches, tings li dat. Need guide for Hana-side, and he da bess. Wen you wan go?"

"Midweek might be best to avoid the crowds," suggested Mattie.

"Get no crowds Hana-side. Dey always too many kine cars on da road down dere, but not cause dey too many people, but cause too small da road."

The more he talked the thicker his accent grew.

"Okay, I'm up for Hana…and sunset on the mountain. How about good shows, nightclubs, or entertainment on the island?" said Chloe.

"Is there a gym in the hotel?" asked Jill. "I have to stay on

31

my workout if I'm going to be drinking mai tais all week."

"Yep, stay right behind da slide to da pool. Nice one too, but we give ono massage on da boat. Extra twenty-five. Professional kine."

"What do people do Saturday nights?" Jill asked.

"Willie K at Hapa's, right down da road. Stay always fun dere. Wan I pick you up? 'Round nine?"

"Great, we'll be ready." Jill was speaking for the group by now.

"We can't stay out too late," said Mattie. "We have a sail tomorrow."

"Okay, I stay go; you stay stay; I see you latah, 'bout nine," Kimo walked towards the door.

"Not so fast, cowboy." Chloe and Mattie turned wondering what Jill was up to. "Didn't you forget your aloha?"

"We never forget d'aloha, ma'am," he said, grabbing Jill and giving her a big juicy kiss. He smiled broadly, then shut the door behind him.

"Well, aloooooha! I like this place already," Jill said, slumping against the door and grinning ear to ear. "It's my kind of people."

seven

HAPA'S

It was nine-thirty by the time Kimo called up. The girls had just showered and finished off a gourmet pizza they ordered in the room. Sometime about sunset, hanging over the lanai railing oo-ing and aa-ing over the mai tai sky and their perfect Arabian kingdom, their excitement caught up with their jetlag and simply wore them out. They passed out until well after dark.

Good thing too, since it was still Saturday night, and they'd been up since four am Hawaiian time. Kimo met them in the lobby, fortified with a friend from school, a haole kama'iiana (translation: white mainlander who's lived on the island a long time – long enough to be like local). Chad ran a computer business in downtown Kahului. Kimo thought the girls would find Chad amusing or interesting or in some way engage them beyond Kimo's limit, which he felt he already reached earlier that afternoon. Plus it was tough speaking normal English, and Chad could speak their language. Also Chad's dancing made Kimo look really good, and he needed to look better for the three babes from the bay.

By the time they reached the club, it was hopping. The musicians were on a break, and some old Pink Floyd CD rattled the place. A table full of Kimo's friends hovered over the girls, hanging on their every word, which couldn't be heard anyway. Still they were new blood and received appropriate attention. Jill had Kimo on the dance floor immediately, and Chad lingered, avoiding it as long as possible, talking computers with Chloe – who didn't quite understand everything the way Jill might have, but was interested in the way his sandy brown hair framed his square jaw line, his mouth tilted towards the left side of his face, and *gawd, could anyone have bluer eyes?*

Mattie was left with three other local blokes – sweet, brown guys who were totally interested in her…and the Super Bowl Game they would miss tomorrow on their sail.

"We en tape it to watch latah," Mikala said. "You can all come ovah aftah da boat trip. You girls like football?"

"Well, we tolerate it sometimes. Jill wouldn't miss it, except that we're here for only a week, and we each promised to give up our normal obsessions to have some fun together. It's our first time in the islands you know." The last said with a hint of flirt, which pushed Mattie out of her comfort zone but had the desired effect. Or maybe it was the volumes she spoke without words – her tiny adorable body, topped with a cherub's face and surfer Barbie hair, long, straight and blonde. And the young voice that reminded men of their first time and endeared and bonded them in a curious way.

"Buy you one be'ah?" Mikala leaned in towards Mattie as Willie K came back on stage and the other four returned to the booth.

"This one wears me out," said Jill, tugging on Kimo's arm. "And we haven't even started." Her flirts were always over-the-top obvious, but somehow captivated everyone.

Chad was being attentive to Chloe when he wasn't 'hi babe'-ing every other woman who walked by on her way to the bar. Chloe was well over his geek talk and just wanted to dance.

"Are you coming tomorrow?" she asked him, hoping he'd say 'no' and relieved when he did. "I've got some deadlines I buggered out of tonight, so I can't…really. But I'd love a rain check later in the week. I'll call you."

"He scared da water," said Kimo, trying to help him out, but making things look even worse, especially to Chloe, the varsity swimmer.

"This guy is good," said Mattie, warming up to the sweet

sounds of Willie K who was into a slack key riff, singing falsetto.

"He pretty famous he'ah on Maui. In Hawaii. Does plenty gigs on da mainland too – concerts li dat." Kimo somehow always ended his sentences sliding back into thick pidgin.

"It's cool, Kimo. We understand you." Jill grabbed his bicep and tilted her face up to him in an attempt to reassure him he was still in the game. The guys nearly fought over the trio on the dance floor, strutting their testosterone and preening their feathers.

Eventually they settled down, neither trying to impress one another nor jockey for position, simply enjoying the music and ordering another round. By one in the morning Mikala invited them all back to his place on the beach. Scott and Kepa had already left with a couple of local girls they knew, which left six, three couples.

"Thanks, but no thanks," said Chloe. "We've got a ten o'clock pick-up tomorrow; it's four our time, and we need our beauty rest."

"Okay, but you no need. Maybe you need something else 'stead...(*ha, ha, chuckle, chuckle*) " I still taping da game tomorrow. Dinner my place?" Mikala asked again, hoping to change minds.

"We'll see." Chloe shot right back. "We've got a pretty tight schedule. We'll let you know tomorrow, okay? She wasn't so sure of herself around these guys; they weren't like men from the city, and she wasn't sure if they'd get mixed messages or wrong ideas. And as usual she was being protective of her brood.

Jill, normally in the middle of every conversation, was deep into a liplock with Kimo, finally coming up for air.

"Let's blow this joint." She used slang to deflect attention from her extremely bright and well-educated persona and act more like a regular bloke.

"I'll bring da car 'round," Kimo responded, right on cue.

In fifteen minutes they were trying to get the card key in right side up and stifling laughter.

"We need ground rules," said Chloe, and they each understood what she meant. "We have one week, and I for one don't want to spend it hanging out with the boys, drinking and watching football. Anyone with me on this?"

"Sign me on," said Mattie, removing her sandals. "Not that it wouldn't be a completely different adventure than any we imagined."

Well, I fully intend to get more of Kimo's package, so you girls do whatever you want while I inspect the jewels."

"Oh, come on, Jill. You're not that horny!" said Mattie.

"Wanna bet?"

"I still want to see the volcano, find some nice beaches, and Maile says upcountry is nice, whatever that is."

"Who's Maile?" said Jill.

"The guest-attendant-slash-maid," Chloe responded, struggling with her buttons.

"I know we need to lay out an agenda, but not now, I'm tipsy…and tired." They all were.

"I'm with you, Mattie. How about over breakfast…right here. Eggs benedict and fresh papaya hanging out on the deck," said Chloe, filling out the order form and hanging it on the doorknob, checking the spaces beside the New York Times, the San Francisco Chronicle and the Maui News.

eight

TRIMARAN

The whale-watching, sliding and snorkeling, tequila sunrise, all-the-hunks-you-could-possibly-wish-for boat trip was as great a time as they'd had in awhile, as fun as a day could be without being illegal. Jill and Kimo were practically doing it...everywhere. In the water, on the deck, in the bathroom, on the bar. It seemed to excite everyone else just having them around. Mattie was sweet-talking back to Kepa, trying all the while to keep his hands off her. Chloe was deflecting advances from the others while reveling in all the attention. She needed help with her fins, her drink, her binoculars. How could a gal seem suddenly so helpless, especially Chloe?

"How come they don't grow em like you guys back home?" she asked as they lay, collecting sun, while the Hawaiians hung out under the tarp. Simple question. Long pause. Stumped the audience.

"Haole guys just too much into dey heads," Kimo suggested. "We pure physical."

It was as good an explanation as anyone offered. Kepa backed him up, "yea, and dey use all dem high fallutin' words, you know...hieroglyphics."

"It can't be that simple," Mattie joined in.

"Yep," said Jill, "pure physical, and aren't we ready for some after all the mental gymnastics we do back in the city?"

The return trip was filled with that kind of banter, each positioning for what comes after. They saw humpback whales, females with their calves, males showing off and chasing the females, breaching and slapping their fins, spouting when they surfaced. Spinner dolphins frolicked alongside the trimaran, filling everyone with a natural glee. The fun factor was definitely off the charts.

But gentle vacillations began as soon as they docked.

"Remember the plan," reminded Chloe, nudging Jill.

"But I want to see the game," she protested.

"Yea, we know what you want," said Mattie, miffed that the plan was already shifting.

"Ok, okay. I'll take a beach walk with Kimo," she said, grabbing his butt and winking at him. "He can't go on property, but there's plenty of beach beyond the hotel. I'll meet you two for supper at the little Italian café at seven, ok?"

It took some convincing, but standing firm, despite huge 'mahalos' for the 'absolutely fab time', they were able to get out of an evening of popcorn, football and who-knows-what with the pure physicals. Already Kepa and Scott were begging for future dates later in the week starting with tomorrow, but all the guys worked, and the girls were way too busy to commit before they had more options. Besides their plans called for a trip to Hana.

It's tough when you're having fun to let go, but the plan did not include hanging out all week with these guys. It was unanimously agreed earlier that morning that they would do the island, not the guys. In fact Mattie wanted something else, and Chloe was determined to give it to her. Now if only she could figure out what it was.

nine

CAFFÉ CIAO

The message light was blinking, and the girls were already gone when Jill returned to the room. She had spent two hours torturing poor Kimo, petting and flirting and deciding not to go there after all. Even though they had found a sandy cove all to themselves, with a backdrop out of Hollywood, going all the way all of a sudden seemed so very high school and was finally somewhere she didn't want to go. Not there. Not then. Besides she loved leaving them hanging, wanting more. It was a practiced skill, and when she left Kimo on the beach, she left him panting for more.

Jill picked up the phone and listened.

"Hi, Jill. It's Michael from the plane. I hope you're settled in and having a great time. I hit the ground running, but I still need to eat. How about dinner? Monday. Tomorrow night? Call me, ok? I'm at 572-4077." His voice was low and articulate like a radio announcer's, giving just the right rhythm and weight to each word and phrase.

She hit 'erase', scribbled the number on the pad by the phone and jumped in the shower. By seven fifteen she joined the other two downstairs in the Italian Bistro.

Leaving Mattie to the privacy of the room for a phone call, Chloe arrived first at the bistro. *Perfect*, she thought. Floor to ceiling shelves were crammed with exotic foods, spices and condiments. There were homemade pastas and sauces, cookbooks, wines, salamis hanging alongside peppers and cloves of garlic. A global selection of well over two hundred cheeses, twenty varieties of extra virgin olive oil, balsamic vinegar from Modena, stuffed grape leaves and olives, prosciutto-wrapped figs – all crowded shelves, along with jars of specialty items – Maui mango chutney, feta goat cheese in olive oil, roasted garlic dijon, passion-fruit jam, and lemon curd. *Lemon curd! I could live here*, Chloe thought, ordering an espresso. Once Mattie arrived they ordered a bottle of Chilean red and were well into it while maps and brochures sprawled on the table, fighting for space with nibbles of antipasto.

"On local time already?" Chloe said, looking up as Jill arrived. "Musta got some Hawaiian in you." She always gave Jill a hard time about her endless flirtations and choices in men. It went clear back to their college days when Chloe was still a virgin and Jill was always trying to fix her up with her excess beaus.

"Au contraire. And nice to see you too." Jill hugged Mattie and blew a kiss across the table to Chloe. "Michael called."

"Michael?" Mattie gave up years ago trying to keep Jill's boyfriends straight. She and Jill grew up together in Marin and were friends in grade school. Ever since then their relationship had a protective, caring, little girl tone, but Chloe was the glue that kept them bound together in adulthood.

"The guy on the plane. Remember, the environmentalist?"

"I don't remember you introducing him."

"Well, I guess I didn't, but you peeked. Tall. Dark. Hunky handsome."

"Oh, yes, I remember. What's up?" Chloe asked

"He wants to take me to dinner tomorrow. Do we have plans?"

"Chloe and I were fine tuning the itinerary just now. We're thinking a drive around tomorrow, leaving early, just to get our bearings and scope out the island. Lahaina. Upcountry. Maybe into the city. What's it called? Kuhahalaylay or something long, starting with a K."

"Like nearly everything else we saw on the map," Chloe commented.

"Humor me," said Jill, picking another olive and spreading hummus on the last bite of crispy pita. "Now can we order? I'm starved."

ten

DENIAL

By nine the next morning they had ordered room service, taken turns in the bathroom, dressed, had coffee and eaten, packed bathing suits and towels and plenty of sunscreen and were heading back across the island towards the town that started with K.

"I can't believe it's winter and we're in shorts," Mattie started. "All this sun just makes me smile."

"Yea, my body's jolly too," Jill said. "Can't we just find a beach?"

"Come on, we have our plan," Chloe said, gathering up her little litter. Everyone says we have to go upcountry, so that's where we're going. Besides, all the surfers hang out in Paia, so the eye candy should hold you for awhile."

"Does anyone's cell phone work here?" Jill asked, searching for bars. "Mine's good for nothing. Like a limp dick."

"I've got reception," said Chloe. "I checked the office this morning. No problem. Wanna use mine?"

"I guess I need to get back to Michael. Hot date and all, but not now. I'll call him later."

Mattie was amusing herself. "Michael, Mattie, M & M…sounds sweet; maybe he's got the wrong girl."

"Don't even go there you flaxen landmine." Jill reached over, swatting at Mattie. "He's mine. My type or not."

"Okay then. We get the next two." Not that Jill hogged them all, but she did tend to monopolize most of the men they met when they were together. It was simple. She came on to them.

"Guys are so easy, Mattie. Just pay attention next time one catches your eye. Look at him. Smile. Bat your eyelids. I know it's cliché, but it works. We think they're complex and will figure us out without our even having to give hints. They don't. Won't. You have to make it easier."

"But then they think all you want it sex."

"Wrong again, little one. That's all *they* want, whether you come on to them or not."

"You do tend to hold back, Mattie." Chloe joined in Jill's defense.

"Oh, as if you don't?" Jill was on the offense again.

"I mean, well, maybe we both seem more reticent, compared to you, Jill. But Chloe never even notices guys. They'd have to literally bump into her, like that guy did at Macy's, then court her for weeks. Actually that's how Tom and I met. At a food court, and look where that got me." Mattie was feeling a little sorry for herself.

"Oh, just get over him, Mattie. He wasn't worth your love. I never mentioned it, but"

"Jill, are you really going there? Hey, who's got the map?" Chloe was deflecting again.

"Yea, I'm going there. Mattie should know the truth. For her own good, since after all this time she's still pining over that two-timing, or maybe ten-timing…"

"What?" Mattie peered over the seat at Jill. "Say it. Just say it."

"Well, you should know that Tom was seeing other women long before Pamela."

"No way," Mattie insisted.

"Way, darling." Chloe said.

"Long before he came on to me." *There I've said it*, Jill thought.

"He what? He knew we were friends. I introduced you for gawd's sake."

"Just listen, Mattie. Tom was going out the whole last year

you were coupled. I ran into him at Gumps one day, canoodling with some redhead. Then Chloe saw him on the wharf, making out over oysters at Alioto's. He even asked me out once. Imagine the balls to do that. You were on a FAM trip to Sydney and the Gold Coast, and he knew it, so he called to see if I wanted to go to the movies with him. I told him off. And that was way before the girl from Phoenix he met at that conference."

"And neither of you said anything?" Mattie whispered in disbelief. "What kind of people would betray their best friend?" she looked sadly at Chloe.

"We talked about it, honey, but by then you were so into him. Tom this and Tommy that and your hopes and wishes all rolled up into some romantic future projection. We just figured you'd find out yourself soon enough then we could better support your loss."

"Yes, it never occurred to us it would take another year for you to discover his tendencies. And if you defend him over us, you're dead." Jill knew Mattie would try to put some sort of spin on this, but she didn't.

"I guess I knew. I just didn't want to. We all talk ourselves out of things that are right in front of our faces. Sometimes he would be text messaging someone and say it was business when I knew by his look it wasn't. There were always girls leaving messages on his tele. He used the same excuse. Still I never addressed it head on for fear it was true."

"So you understand why we didn't either," Chloe said.

"Yea, I guess…" Mattie took a deep, sucking breath.

"Oh, he's so history!" said Jill. "No guy is worth weeks of mourning. Maybe hours. Okay, a couple of days, but weeks? It's not human."

"I got it, Jill. I'm over it. "

"Sounds a little bitter to me, Mattie. Anyway Kimo's mine," snickered Jill. "You get the next one."

"We're in the city already. How about Border's? I need another coffee." Chloe was tired of driving, and it had only

45

been twenty minutes.

eleven

BORDERS

While Chloe ordered, Mattie stood at the magazine rack, peeking through a *Travel & Leisure.*

"Going on a trip?" he asked, holding a *Scientific American.* His voice was like a low, smooth jazz riff. She turned. He was a George Clooney look-alike, taller and ten years younger. *Mmmm*, she thought. *Very yummy.* Their eyes met like a geological conference of turquoise and jade, and for an instant something flickered in the space between them like an invisible electrical current, arching towards a negative pole, like a battery being recharged, or the silent daffodil oath between winter and spring.

"No. I'm in the business." Mattie collected herself, keenly aware of her molecules being rearranged.

"Travel writing?"

"Travel traveling. I'm a travel agent. Mostly I book tours and cruises. The airlines and the Internet have taken all the profits away, but I love the trips and it's a family business. What are you in?" Mattie was already taking Jill's morning relationship Rx: 'Be approachable. Be bold.'

"I'm saving the planet," he explained. "Just call me superman."

"Well, that's an interesting come on. How can a girl resist." She did it. She actually did it. Batted her eyelids as if Jill was coaching from the sidelines.

"I didn't mean it that way. I'm an environmental scientist, specializing in..."

"Invasive species?" Mattie cut him off. "And your name is Michael."

"And you're psychic."

"There you are," Jill spotted Mattie. *Woops, I forgot to call him back,* she thought, spotting Michael. *I guess I got a little sidetracked with Kimo.*

"Hi, girl." Michael spoke up, trying to remember her name and prying his eyes away from the blonde with electric blues.

"Oh, you met my friend, Mattie."

"Not officially. Just checking out reading material. I had to pick up a few things for work." It was as if he'd been caught with his fist in the candy jar.

"Picking up blondes is work-related?" Jill was clearly miffed. Mattie and Michael both wore strange, caught-in-the-act expressions, though their conversation seemed innocent enough.

"Give him a break, Jill. He was not hitting on me." Shivers ran up her arms from the lingering current. Her breath was shallow and rapid.

"Well, I sort of was," Michael confessed. "Especially after that flash that came from your amazing eyes. Jill never called me back in two days, so I figured she was into other things, and we were having a barbecue tonight, sponsored by the State Department of Agriculture, so I was working up the nerve to ask you up. Why don't you both come?"

"There's three of us," Mattie said, happy he asked and projecting already.

"Aside from a few wives it will be an all guy thing, so the more women the merrier."

Jill shot Mattie a look, shrugged and said, "Do we wear overalls and mud boots?"

"It's upcountry, so you'll want more than shorts and maybe sweaters, but there's no dress code. Let me write the address." He took out a ballpoint and printed an address, drawing a map from Borders to the house. "It's an estate. You can't miss it. See you then." He nodded towards Jill, stared straight into Mattie's big bright blues and walked away towards the counter, staggering slightly as if an inner ear condition was affecting his balance.

"I said he was mine," Jill said under her breath.

"And that I got the next one," Mattie replied, raising her eyebrows and smiling her hopeful little girl smirk.

"Oh he's so into you. Are you that daft? Now where's Chloe?" Jill could be quite generous when she wanted to, usually with family and friends.

They found Chloe moments later at a book signing near the center of the store. A local author was reading from a recently published novel he'd written to an audience of about fifteen, and Chloe was grilling him in the Q and A.

"When did you start writing? How long did it take you to find an agent? Did you ever self-publish?"

"Whoa, Red. Well, I guess I began in grade school. I used to write plays for my second grade class. By junior high I was writing poems and short stories. Silly little things really, but it got me in the habit of writing every day before school. I still write early in the day."

"Me too," said Chloe. "Even when it hurts." She smiled her flashing, all-teeth, win-'em-over smile."

Jill grabbed her, whispering. "Oh, my gawd, you're flirting. What's got into you? And where's my coffee?"

"Hi, girls." Chloe turned, picking up a little tray of lattés from the empty chair beside her.

The author signed a few more books as the huddle of supporters dispersed and he walked over to Chloe. He wore faded jeans and a brown plaid shirt, boots and a Panama hat. He was about Chloe's height but clearly older, with light brown hair and eyes like melted chocolate.

"No, I've never self published, and it took me forever to find an agent. But she's a keeper! Jed. Jed Armstrong." He held out his hand.

Chloe took it, but did not shake it. Instead she held it gently, looking up and giving him her Julia Robert's grin.

49

"Okay, you two. That's enough pda right here in the middle of Borders."

"Why, Jill, it never bothered you before." Mattie noticed too. There was clearly something going on between Chloe and the author.

Probably a marriage of minds, Jill thought. "Why don't you bring him along?"

"What?" Chloe was confused.

"We're all off to a big Hawaiian barbeque tonight. Bring a date. It will mean more choices for me."

Before Chloe could interject any comment, Jed spoke up. "Why thank you, little lady, I'd love to come. If that's okay with you, Chloe." He tilted his head looking deeply into eyes he recognized as the color of New Zealand jade – which they were when they weren't aquamarine. Like precious gemstones, Chloe's eyes did a green – blue – green thing, depending on her surroundings and her mood. She never knew however, which is why she stuck to soft neutrals in her eye make-up.

"It's a date then," said Jill. "Around seven. I'll copy the map for you." She leaned over to copy the directions on the back of one of Jed's bookmarks, and Jed looked over her shoulder.

"I know the Baldwin Estate. Are you sure it's okay?" He was asking Chloe, not Jill.

"It sounds fun," said Chloe, wondering if he had hair or a bald spot under his hat.

"Shall I pick you up?" *Well, he's been raised properly,* Chloe thought. *Even though he's a little rough around the edges.*

"No. Thanks, we'll meet you there."

He handed her a copy of his book and found her eyes again. "It's signed. I think you'll like it."

"He's smitten," said Jill as they left the bookstore. "Even though he is an anachronism. And Mattie stole my Michael. How's that for a quick stop? A minute ago I had a hot date tonight. Now I'm the only one without one."

"Well, it shouldn't take you long," said Chloe, buckling up

and searching for a blues station.

"Don't feel sorry for Jill," said Mattie. "She'll have all the beef at the barbeque."

twelve

PAIA

They made a quick dash into Pier One and the Sports Authority before leaving the Marketplace. Jill insisted. It was her kind of store, and she was after a pair of Nike Air Pegasus when she ran into the most awesome collection of Sketchers, then checked out the tropical workout fashions and half an hour later left with bags of shoes, tights, shorts, shirts and a couple new bikinis. "There's no place like home," she said, smiling as Chloe hustled her back into the car and drove out along the north coast on a picture perfect day, past sugar cane fields, a golf course and…

"Stop. Turn left!!" Jill banged Chloe's seat. "Look at that beach…the sun…hunk heaven."

Chloe obeyed orders and pulled into Baldwin Beach, parking near the lifeguard stand.

"Oh, Chloe. Let's have a swim here." It was Mattie. They gathered up their beach gear and headed into the 'wahine' block to change. Within minutes they were slathered up and laid out on a stunning stretch of white sand, teasing each other about how pale they were. As white as Alaskans. As white as shark bellies. Other than Jill who had a base already. A cruise ship passed on the horizon, heading towards the island of Molokai. For a moment Chloe thought she could see waterspouts and a cat's paw. And the whole hydrologic cycle…just there.

"I don't know if it's hunk heaven, but it's heaven." Chloe rolled over, taking it all in and trying to find the perfect word.

Mattie and Jill ran down the beach towards the tide pools

and eventually entered the water, gingerly at first, and then jumping and splashing like spastics. The sea was unbelievably clear and warm, surprising them both. Jill had never in her life been in warm seawater before. Although she dearly loved the ocean, it had always been cold. In Santa Cruz – where she learned to surf or Manhattan Beach down in L. A., and even there she needed a wet suit. *I guess I don't know everything*, she thought, realizing how rare it was to have a thought like that. Time passed with the troika feeling their youth and good health, happy just being alive.

By mid day they put the top down and cruised on into Paia, a tiny old plantation town of small storefronts with pitched roofs and not a building over two stories, most of them old with shiplap siding and hip and gable roofs. It was the kind of town people used to live in before big cities and suburbs, the kind of town that was probably still a community.

They pulled into a parking stall near the corner and walked into the Fishmarket where they ordered fresh mahi-mahi burgers and fries. Chloe loved the place instantly. It smelled good, and she could watch the cooks as they grilled and fried, throwing up orders and shouting numbers. Although the order line snaked its way through the restaurant and nearly back to the sidewalk, it was moving quickly, and by the time they reached the counter and ordered, Jill had found places for the three of them at a long communal table by the window. In twenty minutes they were out the door and back on Baldwin Avenue. Fat and happy.

"It's starting to look like a shopping town." Mattie had spied a couple of boutiques on the way into Paia. She was right. It was a glorious town for all those great finds no one would be wearing back home, and they spent the better part of the afternoon taking advantage of every 'sale' sign, updating their wardrobes and looking for 'just a little something for tonight'.

They had already made one pass back to the car to empty their arms of shopping bags when they saw the Cakewalk

Bakery – with pumpkin & chocolate chip muffins in the window display, pulling them in. Chloe bought a bag full 'just for tasting', then asked for some recipes and a takeout menu. Her love of cooking meant her antennae were always up around food. It was how her culinary expertise developed. That and her back yard garden, the one she'd nurtured since childhood. Chloe loved that she lived in a city that had more restaurants per capita than any other. At nearly any time day or night she could dine in the trendiest gourmet in-spot or find exotic ethnicities like Tasmanian cuisine or her favorite Jamaican hole in the wall.

Licking the crumbs of gingerbread and lemon squares from their fingers, they entered The Enchantress. They nearly missed it, except for the fancy feathered masks in the window.

"Great merchandizing," Chloe said as she pulled the door open.

"Ewe. Could there be a more girly store?" Jill hesitated as she entered. It was obviously not her thing, more like a hundred eighty degrees from Sports Authority. But it was so Mattie.

"It's so romantic!" Mattie stood jaw-dropped – candles and sparkly lights and mirrors and beads, feathers and gowns, satins and embroiders. "Look at this," Mattie directed Chloe to a rack of beaded babe dresses. "Aren't they gorgeous?"

"If a woman couldn't find something here to counter the business suit, she'd be in serious trouble." Jill was being supportive, though bored with the whole scene.

"Your closet could use a few things like this, Chloe." Mattie knew Jill wouldn't touch a thing in the place but was trying to encourage Chloe into being a partner in spree.

"Yep, it's Mattie's style, but we're the ones who probably need this stuff." Jill confirmed similarities between herself and Chloe while complimenting Mattie's taste. Chloe shot Jill a smile, grateful that Jill was easing up on Mattie. She had had the talk with Jill before getting on the plane. This trip was for Mattie, and Jill needed to be more aware and back off when she would normally put some questionable spin on Mattie's naive mindset or dash her often-vulnerable sensibilities. Mattie lived in an Anne Frank mindset, thinking that deep down, in spite of everything, people were really good at heart. No one wanted to change this about her, even if it wasn't true.

"I wonder if they know where to find strappy little sandals. Babe shoes, island style."

"We have a few things." One of the goddesses behind the counter spoke up. "But Sandals in Paradise over in Kihei has the best selection. Or the outlet store nearby in the Gateway Plaza. Where ya staying?"

"We're across the island at the Fairmont," Mattie spoke up.

"The Kea Lani? Great. Where ya from?" A statuesque brunette with sparkles on her cheeks and through her hair came out from behind the counter – earrings jingling, breasts jiggling in a shimmery low-cut top – and met Mattie at the rack she was now pillaging through.

Three voices answered in unison:

"San Francisco." (Chloe)

"The Bay Area." (Mattie)

"California." (Jill)

"I used to live in Redondo Beach, down south. These are all on sale," the salesperson went on, "twenty-five percent off the tagged price. Turquoise is your color," she said, pulling a dress out from the display and holding it up against Mattie.

"Yes, I know. People always tell me I look great in this color."

"It's her eyes," said Chloe, turning to check out an angel in the glass case. It was crystal, sitting on a lotus pad, and she knew someone who would love it.

"How's this," Mattie asked, having slipped on the tiny, spaghetti-strapped, beaded blue dress, twirling around.

"Oh, honey, it's you. It's so you." Chloe hugged Mattie, twirling her around again. "Check out our girl, Jill."

"She's not my girl. She stole my man," Jill pouted, making a face. "But the dress is awesome! So hurry up and put up your plastic."

"What's your rush, Jill? We're slowing down here, remember? Island time."

"Oh, yea, Chloe. Like you're slowing down. I've never seen you move so fast. You gotta date already with a stranger you just met. For you, that's fast." Chloe had a number of relationships since leaving university, none too serious, except Paris, but that one burned out as fast as it caught fire, and everyone knows that whatever you do out of the country doesn't count. Mostly she worked too hard to pay proper attention, and there was always something. Often her dad or even her mom didn't like them, and for some reason that made a difference, and since her father died she couldn't begin to commit to anything.

"I'll know when I meet Mr. Right. Not Mr. Perfect, mind you, but Mr. Right for me. I know I will. I just haven't yet."

"Jill, don't give Chloe a hard time. You're the man magnet of all time. I never knew anyone who went through men like you do. Not that you can't play the field, but you don't need to own it." Mattie took a rare stand in defense of Chloe then smiled, realizing she had indeed stolen Jill's man. "But I am appreciative of your tutelage and instruction."

thirteen

HO'OKIPA

Halfway down the block they found a bank with an ATM in front, and they would have continued their spree if Chloe hadn't insisted they stick to the plan. Herding them back into the convertible, she continued driving along the beach road, coming quickly to Ho'okipa, the windsurfing capitol of the world. Turning in, Jill went crazy.

"Let me out. Let me out!!" She leapt from the car and, grabbing her binoculars, lopped towards the water's edge where dozens of windsurfers gathered, heading in or out with dozens more out beyond the shore break, kite sailing and windsurfing.

"Now we're talking," she called back. "Come on."

"Go ahead, Mattie. I need to get my camera and lock up the car."

"Great idea," she replied. "In fact this whole trip was a great idea. It is so good to be away from our dreary city. Say, have you seen my sunscreen? I had it at the last beach." Mattie fumbled around the car, feeling under the seats and finally dumping her entire bag out to no avail.

"Yep, glad I brought my camera today. Everything's so technicolor. Look at the quality of light, the purity in the atmosphere. The blues are bluer. Skin tones are not only more tan but more alive. Pinch me. I'm in paradise." Chloe was effusing again as she and Mattie joined Jill at the water's edge along with remnants of waves, licking their toes. Jill was already engaged in conversation with a well-built, streaky-blonde surfer, rigging up his sail. He was busy explaining the different breaks,

and why the wind was better at the west end and surf better –
"see where the surfers are?" pointing to the far end of the bay –
on the east side.

"Oh, I get it," Jill returned. "And all the cute guys are at
this end." Her lids started their conditioned flutter.

It went right over surfer dude's head. Or he was used to
come-ons from beautiful woman and just didn't get it.

"Are you staying around here?"

"Nope, we're across at the Fairmont."

"Gnarly. Do you do yoga?"

"No, but I lift weights. Does that count?" Jill shrugged.

"Oh sure, it's just that you have the body…"

"Now who's flirting?"

"Not. Just telling it like it is. It takes a lot to keep in shape.
Not that great bodies can't have good minds…"

"Yes, there is that stereotype." Jill was being unusually
agreeable, but Dan was oblivious to it all as he continued an
unneeded defense.

"Actually I went to UH for a while and worked in my
uncle's business, but now I'm on the circuit."

"How good is that?!" Chloe approached. "Can I get your
name?" She immediately became a journalist, shooting a few
pictures of the obvious star, some with Jill hanging on him,
sucking in her non-existent stomach. Then she broke into an
interview, so within minutes they had the draft of his life story
– Kama'aiana kid makes good in alternative lifestyle – and knew
he was single, came from a big name local family, and had
bagged nearly half a million total in last year's purses and
endorsements.

"Nice work," Jill whispered to Chloe. "How come we've
never tried that before?"

"Don't be cynical, Jill. I really am doing some freelance
work while I'm here. Just for practice. One never knows."

"Anything we shouldn't miss while here on Maui?" Mattie
asked Dan.

"Well," he looked at Jill, brushing her perky little nose, "I wouldn't miss a date with me. How about tonight? I'll pick you up in my new beamer. We'll do something fun."

"We actually already have plans tonight...some party upcountry, but tomorrow would be great."

"Give me your room number or cell, and I'll call you in the morning." He tucked it into some sort of waterproof container and headed back to the shore. "'Loha," he shouted back.

"How easy was that?" said Mattie as she and Jill retreated to a little spot she had carved in the sand while Chloe circled the cove, shooting a few more photos. "I've seen you in action dozens of times, but it seems to get easier and smoother every time. How do you do it?"

"I guess he's okay. Famous name and all that. Sure is cute enough."

"And fast enough. It must be a pastime here, local guys picking up tourists. You'd think the local girls would be enough. They're everywhere and they're all goddesses. Have you ever seen such gorgeous women?"

"Hey, I'm the bi," said ?Jill. "I'm surprised you even notice."

"How could I not? They're all sporting bikinis and the most fab bodies."

"Yoga," was all Jill said, scanning the beach approvingly. Jill had enjoyed a generous sexual appetite since she was sixteen. Her first orgasm was with a high school girlfriend. They had been studying all things sexual through their health class books and others they found at the public library and were experimenting one day. Through her University years she was an avowed bisexual, having both boyfriends and girlfriends. One of the latter she was admittedly in love with, but Ginger left school midway through their junior year when she found out she was pregnant. Jill was heartbroken for about a month, and after then she was mostly into guys, but she called herself 'bi' for the political correctness of it all, and occasionally a girl would still turn her head.

"Anyone interesting?" Mattie asked.

"Red bikini four o'clock," said Jill. "Tom cruise missile at six."

"Got it. Mmmm."

"Yoga, black shorts," Chloe registered one.

"Ponytail coming this way. Well hello, Maryanne."

They spoke in shorthand the way old friends do, finishing each other's sentences, laughing in all the right places, and using exclamations for emphasis. Not that any of them were hard of hearing, but sometimes they had to stretch to be heard; they had such busy lives and cluttered minds.

"Rock and roll!" It was Jill's way of saying she'd stayed too long already. She'd seen the whales on the horizon, watched the windsurfers come and go and figured out exactly how they carved those particular definitions in their bodies, captured enough sun (all the while filtering it through SPF-30) on her delicate winter skin.

Nothing from the others. No response. No motion. Mattie was asleep, and Chloe wrote in her journal:

Like a freight train it came again, building as board monkeys jockeyed for prime position. Then it's there, and they jump on, hitchhiking on air like gods from some Greek hallucination myth. She wrote a surf legend that included whales and whitecaps and a sky so blue it was (for long, steady moments) the truest thing she knew. For awhile she even thought she could hear secret, sacred whale communications. White herons circled, and children danced along the shoreline, and another train came and coffee-colored angels disappeared in the ride.

"I said let's rock and roll. Let's blow this joint." Jill stood next to Chloe now. "Don't we want to babe up before the party?"

"I imagine we do. I could definitely use some prettying up after all this sand and saltwater. I'm positively briny." All three had ventured out between sets, swimming from one end of the bay to the other, hugging close to the shore to avoid the breakers. Jill had even talked herself into a windsurfing lesson with Danny (what kind of guy used a child's name?) Baldwin, famous windsurfer. It had humbled her deeply and sent her gratefully back to her beach towel.

"I'm rested now," Mattie said in a whisper. "The most important part of prettying up is beauty rest. My mama always said girls past puberty need naps."

"Yea, and your mama said to save yourself til marriage, but you haven't got much in that bank." Jill had taunted her old schoolmate for so long, she didn't even notice it. Indeed she had always adored Mattie for her sweetness, the innocent way she made her way through the same challenges that made herself and others cynical and often defeated. When she thought of the perfect woman...for her, it was Mattie-clones she thought of, looked for, in the seasons she was down on men.

"You should talk, Jill." Chloe was defending Mattie again. "You've borrowed out so much you're near bankruptcy."

"Ha ha. Now you're funny. I probably don't do it with guys much more than you two virgins, but I do girls too. So that accounts for a little extra. But my mama said..."

"This'll be good," Chloe chuckled.

"My mama said (again for emphasis)...all you need is love."

"Except that was John or Paul, not Ruby Van."

"Yea, but she got it right. So let's move...love's a waitin'."

"And it's right here," Mattie got up, brushing off the sand and grabbing Chloe. "Come on, Jill. Group hug. Isn't everything just divine?"

"No complaint, saint," said Jill, shaking sand out of her towel and moving towards a little love. Chloe buried herself in, watching the distance as seabirds circled and another set rolled predictably in. It was as if all of Maui was embracing her. *Not unrequited,* she noted.

"Hugs and freight trains. I have gone to heaven."

fourteen

UPCOUNTRY

"Hey, you made it." It was Michael. "I was beginning to wonder if my map was off." The party was just picking up steam when the girls arrived, but there were so few women that they drew immediate attention from a dozen or so men who had already had a couple of drinks.

"Here's your date," Jill delivered Mattie to Michael with a little wink, noting how tempting he looked tonight. *Political capital. I'm building political capital,* she thought. "The directions were fine. Now where's that open bar?"

"What would you like," he said, always the gentleman. "I'll get drinks."

"I'll have a chardonnay," said Mattie, giving Michael her most demure, I-like-you-already look and squeezing his hand. He definitely took her mind off Tom, and looking forward fit her personality far better than looking back. It's just that before now she didn't have much to look forward to, hence the wallowing.

"And a couple rum and cokes," Jill ordered for Chloe who looked about for Jed, wondering if he would make it. Jill was scanning the gathering, pleased to be dateless and therefore free to choose whatever male caught her fancy. It looked promising already.

They congregated on the side lawn of an old Hawaiian estate, which was two-stories, with an eight-foot verandah that encircled three fourths of the home. It had dormers on each end and a heavy shake hip roof. The lights inside looked like an old Christmas card, and they imagined a house filled with families and celebrations. Births and deaths and growing pains. The hosted bar was set up in the breezeway separating the house from a huge four-car garage, with a stable at the far end. The whole scene was lit with torches and twinkle lights, strung tree to tree.

"Hi, Chloe," Jed said, approaching from across the garden. "I'm feeling a little out of place amongst all these cowboys, but like most writers, I guess I'm always doing research."

"Well you look like a cowboy to me. Glad you made it," said Chloe, wondering what kind of person says 'amongst' yet moving towards him and giving him her signature kiss on the cheek. In Paris she kissed twice, sometimes three times, but her habit since childhood had been a single kiss on the right cheek. It was a family thing.

She re-introduced Jed to the girls and to Michael who was already back with drinks.

"I only know one soul here," said Jed. "What kind of group is this?"

"It's all the ag guys – environmental wonks, U of H and County Administration. I'm a consultant here on the County's dime. Actually I think the state's picking up the tab or most of it to catch some federal funds. Seems they have a problem with frogs and a kind of plant that grows above four thousand feet. Invasive stuff. Miconia is degrading the diversity in Maui's rain forests, eroding the natural watershed. Fireweed management is tough too, and there's the diamondback moth, ruining cabbage crops. Then there's always the challenge of controlling fruit flies and GMOs. Genetic engineering's sort of run amuck here on Maui, and the voters are not happy."

"Coqui frogs. They drive me crazy." Jed found a kindred soul. "We've tried all sorts of things to eliminate them. We've even mobilized the citizenry to use citric acid, but without a natural predator, we're swatting at flies. They're only two inches long but sound like foghorns; they eat insects but not mossies. Can you fix them?"

"We're working on it. Doing an assessment of all the species that have come in during the last ten years or become noticeable during that timeframe. Everyone's worried about the havoc to Maui's fragile ecosystem."

My hero, Mattie thought, approving of his efforts and his career. Tom had been a stock wonk and struck her as never committed to anything except the bottom line – his bottom line. He had always struggled with ethical dilemmas. *Like lying to me.*

"La di da..." Jill rolled her eyes. "You kids have a fun time with all this talk. I'm off on a hunt. Gotta find me an invasive specie of my own. Is specie the singular of species?"

She drifted off towards the bar, keen on a man standing with the in-crowd surrounding the Mayor. It was obvious who was the Mayor; everyone was kowtowing to him. And it was, after all, his party.

Her target was tall and beefy and looked completely at home in cowboy boots. His nametag read: "Andy Olsen".

"You don't look Norwegian," she said, investigating his dark brown eyes.

He turned from his conversation. "I'm not. Well, I guess a part. From way back. Mostly I'm Portuguese. Got a good dose of Hawaiian a couple of generations back too, and it's been all poi since."

Jill cocked her face to one side, a little confused by his terminology.

"Poi – all mixed up. Andy," he said, extending his hand. "Andy Olsen, sixth district. Are you with the County?" His dark eyes pierced right through her like heat. Then his generous mouth crooked into a broad smile.

"No, I'm Jill and I'm apparently with you. Formerly of San Francisco." She laughed deep-throated and slightly embarrassed. It was so like her to blast right into a conversation without properly accessing the situation first.

"This is our Mayor, Alan Kimura." Andy introduced them, then ignored her questionable manners and took her arm, leading her away towards the food table. "I'm starved. How about you?"

"I'm always hungry, and thanks for the save. I don't do proper decorum very well. Protocol and all that. Too used to being my own boss I guess. Was I supposed to curtsey?" she fumbled and snickered. "And what is it you do, Andy?"

"I'm a retired rancher. I'm running for the State House later this year, and I sure could use your vote." He winked at her and grabbed two plates.

It was typical upcountry barbeque fare: a whole pig (cooked underground in an imu), roasted chickens and turkeys and a couple slabs of beef, elk burgers, Portuguese sausage, wild boar, and a few salads on the side. A half a dozen pots of sticky white rice, but mostly meat.

"It's a low-carb dream," said Jill. "Manly fare."

"My brother and I caught the boar," Andy gloated. "Try some."

She let him feed her, opening her lips, licking them. "Well, gosh, we don't have any hunters back home. I'm a city girl." She tilted her head just so. "And I didn't even know there were wild things on the island. I guess I thought it all came sanitized in neat styrofoam packages or served with tiny little umbrellas."

"Nope. We've got real cowboys and ranchers and farmers. We raise real cattle and pigs and goats and..."

"We're not eating baby goats are we?" Jill was beginning to pick through the slabs of animal carcass the servers had piled on her plate.

"Don't worry, little lady, I'll let you know when they dish out the mountain oysters. Now come over here and tell me about yourself." He led her to a table and began coming on to her in such a way that she couldn't tell if he wanted her vote or her body.

Mattie had managed to get a little time with Michael, who was still in work mode, mixing with the pols and responding to queries from the agriculture guys.

"I'm sorry," he said, turning his attention back to Mattie. It was an honest apology. "I just get so caught up in my stuff. Especially when others are seriously seeking information. It is after all an election year, and information is power. Can I get you another drink?" A broad smile illuminated his ruggedly handsome face. Mattie noticed each nuance, loving the beautiful low lilt of his voice, how it caressed.

Michael gently slid his hand in hers and led her towards the bar. It was his way of saying he was ready to hang with her now.

fifteen

REAL ESTATE

Chloe and Jed wandered off towards the house, where they sat on an aging wood slat swing, hanging on the wide verandah. "It's night-blooming jasmine," Jed said when she commented about the saccharine scent. It reminded her of exotic palaces and peacocks, intimate nights with incense, sheiks and bedouins. "Another drink?"

"I can't do rum and coke. It's just too sweet."

"How about a Maui Sunrise? Your place or mine?" It was his attempt at humor. "Actually I think I put a couple of those in one of my books. But seriously, I'd suggest the red. Our host is a wine snob, and the wines are bound to be good. Plus I love red wine."

"Thanks, Jed. Reds are my favorite too. Ever since Paris." Light banter wove into Chloe's trip to France, her tortured artist's soul and her work-a-day life in real estate brokerage.

"You won't believe it. I'm a realtor too. Or was, a few years back before my books starting selling. You think your soul is tortured. Wait til you try to get something published. It's worse than divorce." He had been twice divorced, and it showed in tired little lines around his bear-brown eyes and the way he carried his shoulders. He wore a Panama hat so unless Chloe tried, she didn't notice the slump to his eyebrows – a sure sign of holding some secret burden. They observed each other as writers do. *He carries more baggage than the average train.*

"I thought because I knew how to write, I could be a writer," he continued. "But you need to know the business of writing, not just the creative part. First person contacts help. And a lot of plain old fashioned luck."

"But aren't there more books and movies being made all the time?"

"Yep, and more competition for agents and publishers. And just when you thought Time Warner was a great entertainment/cable/movie company, it got in the book business. I think they publish more than the big houses now. Still you'll need an agent."

"Well, I need a book first, don't I?"

"No, not unless it's fiction. That's actually how I broke in. With a non-fiction book about how to buy tropical real estate."

"Is it a secret? Isn't it the same everywhere?"

"Not really. It changes state to state, and of course it's way different in Tahiti, Fiji, other places I've worked."

"Seriously, you've worked outside the states?"

"Did about fifteen years peddling all over the South Pacific. Sometimes the highest and best use for a plot of land was that it held the earth together. I ran into a coup or two, had some tribal leaders unilaterally take properties, lots of shenanigans. I had these clients a few years back from Newport Beach, some upscale place in southern California. He'd made millions on a tech company, and his dream was to own an island. We had a consultation in which I advised places to avoid, along with other things. You know – what to do, what not to do. I thought he retained me for my expertise in the islands."

"But he thought he was god's gift to investment, so he made his way solo to the Marshall Islands – one of the places I said to avoid like the plague – and negotiated himself a small atoll, thirteen islands of bird sanctuary circling a shallow lagoon. Thirteen should have been a clue, but like everything else, he missed the signs and instead penned a lease, then moved container loads of construction materials, commercial kitchens and dive chambers across the globe to build his Pacific dream resort. It turned into a bloody nightmare when one of the chiefs came forward saying he had not and would not sign the lease. It went all the way to the Supreme Court. The finding was the kicker. The court ruled that the lease was valid, i. e. the tribal chiefs could keep his millions, but he could not develop. He lost everything "

"Called me six months later with his tail between his legs on the fierce end of a bitter divorce – she never shared his dream and decided to stay close to Rodeo Drive before he blew his millions. Last time I heard about Spencer, he'd spent the last of his money overpaying for a freehold island in Fiji and was seeking Japanese money to help develop it, living like a hermit on his deserted island, catching fish and occasionally having supplies flown in. Growing old alone."

"People still can't understand why I left my career. I think I just got tired of it all. The money was good; I loved the lifestyle, but I missed my children…from my first marriage. They're here on Maui, a son and a daughter, both teenagers now. I wanted to be back here after living in Tahiti for a few years and Fiji for two. I lost a couple of big sales there during the coup, but had a bonanza of listings afterwards – expats fleeing for the last time – and some of the best resort properties in that nation. But I always wanted to write."

"Me too," Chloe smiled. "Always."

"And with a little saved up, I figured there was no time like the present. So I dumped most of the inventory and came back to Maui on a one-year sabbatical – to test-drive my obsession with words. That was six years ago."

Chole commented, "I took over my Dad's brokerage company when he died. He was third generation real estate, and I'd worked there part-time since I was fourteen. I guess I felt it would be disloyal or something to leave. So I've stayed…for years. I know I can't do either part time."

"How many agents do you have?"

"Forty-seven last count. We're a pretty small company for our market."

"And you're the managing partner?"

"Yep. Buck stops here." Chloe smiled again, shaking her long locks and tucking wayward curls behind her ear. "My mother owns half the company, but golf's her thing now, and I just have to be there. All the time. You know the game, Jed."

"Well, Chloe, you really don't. You could hire a broker to manage the sales agents and/or the company. You could sell shares in the company to your agents then let them hire someone. You could probably sell the company altogether for a nice sum."

"But I need to decide if I definitely want another life, don't I? I mean I have to be absolutely sure I want to get out of real estate."

"That was tough for me too. I was addicted to the deal."

"Spot on. It's beyond the money and the fame. It's the rush," Chloe remembered, as she often did, what she really loved about her job. "There are rational reasons workaholics work so much, but the real skinny is that they love their work. I certainly do. But you're right; I have all sorts of choices."

"Maybe you could try some time off. Hire a replacement for your work (or a couple as was my case) and give yourself time to write and figure it all out. Keep your license current. That way you can always jump back into the game without having lost too much traction."

"I guess you know the ropes. I could use a mentor in all this."

"Find a writing group, a coach too. Give yourself every possible reason to succeed. My guess is you'll get the rush of writing and never go back to what seems now like a pretty great job. I mean I worked all over the Pacific. I brokered little boutique resorts and private islands. Talk about a great job! Still, all I wanted was to write. I used to write waiting for little puddle jumpers, while stuck on an outer island or not able to photograph because of a downpour. I actually wrote my first novel during one of the busiest years of my life. I traveled to forty islands that year and closed three hotel deals, a couple of New Zealand wineries, and a rosewood forest in Papua New

Guinea. Still, waiting in thatched huts for a launch or at a runway's edge for a delayed plane gave me plenty of time. Start where you are. Do what you can. And eventually you'll find your way."

"That's so encouraging. Most of my friends do everything they can to talk me out of leaving my career. I'm not sure I'm ready, but I guess it's okay to plant seeds for the future."

"Everyone envied my job, and I loved it too, but I think if you discover another mission it's acceptable to switch horses mid stream. I mean we can swim, can't we?"

"Entrepreneurs always believe in the future. It's in the blood. Besides I've always landed on my feet before."

"Are you still talking farm animals?" Mattie approached. She and Michael had pecked at their food, talking softly about friends and family and things important to both. "We're going to take off. There's some jazz down the road, and Michael says he's been hanging with the guys twelve hours already today. He'll get me home."

"Have fun, sweetie. I'll tell Jill – who hasn't been seen since arrival. Did you see her?"

"I wasn't looking," Mattie admitted, looking happy. "Catch you later."

"Aloha, Mattie. Michael. Nice to meet you both." Jed said.

I like a guy with manners. Chloe thought. *You don't find them very often. At least the guys I know. They're so into themselves, they hardly notice anyone else. How refreshing – a real man. A nice man. Oh girl, be careful. You just met this guy. He lives on Maui. You're in SF. Whoa, future tripping already…I'm pulling a Mattie…and I just met the guy!*

She leaned into Jed's shoulder, speechless for a change, took a deep soundless breath and relaxed into the moment.

sixteen

M & M

Mattie and Michael enjoyed a sweet evening. You would think they might; the ingredients were good – initial chemistry and attraction, geographical desirability, gemstone eyes, not to mention mind melding and electricity. Still they had all the hurdles to jump through when boy meets girl, and as both had already learned, nearly everything conspires to keep couples from succeeding.

Her parents had divorced when she was only eleven, so although they each started behaving better once separated, her mom and dad continued to hold grudges, and the kids were collateral. It got better over time, but Mattie's over-reaction still was to trust everyone, give them the benefit of the doubt, hang in and hold on, even in the light of a coming disaster. She had suspected from about three months into her relationship with Tom that a stage five hurricane was coming and would eventually break down the levees she had carefully constructed to keep out the flood.

One cannot spend forever in denial, despite the occasional comfort it allows. So she spent the weeks since last seeing Tom trying to understand more lucidly where she got caught up, where the faulty bricks and mortar had kept her levy from holding. Not that knowledge is any protection from future relationship disasters, but at least she carried the immunity of the recently separated, so she was not afraid. But was there a beginning or end to her confusion? Or the cluster of emotions that gathered in her heart and hid behind aqua eyes?

"Earth to Mattie," Michael brought her back with his syncopated bass voice and a hand, placed carefully on her forearm. She was somewhere between a new realization of her strength and a jazz riff that caught her by surprise. They both loved jazz. If truth were told, she loved blues more, but the music was sensual and hot enough to melt any insecurities, any hesitations.

She leaned in and focused on his face, square and balanced, lovely without being too pretty. She wiped foam off his upper lip.

"Cappuccino." She softened, brushing his lip again just for the heck of it and because it quivered ever so subtly when she did.

"How can I spend the week with you when you're here with your friends and I'm working?" He wanted more already. Had since their first meeting. Had carried that longing around with him all day, through meetings and research and knuckling down.

"I think we'll find ways," Mattie glowed. She could feel his desire. No one had wanted her this much in years. Not Tom anyway. She knew he hadn't, but she had invented in her mind that he had, so by the time she finally realized he didn't, she had forgotten that he hadn't all along. She didn't count the endless lookers, the guys where she featured as lead fantasy, men in bars or on the streets or popping in and out of the agency, undressing her and taking her to dark foreign places in their minds.

"I don't think we have anything planned for tomorrow, but sometime this week we're going to Hana and spending the night with an uncle of Jill's friend."

"Let me know when. I have a day's worth of work in Hana, so maybe we can hook up there. And I'm free tomorrow night, so how about dinner?"

"I'd love to, Michael. Maybe I'll even eat. All that meat sort of turned me off, being vegetarian and all, although I've lived on rice and salad before."

"You didn't say you were veggie," Michael was pleasantly surprised. "Me too. I guess I just thought you were picky. I know a great veggie Vietnamese joint. We'll eat a real meal tomorrow. Promise."

"It's after midnight; maybe I'd better get back. And you need sleep too." *Good thing I got my beauty rest* sailed through her thoughts like a golden heroine in a Peter Max drawing, and she was off in some reverie again. Neon tracers every spectrum in the color wheel trailed after the sailboat, leaving reflections in the water from cosmic clouds drifting across a marmalade sky. Thoughts interrupted her pictorial fantasy and jumped to this sudden stranger and why he seemed so like someone she'd known forever. She didn't believe in love at first sight, having never experienced it nor seen it work out in the long term for those who had, but even non-believers get swept up in that precariously delicious force that brings souls, mates or not, into harmony.

"I'm sorry. I can't seem to focus." She apologized. "Did you slip something in my drink?"

"Yea, it's my secret love potion," Michael joked. "It opens brain synapses and floods them with dopamine."

"I'm serious. And I haven't had that much to drink. Is it possible for the body to feel jetlag two days later?"

"No. It must be something else. Go with it. I'll take care of you." Michael was a nurturer. Rare for a scientist, but bred into him at a very young age. It was always Mikey and his mom against the world, so caring and sharing came naturally. He had a brilliant, scientific mind yet remained completely open to the mystery. Like work ethic engenders rationality, once he understood the love ethic, he could not help but open to mystery. He was a mystery himself. And everyone he knew and nearly everything he knew. Most of his mentors and almost all of his students believed in inexplicables. Now here before him was a mystery so precious he just wanted to treasure it, open to it, believe again.

After leaving the club and the club sodas, they returned to

the Fairmont and walked along to the sound of violet waves caressing the beach for nearly an hour. When they saw the lights of the hotel not far in the distance, Michael finally wrapped his arms around Mattie, snuggling into her hair, which smelled like fresh ginger and kiwi honey. They stood in the sand, holding each other, quietly impelled by a vast conspiracy of stars, which, curving around them, reflected in the flat sea and joined them inexorably to each other, the cosmos, and their silent, brilliant conspirators.

It was nearly three a.m. before Mattie finally kissed Michael for the very, very very, very very very last time and knocked quietly on the door to the suite.

She had forgotten her key card.

seventeen

ROOM 1210

Chloe was up early the next morning, at the desk, clicking away at her keyboard when Jill woke.

"You have a million messages," Chloe said in a whisper, pointing to the telephone.

"Good morning to you too. Didn't we have fun last night with all the cowboys?

"In a minute, Jill. I'm handling some work for the office. Deadlines. At least we have wireless access up here."

Jill walked over to the phone and punched '7' for messages. She listened all the way through before scribbling them on the logo'd note pad. There were ten, seven for her: Kimo, Kimo, Dan, Lori, Kimo, front desk, Eli, Andy, Jo, and Michael.

Kimo wanted another date, had to see her, then called again, 'just in case I forgot to give you my cell number'. Dan wanted to take her to dinner and the movies Wednesday after the surf meet. 'I hope you can make it' was followed by a number and 'you're a hot babe for a city girl'. Lori, Chloe's PA, left a long, line item, bulleted message, which Jill assumed Chloe was on to, working furiously on her laptop over in the corner. Kimo again, from the pool cabaña, 'I miss you, call me.' He sounded a little frantic then gave his uncle's number again to book excursions and a room in Hana.

Leilani, the front desk clerk, had found a gold bracelet near the pool with M. Wilson engraved on the back and was surprised to find a guest in house with that name. 'Would

81

Mathilda please call the front desk?'

Eli, Jill's website assistant, left a long message in tech-speak about busted motherboards and a server failing just when the other needed regular maintenance, and asking if he should do it anyway, putting them a day behind on their workload, or what?

Cowboy Andy called to say what an enjoyable time he had with Jill and wondering out loud when he could see her again. He left his cell number.

Jolene, Mattie's aunt, went on and on wondering 'how you three are doing' and reminding Mattie she had not called to confirm arrival...'not that you forgot...or that it's even important, but we still want to know. So call us: 415-337-8287' – as if Mattie didn't know her own office number.

The last message was from Michael at four a.m. Deep and slow. "Yesterday was a miracle...or maybe it was you. Thanks, Mattie. I'll call from the lobby tonight around seven. Have an awesome day...unless you have other plans."

"I heard that," Mattie said, awake now, and insistent: "Play it again then save it, would you, Jill?"

"Mattie has a boyfriend. Mattie has a boyfriend," Jill taunted her.

"It's way too early for that," Chloe shot a look at Jill, "and good morning, sleepyhead. Was it good for you two?"

"It was amazing," Mattie replied. "I'm a smitten kitten."

"Well then we all had fun. Jed nearly talked me into selling my company before plying me with too much red wine and trying every which way to get me to go home with him."

"She didn't. She came home with me. Slept with me even." Jill wished. Mattie had won the straw pull for the separate bed, so Jill and Chloe shared the king.

"You're such a tease this morning. Didn't Andy make a move?"

"Well, yes actually, but I decided since I was more into surfer Dan, I'd save myself for him. I mean have you EVER seen a body like that?"

"Which one was Dan?" Mattie asked, thinking back to

Kimo's friends and all the other guys they'd met since arriving. *Has Jill ever saved herself?*

"The surfing Baldwin. The Ho'okipa Hunk."

"Oh. I thought you were into Kimo. Now I'm all confused."

"Dan's a Kimo with family money. Besides, he speaks better English." *Not much better,* she thought, *but at least I can understand him.*

Chloe closed her laptop and turned around. "You call that English? Okay, Moe and Larry, who's on first? What's on the itinerary today?"

"I need serious beauty rest," said Mattie. "I think I was out pretty late."

"Two forty-seven," Chloe said. "A. M. And why don't you pick up a spare card key when you retrieve your bracelet."

"Wha…" Mattie looked down at her bare left arm. "Where'd you find it?"

"The hotel staff found it on the beach. They're holding it for you at the front desk."

"Oh, thank gawd. Dad gave me that for my twenty-first birthday."

"I think we need to decide IF we're going to Hana and WHEN. Otherwise Kimo will keep calling, and I really got my fill of him the other day. Don't get me wrong; he's a nice guy, but now I have better fish to fry." Jill winked, "so I'd best get busy."

"How about Thursday-Friday for Hana? We can stay over Thursday night." Chloe was making an attempt at organizing the group which, now that their options were growing exponentially, might find it difficult to schedule at all if they didn't *do it now.*

"I'm good with that. Michael has to go there and wants to meet me. I'll call him after you've made the reservations."

"What if Dan wants to see me then?"

"Jill, that is so NOT you…waiting for a guy to call." Now even Mattie was calling Jill on her nonsense.

"Just call each one and schedule at your will. They're all at your beck and call anyway. Then call Kimo and have him arrange it with his uncle. It will give him something to do other than leaving multiple messages for you."

"Good idea, Chloe. I'll just put on my littlest thong bikini and get down poolside and nurse my hangover from all those bull shots. That way I can kill two birds...actually three if you count working on my tan. You know me, living on the edge."

"That's your cliché limit for the day, Jill. So let's meet for lunch by the pool at around one. I still have some business to take care of and some writing to do. I scheduled a massage for eleven, and Mattie looks like she's back to bed."

Jill left in the tiniest little swatch of fabric, determined to be a total flirt with Kimo, arrange free lodging in Hana, chase away her hangover with a few bloody marys (comped by Kimo or any other pool guy worth his salt) and work on her tan, which, thanks to a couple of days in the sun already, was coming along quite nicely. Today's aim was to expose even more skin, while keeping it all covered with spf-30. After all she wanted to tan, not burn.

eighteen

PLACES

Chloe tucked Mattie in, re-closed the blackout drapes, and took her notebook out on the lanai. The view was astonishing. She scanned the horizon for whales, spotting a pair within a minute and watching them fin, breach and spout for nearly a quarter of an hour. *It's mesmerizing,* she thought, finally opening her pen. The Sultan of Egypt had invented the fountain pen over a thousand years ago. Mont Blanc perfected it. If Chloe was writing, she figured she'd better start with perfection. Taking a deep gardenia-infused breath, she dove straight into a fresh page.

Before long she had journaled the entire trip from Saturday morning, exaggerating moments which took her breath away. Or can one exaggerate the superlative? It seemed a lifetime of endless moments since arriving in this magical place. Chloe thought of paradise and wondered why some places have holds on us and others don't and why some trips are more like pilgrimages. She scribbled 'Paradox of Place' in the margin, remembering a trip her Dad took to New Zealand while he was still alive. It was a story that so defined her dad it had become her own.

He told her on a vibrant summer Sunday while they were weeding together in the kitchen garden, waxing on about how awesome it all was down under, especially a side trip he'd taken. *What was the name of that tree, the Father of the Forest?* Chloe's dad, having always had a mad love affair with redwoods and other trees, insisted on taking a back highway to see a famed kauri tree. Tilly knew better than to argue so they drove two hours out of their way to a dusty parking lot in a small forest grove where he rushed down a pathway – while Tilly looked around for a noted refreshment stand. He walked for ten minutes through a meager stand of trees, a poor excuse for a forest but abundant with tree ferns and flowers. "You *could* see the forest through the trees," he had emphasized. Just when he was thinking of all the other forests he'd visited, each a hundred times more memorable than this, he turned a corner…and lost his breath.

There, across a small fern glen, stood a tree so massive, so unimaginable, so alive, he couldn't move from the sheer presence of it – a phenomenon, pulsing there in the clearing. A giant alien creature. A tree you could bungee jump from. The yang of trees. As he stood silent for minutes his breath eventually came back, in fact seemed to synch with the tree – Te Matua Ngahere, 'father of the forest' – and a whole moving universe. Then Tilly came running up, guidebook in hand, reminding him that thirty-seven species of birds lived in that tree.

Though she had never visited in person, Chloe thought of that tree and of Stonehenge, the pyramids, Crater Lake and Machu Picchu – and a place she had visited once in Oregon where some sort of vortex conspired to make things appear as physical laws said they couldn't. She thought of Santa Fe and Shasta and other places that had unusual pull, especially for artists. The Great Astrolabe.

A lilting breeze caressed her curls, sun-streaked already, and she tossed her head, re-focusing on the scene before her. In one breath she was back to the present. She heard shrieks of joy from a couple of children down at the pool. When she listened deeper, she could hear the ping ping of tennis balls on a court she hadn't yet noticed. She made a mental note (to-do lists were a habit) to get Mattie or Jill out for a game later on. The beach beyond the pool and cabañas glistened by the magic of mid-morning sunlight, and beyond, a wide swatch of aqua melted into true blue then cobalt, out where it cut a fine line joining the sky – which was robin's egg blue and perfectly cloudless.

How fortunate we are. She grabbed a thought, finding it impossible to look and listen without editorializing. Still it was worth the exercise, and she went back to her breath, which had a way of taking her back to feelings and a more intuitive way of seeing the world. *I'm tanning* she thought. *And need a manicure!* She looked again at her hands, even more critically, remembering now that she had not had time for one before leaving, and Mattie had mentioned getting manis and pedis on the island. She wrote: 'manicure appointments' and 'tennis' on her pad, thinking all the while *not very creative. Maybe I'm not a writer after all.*

Mattie joined her with a tray of coffee and danish she ordered from room service on re-awakening. "It's Chad," she said, handing Chloe the phone then whispering "from the club".

"Good morning, Chad. What's up?" *He probably is. Gawd, I hope he doesn't ask me out.*

"Just thinking about you. Got any time this week?" *Damn.*

"We've planned most of it already, Chad. Let me see what I can do, okay?" *Don't hold your breath.*

"Call me then," he said and hung up without waiting for a response or leaving a number, obviously used to rejection.

Chloe put down the phone and turned to Mattie. "Remember that guy a few years ago who registered a star in my name?"

Mattie set the tray down on the table and poured Chloe a cup, black. "Wasn't that Glen or Ben or something?" She took a bite of cherry danish.

"Glen. Cute, sort of nerdy guy. Crazy about me."

"And?"

"And it was a sweet gesture and all that, but I never warmed up to him. He reminds me a little of Chad and all the other guys who like me, but I'm not into them. At all. It's like my responders are off or something." She took a sip and then another once she realized it wasn't too hot.

"We can't help who we fall for, who we're attracted to. Your Mr. Right for You will come. Or he won't. No use worrying about the ones who don't do it for you. I mean just look." She swept her arm across the view. "It is so gorgeous here, Maui could be Mr. Right."

"I never thought it would be this obvious," Chloe said, fully diverted. "I guess I always imagined some saint at the gate, checking us in. Not immediate entrance to a wholly golden world."

She finished her cup and poured another. "So how was Michael, really? Other than smart, cute and completely into you."

"Chloe, I think I'm in love. Don't you dare tell Jill. She'll spoil it all, but talk about immediate. Well you saw the sparks at Borders. They ignited into the sweetest fire. Not a conflagration, mind you. We are behaving. But like a glowing cocoon, holding us in, warm and inseparable. We breathe each other's breath and hang on every word. His eyes are peacock, the greenest green, a meadow I melt into every time. The tiniest flecks of grey frame his face, that face I've known forever. It never mattered before that I liked someone's politics, not like you, but there he is – on the right side of everything. And his voice. Oh my god, his creamy vocal chords vibrate just right. He's a melody. A symphony."

"Yes, but does he pass the kiss test?" The three had come up with a kiss test years before, around the kitchen table after Jill complained one night about her date being a horrible kisser.

"That's an oxymoron," Chloe had argued. Jill went on, "but a good kisser's a good hummer." Before long they had delved into the science behind great kissing, finally coming up with a sliding scale, which had held through copious dates, boyfriends, and the test of time.

"A ten," Mattie said, quietly and without fanfare. "A ten plus. To say I'm over Tom would be a gross understatement."

Chloe had never seen Mattie like this. "Are you sure, honey? We don't want to be saving you from your saving trip."

"He's my savior, Chloe, and it's all good." She smiled broadly, a smile that explained everything to Chloe.

"I believe, Mattie, I believe. Now pass me an almond croissant and another refill." She picked up her pen, poem in mind. "I'm trying to save myself here."

nineteen

BLISS

Mattie was leaving as the massage therapist arrived. She showed her in, calling to Chloe on the lanai.

"Aloha," the sturdy woman started. "I'm Bliss from the Spa. I'm actually from the lost continent of Mu, but they don't want me saying that to hotel guests."

She actually believes that, Chloe surmised, showing her into the suite, clearing a space for the folding table. "Great name," Chloe replied. 'Is there a first name too or..."

"Nope, just Bliss. Isn't it enough?"

"Hopefully."

The massage therapist named Bliss from Mu looked average enough – about five foot seven with stringy brown hair that needed cut, color and style. She had that haggard look of single moms everywhere, aged before their time from running on adrenaline. Chloe felt a little sorry for her, watching as she heaved open the table and arranged blankets and sheets with a heating pad between them. She then spritzed the air in the room with a spray that smelled like lilacs and mountain streams. "Clears the energy."

"I do mostly lomi lomi with a little Swedish and some Thai. Would you like a guava lava on your face while I work on your front?"

"Sounds yum," said Chloe, removing her pareu and climbing up on the draped table.

Bliss startled Chloe with a chant. It must have been some sort of Hawaiian invocation to the gods. Or maybe she was

91

calling her homeland. Then the sounds of Indian sitars and wood flutes began. "It aids relaxation," she said, clicking on the baby boom box. Soon enough she was 'pulling energy from the source' and palpitating Chloe's lymph nodes then plying her muscles, pushing here, pounding there, kneading away the cares of the world.

Chloe was suddenly in a round, gilded, windowless space, flooded with incense, sandalwood and spice. She was flying over Buddhist monks who sat in the room on maroon cushions, chanting in prayer. She flew low and horizontal. *Strange*, she thought. *I usually fly vertically, like Mary Poppins.* But now she flew like Superman or monarch butterflies. Rising with the heat of the prayer-breath she circled ever wider until the walls of the temple disappeared, and peaks and mountains rose like the lost continent of Mu, poking up through layers of cloud cover.

A red dot, like the beam from a laser pointer, appeared on the mountain slope, and she flew towards it as a moth to flame. Instinctual. Magnetized. Enlightened by a message burning into her brain directly behind the retina of her right eye. *What was it?* Landing on the red dot she immediately grew warm and wet and dense as if assimilating the orgone energy of some distant planet, the ether, the élan vital, ozone, gravity. She began to glow with some primordial cosmic goo. Orange first, then red. Then the whole blue spectrum entered her aura, and before long she was a rainbow of color and light and some primeval moisture, doing backbends and downward dogs, arching like rainbows over a hillside and a small white cottage surrounded by blackberry bramble and lemon trees.

Drawing a deep breath the sun came out, and her vibrant, multihued body dissipated into the ferns and figs, honeysuckle vines and the rich black earth – out of which sprouted one singular violet rose.

Chloe woke with a shudder. Bliss was kneading her low back, stretching the piriformis muscles and putting pressure on the meridian points just below the kidneys on either side. Chloe lay there, remembering snippets of the dream and wondering how long she'd been out.

Bliss was stroking now from her feet to her shoulders – soft syncopated feathers, up and down the province of her body, which had blissfully morphed from bones and flesh into a squiggly cosmic substance. *Jell-O.*

twenty

JUGGLING

Kimo spied Jill immediately and walked over with towels and iced lemon water.

"Hey, girl, where ya been?"

"Oh hi, Kimo." *He's ubiquitous,* she thought. "We've been all over the island."

"Working on da tan, I see." He noticed her shade deepening and her tight buttocks, split only by the tiniest thong.

"We went to a party upcountry last night. A bunch of ag guys and environmentalists. The Mayor was there and a friend of his, running for office. Have you heard of a guy named Andy?"

"Naw. I no get da politics." His mood shifted. "You decide fo do Hana?"

"We're up for it if we can stay somewhere cheap. This place is draining us."

"Well, your bar's on me today. What'll you have?"

Around my finger, she thought. Jill was in incredible shape. A lifetime of great physical habits showed, and Kimo noticed. Like most men, he noticed. And appreciated. It was one of her main tools in the tool chest of male manipulation.

"What do you recommend for a hangover?"

"If you en chase a few last night, you gotta do piña colada."

"Perfect then. How about some extra fruit? And maybe you could arrange a room for Thursday night with your uncle.

We've decided to travel around to Hana on Thursday and come back Friday, if that's good."

"He goin' make time fo yous. If no can, he wen arrange tings with some uddah braddah from da family. He da bes guide though, s'pecially if you wan make hike. And Emma's one ono cook too, 'less you wan fancy food like da kine Hotel Hana Maui."

"Local food is fine. Why don't you confirm everything then draw us a map. We'll need his cell number to connect once we get down there."

"Sure. I get your drinks first." He moved back towards the bar, wondering who Andy was and if he was the reason she hadn't returned his calls. *Maybe I call too much,* he thought, thinking himself a tad foolish, fawning over her the way he had.

Jill sat up, thinking about Dan and Andy, and wondering why she always wanted what wasn't right before her, like Kimo, now. She had been in love once, before she learned the benefits of controlling guys, but that was back in college. Since then she'd had dozens of lovers and a few boyfriends, but she'd always called the shots and frankly, liked it that way. Especially after watching friends and acquaintances lose themselves – and their friends – in relationship. She had to admit she really didn't trust men at all. Not their motives, not their desires.

"I hope you no tink I come on too strong," Kimo said when he returned, drink in hand, a plate of fruit on the side.

"Au contraire. I was the one dealing out the come-on. You just followed my lead."

"It was fun. Wanna do something later?" He was a yo-yo now, being played and spun.

"We have plans tonight, Kimo." There, she'd said it. Lied to him. In fact she was hoping Dan would get back to her. She'd left a message on his cell, and she wanted to be free in case he called. And she knew he would. They always did. She'd called Andy back too, leaving some lame, politically correct message about what fun it was to meet him, bla, bla.

She looked up at Kimo, inspecting his muscular physique.

"Maybe when we get back from Hana. We have a busy week planned already."

"Well, you know where fo fine me. Enjoy da piña colada." Kimo smiled stiffly, feeling her brush off and wondering why. *She was so into me.* He thought about Saturday night and Sunday and how easy it would have been to nail her then. *She sure looks good. I'm not giving up. Not yet.*

Jill's cell phone rang. *Oh great, it works down here by the pool.* "Aloha," she said when she saw the local number on the screen.

"Is this Jill?" the voice sounded deep and educated with a local accent. It was Andy.

"Hi, Andy. Glad you caught me."

"Busy, are you?"

"Yea, busy working...on my tan." She looked down her legs approvingly. Her toes needed attention, but her legs looked fabulous.

"I was wondering if you wanted to go out to dinner. Maybe Thursday?"

She hesitated. "We just made plans for Thursday. We're all going round to Hana for a couple of days."

"Staying over at the Hana Ranch Hotel? You'll love it. Maybe tomorrow then. Would tomorrow be good?"

"Maybe. I'd like that, but I'll have to check the girls' plans just to be sure." She knew of course that she could do anything she wanted, but now it depended on her date with Dan. She still wanted to keep her options open, but tie Andy up just in case.

"Sure. Call me later. In the meantime, I'll look forward to seeing you."

"Me too." She lied again. Well, not really. If Dan flaked out, then she probably would look forward to seeing Andy. He wasn't really her type, but a lifetime of physical work had given him a very nice body, and he did seem juiced over her.

"Okay, then. I'll call you later."

"Thanks Andy. How do you say it? Mahalo?" She put honey in her voice to keep him wanting. She was practiced at this.

Jill closed her phone, took a long swig of the foamy, smooth sweetness *mmmm, piña colada* and did a few sit-ups before lying back down on the beach lounge. *Maybe I'm gay,* she thought. It had not been the first time. She had certainly had careless liaisons with women too. In fact, over all she liked women more than men. But men were so much more easily manipulated. And at this stage, manipulation was her game. Had been for years.

She lay quietly for another hour, turning every fifteen minutes. Her mind wandered back to her childhood and all her brothers, her boyfriends and girlfriends and whom she really loved, if any, and why. To be thirty and still not have it wired insulted her intelligence and her sense of who she was. *If I'm so smart, why can't I figure all this out?*

Kimo brought another piña colada just as Chloe and Mattie arrived.

"There you are," said Mattie. "We didn't recognize you for your tan."

"It's working then," said Jill, lifting her drink. "Mahalo, Kimo. How about a couple for my roomies?"

Thinking all hope was not lost, he turned on all his charm. "Dey on me," he re-assured them, figuring that at least one of them would be worth a good tip. Maybe a mercy tip. Maybe even a date.

"You've got him guessing," said Chloe when he left. "Still holding out for something else?"

"Always." It rolled off her tongue easy, but stuck somewhere between her rib cage and her throat.

twenty-one

GECKO BAR

Over lunch the sheer beauty of the island caught each of them in its spell, which was both wordless and nurturing. They quieted, sitting at the pool bar and gazing out to sea. It was a high form of meditation and a good reason stressed people from all over the world came here to this tiny island. If we consider the power of place, one of the main pulls of Maui is its ability to re-create people and for a brief duration to take them, calm them, and fill them with a gratitude that balances, enlivens and restores. Maui was a joie de vivre factory.

They scanned the horizon for whales and watched a few boats slowly making their way to and from Molokini or Lanai, filled with tourists soaking up sun and the natural paradise of the south Maui ocean. The whales were still here. They came to the islands in pods from Alaska every winter to calve and mate, usually arriving in November and leaving about March.

"Let's go to the aquarium," suggested Mattie. "I read about it in the guide. It's supposed to be nearby and has one of those walk-through tunnels that make you feel as if you're in the water with the fish. I visited one once in Australia, up on the Gold Coast, and it was unbelievable."

"I'm clear for the afternoon. Let's go today. How about you, Jill? Can you juggle your guys by cell phone?"

"If cell phone turned into phone sex I'd be better, but I'm good to go. I've probably had enough sun anyway, and Dan and I keep missing each other." She was looking down at her phone, wondering how in the world she could have missed his call yet again.

Lunch arrived. Chloe had a fresh fish burger and small salad. The bartender had recommended the ono, and she was game. "I almost always take the recommendations of the wait help. They know what's fresh and good."

"And sometimes it's what they've been told to sell. You know – get rid of the fish before it goes off." Jill articulated it in a gruff chef's voice. She had a point.

A huge Greek salad came out for Mattie. "I need to save the calories for dinner with Michael."

"I ain't saving nothing," said Jill as a bacon-blue cheeseburger and fries were placed in front of her. She reached across the bar for the ketchup and swamped everything on her plate with the blood-colored condiment.

"You're so gourmet," Chloe commented. Watching people season food without honoring the cook with a taste first was anathema. She grunted then took a bite of fish and turned to Mattie. "So you're on tonight with Michael?"

"We're going to town to some Vietnamese place that specializes in vegetarian food."

"Well how sweet is that? Then he's vegge too?"

"Good thing you got him then," said Jill, gulping down her burger. "Besides I can't even juggle the ones I have. I actually thought I'd come here and spend the week with Mr. Right for Me – a hunky sexaholic who liked to feed his women. Instead I can't seem to connect, and I'm feeding myself. Maybe my timing's off from the long flight. Or the sun."

"Was that the plan?" said Mattie. " I thought you brought me here to find one to help me get over…"

"Yea, yea. I know it's cliché but true. So true. The best way to get over a man is to get under another. Works every time."

"Well, that's advice you could very well give, Jill." Chloe went on to mention that she had fully intended that they just play together, but if they want to spend most of their time with strangers, that was fine. She, after all, came to write, and it would give her more solitude if they were each out and about.

"But I thought you hit it off with the writer last night," Mattie said.

"Oh Jed was nice, but we mostly talked about the writer's life. I'm not here looking for a man. A few free days are all I need to recharge my batteries. But I'm recharging for work."

"It's like that magnet on our fridge," said Mattie. "The one with the nineteen fifties June Cleaver woman, patting an old, empty upholstered chair. The caption says 'she liked imaginary men best of all'. That's you, Chloe."

Chloe thought about her refrigerator, covered with magnets and postcards, one from Florence, one with little donkeys in some Greek island town, one of the massive redwoods in Muir Woods – all from friends who traveled more than she did. She smiled remembering one on a cluster of plastic grapes that read: 'I like cooking with wine. Sometimes I even put some in the food.' Then there was Rufus, a husky black lab she'd had since junior high. It was an old picture, curling at the corners and needing extra magnets. She had always thought she'd replace him, but the grief took longer, much longer, than she could have anticipated. Besides, who had time to train a puppy?

"You're never looking, Chloe. Maybe that's why you never find one. If you wanted a man enough, you'd have one. Gawd knows you've passed up plenty." Jill was ganging up on her.

"Here's your kind of guy, Chloe," said Mattie, reading from the menu:

"In Hawaiian mythology Maui was the trickster hero of Polynesia. His mother used to work all day making tapa (bark) cloth. For Maui and his mother, the days were too short; there was never enough time to accomplish anything in only one day. Maui wanted to allow his mother to have more daylight to make bark cloth. He thought that if the sun were moving slower across the sky, there would be more hours of light in a day.

So Maui cut off the sacred tresses of his wife, Hina, to make a rope that would not burn once in contact with the Sun. With his rope he caught the Sun as it was rising and beat it with the magic jawbone of his grandmother. The Sun was so weak after the beating that it could no longer run but only creep along its course. In this way, the sunlight lasted longer, and it was possible to work more during the day.

Maui was small but very courageous. He wasn't afraid of anything, even the monster eel Te Tuna. Maui challenged Te Tuna for his wife, Hina. The two compared the size of their phalluses, and Maui won, so Hina confidently changed lovers. He was always trying to impress women. It is said that when he died his blood made the shrimp red and formed the colors for the rainbow."

"Interesting," said Chloe. "Longer days — just the way to a workaholic's heart."

"Yea, that might work. Longer days and a bigger dick. Hmmm." Jill stuffed a handful of fries into her mouth.

"Oh the pleasantries of vacations," said Chloe. "Time nearly stands still caught up in idle banter. Here our three heroines pass the noon hour in the gentle winter sun, satiated with food and island rum. Yum." She thought of one of her favorite authors. *Yum is my mantra.*

twenty-two

OCEAN CENTER

They left shortly after one for the aquarium in the leeward harbor of Ma'alaea. No one could remember the sun feeling so good, so soft. Sure there was sun back home, but it didn't look or feel the same, plus back home it was February after all, not the warmest month in the city. Not as sunless as July, but not as fabulous as here...now.

The aquarium adventure began with an indoor/outdoor living reef, which showcased uniquely stunning tropical fish, coral reefs, and marine habitats. The waterworld showed the evolution of life from algae and sea lettuces to coral – orange cup and cauliflower coral, branch, antler and brain corals – corals they'd seen and most they hadn't. Room after room of exhibits, with written and audio guides, elucidated the experience for Mattie and Chloe. Jill listened in for a while then preferred to have her 'own experience' of the various fish and sea creatures, removing her headset and refusing the canned storyline.

Crabs and live shells, starfish and tritons, shrimp of all sizes, shapes, and luminosities played hide and seek with eels and urchins, wrasse and butterfly fish. A room of live octopus displays was black-lit to amazing effects, graceful tentacles glowing delicately and eerily in the darkened room. The three emerged back into sunlight, arriving at the endangered green sea turtle lagoon right at feeding time, asking questions of the attendant and feeding the hawkbills.

"They're called 'honu' and are coming back here.

Apparently they have breeding grounds in various locations around the state, and on Independence Day, they have a huge release on the Kona Coast." Mattie was keeping up with the audio portion, and filling Jill in.

The Whale Center told stories of the 'gentle giants', their migration habits all over the globe, specifically the Alaska to Hawaii trek they undertook each winter for calving and breeding. It surprised all three that whaling was still going on in various parts of the world like Japan and Norway, allowing the killing of the endangered beasts.

"I read somewhere that Lahaina used to be the whaling capital of the world," Chloe mentioned when they were discussing why in the world whaling would still be a viable industry.

"Most of the endangered species on the list are hunted for the express purpose of making mens' dicks harder." By using hyperbole Jill often defused her comments, but the girls got her drift and agreed without argument. "I dated an ichthyologist once, and he was outraged about it all."

"I can't imagine you with anything icky," said Mattie. "Especially a guy."

"He was a fish dude. Worked at the Long Beach Aquarium. I met him at my cousin's wedding. Brother of the groom or something. Anyway it's all we talked about – fish! Which is why we didn't do much talking." Jill snorted.

Room after room of floor to ceiling tanks told tall tales that land creatures could hardly believe, and they became fascinated and enchanted as each room depicted a deeper descent into the ocean, where new species would appear. Near the end they came upon a wall of large fish, yellowfin tuna, and sharks. A marine biologist was in the middle of a short lecture about the giants of the sea, while the girls were amused by graceful grey and black-tipped reef sharks, little hammerheads, and larger tiger sharks.

Walking through a plexiglas tunnel they got a three hundred sixty-degree view of magnificent underworld. A manta swooped overhead, observing them with its eerie smiley face. No one could remember seeing the face of a manta before. There were unicorn fish and amberjacks, peacock groupers and dolphin fish, giant trevally and more spotted eagle rays.

"Enough!" It was Jill. "I have to come up for air."

"Me too," said Chloe. "I think I'm growing gills."

"I could stay here forever," said Mattie, "but for you guys..."

"Fuckin' amazing," said Jill, emerging into the blinding sunlight.

"Wow, feel that sun," said Chloe, pushing open the door. "Paradise," she purred.

"That was awesome." Mattie took Chloe's arm to steady herself as her eyes accustomed.

"I always thought I was a dolphin in a former life. You know, my being so at home in the water and all. This was like being with my hommies."

"Look, there's a souvenir store. Shopping!" Jill led the way into a huge space with a vast array of everything undersea or Hawaiian: carvings, paintings, sculptures, clothes and jewelry, fish this and fish that and endless knick-knacks in price ranges to grab everyone.

"Try this," said Mattie who had found a dispenser of tropical fragrances and lotions. Chloe left the postcard display temporarily, spritzing on a sample.

"Mmmm, gardenia, my favorite. Maui in a bottle."

Jill's cell phone rang and she took it outside, hoping for better reception. It was Dan. "I didn't know if you were avoiding me or what," he said.

"Just playing with you. Tag. What's up? Are we still on for tonight?" Jill was hopeful. In fact she'd hung a few hopes on seeing Dan again.

"I can't tonight. The wind surfing championship is tomorrow and I'm being filmed for a documentary."

Jill wondered what all that had to do with eating dinner, but held back.

"But I'd like to see you tomorrow after the event. It's at Ho'okipa, by the way, in case you and your friends want to come. It's free."

"We'll try. I'm not sure what the girls have planned, but it would be a first for all of us."

"Let's meet afterwards in town? Do you know the MACC?"

"Don't even hint that you're taking me to a Mickey Dee."

"I do have a little class, girl. I'm talking about the MACC, m-a-c-c, Maui Arts and Cultural Center. It's in Kahului along the ocean road by the college. He started to give her directions, but she cut him off.

"I'll find it."

"We'll have a bite then see the film. *Source Code* is showing. Supposed to be an interesting film."

"Oh, great. I haven't seen it yet. And I love Jake...ever since *Brokeback*," she said. "And he rocked in *Love and Other Drugs*. But then so did Anne Hathaway."

"You're not born again or something are you?" He was nervous now, thinking the film might be anti-religious or something like *The Da Vinci Code*.

"Dan, you don't need to worry about me. I'm bi and I live in San Francisco. I'm the furthest thing from a bible thumper you're ever likely to meet. I'm looking forward to the movie. And seeing you again." She was unusually polite. Dan was her best alternative so far, and they had days of potential pleasure ahead.

"Good. Six-thirty in the courtyard then."

"I'm breathless. And good luck at the championship."

"You'll bring my good luck, babe. See ya then."

Jill told Chloe and Mattie later what a whuss she thought he was, saving himself for the tournament. She went on with a wink in her voice. "I may have to punish him a little for that."

Mattie and Chloe had filled a couple of shopping bags with trinkets – Maui postcards and fish magnets, some tuberose lotion and plenty of mac nuts for family and friends back home. And for Chloe's kitchen of course.

twenty-three

SPORTS PARK

Walking across the parking lot, Mattie noticed a sign at the far end. She was jumping up and down like a kid. "Mini golf! They have mini-golf!" Her dad had taken her as a nine-year old to play mini-golf, and she'd loved it ever since. Mostly it was all about fond memories of her dad and her childhood. And something she was good at.

Over the years she had found fewer and fewer mini-golf courses as, online golf and indoor driving ranges emerged. She never learned regular golf, despite trying a couple of times. Never could find the time. It became immediately obvious to Chloe and Jill that they were about to take on a round.

They dropped their packages in the car and sun-screened up, walking over to the little park. Within minutes they stood at a little windmill, letting Mattie putt first. Crossing bridges, they shot through tunnels and little gardens of tropical flowers, their scents sending them spinning with expletives of joy.

Naturally Mattie won. Chloe gave her a run for her money, but in the end Mattie prevailed, surprising even Jill.

"Years of practice," was all she said as she let the girls buy her a celebratory mango ice cream at the snack stand. Sitting on the edge of a large pool with chutes and fake waterfalls, they noticed eight little one-person boats tied up along the shore. Chloe looked at Jill who nodded back to her, and before long they each lowered into a little bumper boat, armed with front-loaded machine guns that could spout nearly twenty feet.

Sheer delight and unbounded laughter ensued as they

climbed into the boats and jettisoned across the pool, chasing and spraying each other with the high-powered water guns. Chloe and Jill ganged up on Mattie, forcing her boat under the waterfall for a complete drenching. They were three children again, excited to screaming. The sun and splash, mingling with the miracle of friendship, fed their spirits and hearts with pure glee. Like children, they were probably a little high off the sugar rush from the ice cream. Or another perfect day.

Chloe was spraying Jill and thinking about the alchemy of laughter, trying to remember the name of the man who wrote the cancer cure book about humor therapy. He'd watched old videos of the Three Stooges, Jerry Lewis films, Lucy. *You've gotta love Lucy. She could cure anything that ails you. Maybe that's what Susan needs,* she thought, recollecting her cousin who was struggling with some horrible disease. Just thinking about it brought Chloe down. *Yes, she definitely needs some humor. I'll call her when we get home, visit the video shop and drop by for a visit.* For a moment she was thankful to be healthy and blessed with optimism. *Positive genes. And I think I'm in love. An inter-species love. Is that possible?*

Half an hour passed as they squirted and howled and banged into each other. Then a young tribe of eight to ten year olds hopped on the remaining boats and the women were soon outmanned and outgunned.

"That was better than sex," said Chloe as they towel dried, changing into dry clothes.

"Speak for yourself, girl," Jill challenged her. "There ain't nothing better than sex. But right now I need shoes! Where was that shoe place? Anyone remember?"

"Kihei I think," said Chloe. "I wrote it down somewhere."

"I have a date at seven." Mattie spoke up, making sure everyone knew she needed to be back in time to primp.

"Yes, of course. Michael is calling. Veggies for two and all that. How could we forget?" Jill teased her. "We'll drop you off then and go shoe shopping...and then out for steak."

"I have a hundred dollar budget. Find me something cute,"

Mattie was speaking to Chloe. They had pretty similar taste in shoes, and although Mattie's size was several smaller, Chloe knew what to look for.

They were off down the road, heading east back to Wailea, the wind blow-drying their hair, sun on their backs, still giggly.

"Perfect," Mattie purred. "So perfect."

"Fatal attraction, fuck you very much," Jill said, mixing movies and metaphors. "Now don't go all kukui nut on me."

Chloe dove right in. "Pardon my French, but Jill is so tight that if you stuck a lump of coal up her ass, in two weeks you'd have a diamond."

Jill had instant recognition. "Ferris Bueller's Day Off. I win. I don't believe in Beatles, I just believe in me."

twenty-four

JOE'S

While Jill and Chloe searched through rack after rack of island shoes at the outlet store on the backside of Kihei, Mattie showered and prepped for her date, wondering all the while what it was about Michael specifically that she was so drawn to. Yes, he was handsome and charismatic, but a little rugged around the edges, giving him a bit of a bad boy aura. *Obviously or Jill would not have been attracted.* Still he wasn't in fact a bad boy but a gentleman. And a scholar. She made herself laugh. She figured out it was how good she felt when she was with him – validated, appreciated, beautiful. She could tune into her innocence, that very core of herself that stayed with her through years of dating and even survived her twenty-three months with Tom. Michael saw that and liked it, even thought it delicious and rare.

He knocked at the door promptly at seven. She had expected a call from the lobby, which would have matched his propensity for being proper. She was still putting on lip-gloss and an armload of silver bracelettes collected from all around the world. Once her collection was started, friends and relatives always knew what to send for birthdays. Like Chloe's black pearls, they were her signature accessory.

"I couldn't wait," he said, handing her a bouquet of gardenias and looking a little like a kid in a pet store, wanting to pet and fondle.

Mattie peeked up and smiled, warming Michael all over. They embraced, heads buried in each other and in an armload of gardenias. She was glad the girls were out and they had this moment before rushing off. It felt so good to feel safe with a guy. And yet she didn't even know him. Could she trust her feelings, Michael, herself?

"I thought about you all day," he interrupted her thoughts.

"I had such a fun day I didn't think about anything. Chloe and Jill let me sleep in a bit, so the morning went by like highway signs on a road trip. Zip and it was lunchtime.

"I'm jealous. I had to lead a meeting at eight, so getting sleep was out of the question. I caught a twenty-minute power nap mid afternoon, thank god."

"We had the most awesome afternoon. We went to the Ocean Center then I cleaned everyone's clock at the mini golf course."

"I wouldn't have figured you for a golfer."

"I'm not, but my dad got me into mini-golf when I was a child. I've been hooked ever since."

"Did you ride the bumper boats? I took my nephews once, and we had a ball."

"As you can imagine, with a fresh win under my belt, I was the target. Chloe and Jill ganged up on me, and I got the waterfall."

"Poor baby." He squeezed Mattie again, sympathetically. They had wandered out on the lanai, sharing their conversation with the leftover peach and mauve of a happy hour sunset. He held her closer thinking *how strange to feel so close to someone so immediately. How strange ...and how sweet.*

"I know I promised you my favorite veggie Vietnamese restaurant, but if you don't mind, I'd rather not spend half our evening driving. Maybe we could eat a little closer to home."

"I'm fine with that, Michael. Whatever you think."

"Do you like sushi?"

"Raw fish? I love raw fish! And octopus and eel and shrimp." She thought a moment about the exhibit at the Ocean Center. "Although it might be tough after the aquarium today."

"Then I know a great little spot just down the road." And

they were off to Joe's on the golf course, famed Chef Gannon's second Maui restaurant and a top south side choice. The twinkle lights throughout the restaurant brightened their eyes as they dove deeper into conversation and broke bread.

"How long have you been a travel agent?" Michael asked, wondering if this was her life's ambition or a passing thing.

"Ever since I worked part time in college. It's my aunt's agency, and family means a lot to me. They gave me work when I needed it, then I got addicted to the travel and adventure side of things. Friends think it helps to round out my bland personality."

"Bland nothing. What could possibly be bland about you? I figured you for an adventuress, but do you find you use your talents in this business?"

"Actually I'm a good communicator, a great organizer, and now that I'm leading some tours, I find quite a bit more skills come into play. Would I prefer more adventure tours to educational ones? Younger travelers to older ones? Yes, but right now that's where the market is. If you want me to admit I'm working below my skill set, I won't."

"That's not it at all. I just never knew much about your business. I always book my own trips online. I can't remember when I last called a travel agent, and I guess I just assumed your business was dying out."

"Actually like most it's changed. And changing. We don't make any money in airlines or other sectors, but we have lots of old clients who've booked their trips with us since way before the Internet. We do lots of cruises and adventure/ecotourist travel. More and more people are interested in aid travel or trips where they can actually do some community good. You know, dig a well, build a bridge, teach English. That's a growing sector, and one I'm pretty passionate about, but it's probably not growing like environmentalism."

"Well, that's debatable with this administration, but in fact many Americans and majorities of others around the world are keenly interested in preserving and protecting our ecosystems.

Of course we're the monster on the map – the old US of A. We're the number one degrader, and we're in deep denial of the frightful changes we're contributing to."

"Don't get me started on politics. I'm warning you. Don't get me started." Mattie reached over and stroked his arm. He held her hand over his forearm, gazing deeply into her eyes.

"Just as long as we're on the same page." He squeezed it, and then with his other hand touched the corner of her lip where some olive tapenade lingered. "You should know I hold deep opinions about my work and its larger meanings, and I am a political being. I sense you have heat in those areas as well. I guess what I'm saying is that I see James Carville and his wife Mary coming from completely different and strongly held opinions, and I can't imagine living like that. It's important to me to have compatibility in those areas as well as others."

"I couldn't agree more. Still people need their independence, and no one thinks or believes the same as another."

"It feels so awkward – all this small talk – when I feel so intrinsically close to you. Still I don't want to take anything for granted, and I want to know you much better…deeper, more."

"I agree. Maybe we need to back up a bit, and…"

"And ignore what we feel?" Michael interrupted her. "How in the world do we do that?"

"Well, I'm certainly not the expert in these matters. If you ask Jill, she'll say I'm very much a novice. In fact the whole reason we're here on Maui is that the girls thought I needed some real sorting out. I guess I was still nursing wounds from a former relationship. One I now think I should never have been in."

"Bit of a pity party, eh?" He said it with such charm and obvious concern, she couldn't take it any other way. "Hey, I was married for five years, four of them pure hell."

"I bet you learned a lot."

"Oh yea, it was a monster learning curve. Then a huge brick wall, and I crashed and burned. Didn't date for well over a year, and it's been three or four since then. I've had a few flirtations and some wonderful women throwing themselves at me, but I guess I buried myself in my work and my activism and pretty much ignored the opposite sex. But when I saw you, Mattie, something in me came alive again." He leaned in, voice softening. "Something in your personality or your pull, your look or eyes, touched something deep in me and said NOW."

Mattie wasn't used to men speaking to her this way, with real feeling and honesty. She realized that mostly until now it had all been come on in the game to bed her. Michael was different, and she loved that about him as much as anything.

Their main courses arrived, and they ate quietly. Michael had selected a lovely New Zealand sauvignon blanc, which went perfectly with her quick-seared ahi and garlic mashed potatoes. Michael ordered the seafood bouillabaisse, filled with mussels, shrimp and fresh catch. A crunchy French bread dipped in the rich broth brought lip smacking. "I'm so glad you eat fish. I used to be vegan, then I added dairy, then finally seafood. I just needed more protein."

"I never gave up fish, just meats and land animals," Mattie explained between mouthfuls. "I think it was the horrible treatment of animals that bothered me as much as anything. I mean they are sentient beings."

"Don't tell me you're a Buddhist too?"

"I'm not an 'ist' nor do I have an 'ism'. I've studied Buddhism and I enjoy many of its practices, especially meditation, but I dropped labels and churches for good when I left my childhood church."

"Which was?"

"Which was Catholic. And you?"

"I was raised by my mother in Northern California. She had been a hippie, so all world religions were taught me from the beginning. I love the Sufis. Like the Buddhists I can't quite grok god as a concept. To me god is experiential. But I dig Jesus' message, which for me was to love god and love each other. As a scientist – like Einstein, whom you can imagine is one of my heroes, especially when he said 'imagination is more important than knowledge' – I question everything, so falling for any bs is not likely. Albert was convinced near the end of his life that everything couldn't be explained scientifically. Remember that quote about it being possible to explain Beethoven's symphony as wave particles, but it would have no meaning. His god I think was part of the whole soup we're all in together." He got excited talking about his mentor, and his excitement turned Mattie on.

Michael took a small and worn leather book from his back pocket and read, *"A human being is a part of the whole, called by us 'Universe,' a part limited in time and space. He experiences himself, his thoughts and feelings, as something separated from the rest – a kind of optical delusion of his consciousness. This delusion is a prison, restricting us to our personal desires and to affection for a few persons nearest to us. Our task is to free ourselves by widening our circle of compassion to embrace all living creatures.* That's why I do what I do."

"Here's my favorite Einstein quote," she said. *"There are only two ways to live your life. One is as though nothing is a miracle. The other is as though everything is."* Now that's a prophet I can believe in, being a glass-is-half-full person. I'll admit it though. I still don't get the e equals m c squared thing. I mean I get it, but I don't understand it. *I hope he doesn't get into chaos theory or the Heisenberg Principle.*

"We're all into string theory now. Albert would have loved it."

She dropped it like a hot potato, reaching across to offer him a bite of her fish, dipped in a spicy beurre blanc. "It's divine. Try it."

"I grew up sharing food too. Have you ever noticed that there are people who share food and those who don't? I went out with a girl once and when I suggested we share a dessert, she completely freaked out. Didn't return my call, ever again."

"Yea, I know what you mean. I had a guy totally unnerve me when I reached over to have a bite of something on his plate. I mean it was about our fifth or sixth date, and we were getting pretty familiar, and I think it must have been chocolate, but he snapped – nearly whacked my hand off right there. I didn't like the punishment for something I thought was normal, but he wouldn't talk about it either. It was our last date. I used to think it was a big family thing, but you would bust that theory. Some from big families hoard, some share, and I guess it's the same for solo children. Anyway, I'm glad we both came from the sharing crowd."

"My mom and I ate everything Chinese style. Still do. When I see her we order a couple of plates of food and share them completely. Here, try the shrimp." He used a spoon to make sure she got plenty of sauce. "Taste the lemongrass?"

"Don't tell me you cook too." Mattie said, enjoying being fed. The metallic taste of the spoon disappeared in the sweet-sour-lemony essence that lingered.

"I love to cook! Would do that if I weren't doing what I love even more. How about you? Are you a kitchen goddess?"

"Naw, Chloe's the chef. Totally gourmet. Grows all her own organic herbs and greens; belongs to a co-op. But I'm learning, and I can make eggs any way in the world. Coddled, over easy, one-eyed Egyptians. Benedict's my favorite, and I do a mean vegetarian chili. Actually my specialty is chocolate. Anything chocolate. I do an amazing chocolate mousse, if I do say so myself. Truffles, flourless decadent cake, chocolate biscotti, white chocolate divinity, chocolate-dipped strawberries, chocolate-mac nut brownies, Gramma's fudge, chocolate chip cookies of course and the best hot chocolate in the world. Actually it's the recipe from the movie."

"The movie didn't give a recipe." He knew immediately which film she spoke about.

"No, but I tried and tried. I was on a mission, and I found the lost ark of hot chocolate. Binoche left clues. It starts with the right cocoa beans then it's the spice. Just a pinch of the hot stuff."

"I can't wait to taste it. Any of it…all of it. Can I assume you're up for a little dessert then?"

119

The soufflé was rich and light, liquid in the middle, with just enough Tahitian vanilla ice cream to cleanse and cool the palate. It melted their taste buds just like kisses.

Mattie leaned in and kissed Michael, licking a little chocolate off the corner of his lips. "Didn't he also say, '*gravity can't be held responsible for people falling in love*'? Or something like that?"

"Albert would have loved you too." He kissed her back, gently putting a hair back in place while thinking about their center of gravity. It had to be somewhere near the heart.

twenty-five

GREEN FLASH

Chloe and Jill spent two hours in shoe heaven, buying shoes they wouldn't wear often back home – strappy little sandals, mules, and slip on babe shoes, many of which would simply not work in the city for career gals, except on the occasional sunny summer day or casual Friday. But at least they would have fabulous feet this week. And/or be ready for tropical adventures anywhere in the world.

"Okay, I admit it. I have a fetish," Jill said, putting six pairs on her credit card.

"Jill, dahling, you are the Queen of Fetish, Chloe said, loading two bags of her own.

Mattie was gone when they returned to the room, but the sun was lowering, so Jill and Chloe wrapped around sarongs to match their sandals and rushed down to the Gecko Bar for a closer look.

"Sex on the Beach times two," Jill called across to the bartender, settling in for the high drama of another day's end. They grew quiet as the birds chatted and chirped, tweeting and warbling, occasionally breaking into song. The sky dripped peach then mango as a glowing orb descended quickly into the sea. As it began its final dip they observed in silence. Chloe held her breath. Then it happened.

As the last peek of sun disappeared into a violet horizon, a neon-green flash burst like an electric kiss. The sun dipped and a lightning bolt sprawled along the horizon. A witness to the

121

passion between sun and sea.

"Did you see that?" Chloe asked, jumping up. "I've heard of them my whole life but never saw one. You saw too?"

"My first green flash," said Jill. "Better than a hot flash."

"That was it, Jill, and it wasn't the booze."

They were awed and stunned, watching until the whole sky turned from peach to dark violet as Venus rose over the same horizon. Jill ordered another round of drinks.

"I should have brought my camera," Chloe said.

"They say it can't be photographed."

"How silly. If you can shoot a rainbow, you can shoot a green flash."

"Yea, but then you'd miss it."

"Point." Chloe raised her glass. "Here's to you and your shoes."

"And you, finding your muse." Jill was suddenly a poet. "To Mattie, finding love again." Chloe and Jill clinked glasses, sending wishes to their sister on their breath, on the ether, the thought tide, the instinctual, migratory path of monarch butterflies and whales.

They ordered some appetizers for dinner — a basket of dim sum, Asian dumplings with sweet and sour sauce, a plate of fresh ahi sashimi with wasabi vinaigrette, and a mozzarella-tomato-basil salad. By the time they'd finished, a Cheshire moon smiled down on a silver mirror of sea, which blazed its way to the end of the world. Clusters of stars began to twinkle like sequins all over their own private paradise.

Jill and Chloe ended up back at Hapa's, and it was ladies' night. Kimo had left a message while they shopped for shoes, saying he'd meet them there. "What the heck?" had been Jill's response. Dan had flaked, but before he did she had said 'no' to Andy (rain-checked for Friday, unless she and Dan really hit it off on Wednesday), so she was on her own. Chloe had protested — something about finishing the page burner she was halfway through, but after a great sunset, moonrise and food,

Jill successfully twisted her arm. "Just an hour. If you're not into it, you can come back with or without me."

Hapa's was pounding, and the babe shoes went out, ready to dance.

twenty-six

1210

Mattie was back first. She and Michael had lingered over coffee and moonlight, weighed the alternatives of some live blues versus a movie, finally deciding they were both whipped and would call it a night.

"Even I need some beauty rest tonight," Michael confessed, although to Mattie he was gorgeous, tired or not.

He asked the bellman to hold the car up front while he walked Mattie up to her room. When they realized no one was there, they made their way to the balcony and kissed goodnight, the tropical air pungent with night-blooming jasmine, infusing their senses. Moonlight shone playfully through palm fronds onto their Moorish dream world.

"I'll call you tomorrow," he said at the door as she rested her sleepy head on his shoulder.

"Thanks again, Michael. I had a wonderful evening. It would all scare me a little if it were anyone but you."

"I'll take that as a compliment." He winked and kissed her tenderly on the forehead. "Sweet dreams."

Mattie was just climbing unto bed when Jill and Chloe burst into the room in high pitched giggles, carrying on about 'da bruddahs'.

"Mattie. How was your date?" Chloe asked.

"We didn't expect to see you home so early," added Jill.

"We were both so tired from last night, but we had a marvelous dinner. I really like this one."

"Duh, like he's perfect for you." Jill couldn't resist.

"Everyone needs the perfect rebound guy."

"I hope he's more than that," she defended Michael, her feelings, their magic.

"I hope so too, honey," Chloe was sincere.

"We had to fight 'em off at Hapa's." Jill said. "It was ladies' night so all the guys showed up, and Kimo saved us a table."

"The music was great, and I danced my tush off," said Chloe, pulling off her spaghetti straps. "Did you see what we got you, Mattie?"

"I just got home."

"Look!" Chloe brought out a bag from the closet and placed four pairs of shoes ceremoniously on Mattie's bed.

There was a shiny, bejeweled turquoise wedge with two-inch heels, a pair of magenta scrunchy slip-ons, a cute pair of turtle thongs, and leather black strappies with a three-inch platform. Mattie tried them all on. "Oh my gawd, they're perfect! All of them. How much were they?"

"Little presents from your girlfriends," Chloe said, giving Mattie a hug.

"Get serious. How much?"

"Seriously," said Jill, "they're a we're-so-happy-you're-out-of-your-funk present. Even your Dutch friend pitched in," she winked. "Happy Maui. Happy M & M." She grabbed Mattie and twirled her around. "Or is it S & M?" Jill laughed out loud. "Wait, there's more." She winked at Chloe and reached under the bed, emerging with a large white bag with a big red kiss and "Love Shack" scripted on the side.

Chloe giggled. "She made me." Then Jill and Chloe started laughing, big rolling hoots of laughter.

"Oh, I get it," said Mattie.

"No, darlin', you weren't there," said Chloe. "Jill actually embarrassed the sales clerk in a sex shop for christ's sake."

"He was asking for it." Jill defended her brazen behavior. "He-she was tall and sexy and had been flirting with us since we arrived. So what if I teased her into helping me in the dressing room."

Chloe continued, "when he opened the curtain, Jill was standing there stark naked except for a couple of nipple clips and a strap-on. Bare ass naked except for accessories."

"They started laughing again until it became uncontrollable, then they leapt on the king bed, tossing pillows at each other and bouncing around the room.

Mattie opened the bag and peered in. It was a virtual smorgasbord of sex toys. Jill and Chloe gathered around, calming a bit.

"This one's for you, sweetie." Chloe handed Mattie a box, and Mattie stopped to examine the photograph on the outside.

"Interesting," was her initial comment.

"Jill got the nipple clips and some handcuffs."

"Look, they have sheepskin lining." Jill held up the cuffs..."all the way from Australia."

"I got two dildos. A fairly large one with killer vibration and a little finger one with rubber spikes." Chloe held them up admiringly.

"Mine's big and black," said Jill. "My fantasy dick."

"Yours has the clit vibrator and is the deluxe German model. I may have to borrow it sometime. Don't you like it?" Chloe asked.

"You'll like it when you try it," said Jill. "They're not the kind of toys you just look at. You have to actually play with them." She looked at Chloe, and they broke out in snickers again.

"Why ladies, I'm amazed. And delighted." Mattie spoke in her most proper, boarding school voice. "I just need my crotchless panties, and voilà – manless fuck!"

"Well, we're not suggesting you do it here...now, Mattie." Chloe went on, "but I'm sure you'll find your giggle too." She and Jill started chortling again, and Mattie joined in.

"I wonder if we'll change our name to S & M?" Mattie ruminated.

"Not after Sunday," Jill said, thinking Michael was Mattie's Maui present, her awakening. Definitely her rebound guy.

Mattie pondered for a moment as she tucked the shoes and device back into their boxes and returned them to the closet. "I can hope, can't I?"

"Hope away girl, but I say get it while you can."

"That's just not me, Jill. And I don't think it's Michael either."

"Well, it's only Tuesday, so I guess there's still hope." Chloe grabbed her arm, and they all went out onto the balcony, looking out to sea and the moon-swept sky.

When they turned to go back in they were still awash in giggles. Chloe hugged them both. "I just have to journal," she said. "I'll keep the light low."

twenty-seven

HOTEL

By morning they were all back on the same rhythm, sleeping in until nearly eight and calling room service for a lumberjack's breakfast. Mattie stretched in the corner, doing a few yoga postures. She was into a downward dog when she asked, "so what's on for today?"

"Here's what's still on our list: Lahaina, Iao Needle, Halekalakalakala crater, Baldwin House Museum, Surfing Goats, lavender tour, wine tasting..." Chloe was into a long laundry list when Mattie interrupted. "Manis and pedis, please. PUHLEEEZE."

Jill registered her priorities, "more beach, water aerobics, weight training. I need to get down to the spa, and I think pool aerobics is at nine. I'm not getting any sex, so I need to double up my workouts. For workout value, sex is better than tennis and depending on the guy, better than jogging."

"I read you can burn five hundred calories per session," Mattie mentioned.

"Irrelevant, darling. The question is how many mai tais can you burn?"

Chloe continued, "Big Beach, Little Beach..."

Mattie squeaked from her triangle pose. "Darlings, I'm afraid we simply can't do everything in one week. We'll have to prioritize."

"Here's my priority," said Jill. "I'm meeting Dan for dinner and a movie somewhere in the K town. He invited us to his surf meet. Whaddya think?"

"Have you got plans with Michael, Mattie?" Chloe asked.

"He's calling this morning. Should we all go to the movies? What's playing?" Mattie was thinking of Chloe being left out while she and Jill had dates.

"Source Code," Jill said.

"Oh, that flashback thriller thing with hunky Gyllenhaal. I'd love to see it. Can I come too? Chloe was feeling a little excluded when the phone rang.

"It's for you." Jill handed Chloe the phone. "It's your author friend." She winked. It was Jed, asking Chloe if she wanted to go catch a movie at the MACC. After a brief confab with the girls, she said she'd meet him there at 6:30. "That's settled. Now we just have the day to plan."

"Actually, I could use an unplanned day," said Mattie. Maybe a day just hanging around the beach and pool, catching up on my book and my tan. You guys do whatever you want."

"I'm on with that," said Jill, slipping into a tiny blue bikini, striped in silver.

"I have some catch-up with the office, but I'll be down later."

"Okay, Chloe, but I have to catch up on my tan." Jill was part Cherokee and tanned beautifully. The other two, swathed in sunscreen, still pinked first.

"Why don't we pool a few hours then head off to Lahaina. Pack towels and a change of clothes in case we end up somewhere we hadn't planned and have to get to the film."

"Chloe, the scoutmaster, always prepared." Mattie saluted. "That leaves me two to three hours of unplanned." She smiled up at Jill and grabbed her sunglasses. "Catch you later, mom." And was out the door. Chloe turned and grabbed her IPhone, determined to work fast and join the others sooner than later.

It was another lilting day. The February sun was up, but it wasn't hot. Steady trade winds moved the air sweetly over their nearly bare bodies. Chloe finished her work by ten and joined them poolside, reminding the girls to turn over, and applying sunscreen to their backs and legs. Jill had already finished her aerobics class then lifted free weights for about twenty minutes. Mattie did some water aerobics then left for a yoga class on the beach.

By the time Chloe settled they were all enjoying a leisurely morning, sunning and deep in conversation about work, life and love. They each had a book, but neither was reading. Chloe rolled over and read from hers,

"Hawaii is the home of shanghaied men and women, and of the descendants of shanghaied men and women. They never intended to be here at all. Very rarely, since the first whites came, has one, with the deliberate plan of coming to remain, remained. Somehow the love of the Islands, like the love of a woman, just happens. One cannot determine in advance to love a particular woman, nor can one so determine to love Hawaii. One sees, and one loves or does not love. With Hawaii it seems always to be love at first sight. Those for whom the Islands were made, or who were made for the Islands, are swept off their feet in the first moments of meeting, embrace and are embraced."

"That's Jack London's *Stories of Hawaii,* written in the early 1900's. I finished Mark Twain's *Letters.* They loved Hawaii as much as I do; they just wrote it better, but I'm practicing."

Mattie smiled over at Chloe, rolled again and picked up her book, a sweet little indulgence called *Confessions of a Shopaholic.* Jill was halfway through *Tips and Tricks for the iPad 2.* Chloe put down her book and ran towards the beach.

The sun dazzled on the wrinkled Pacific. Like the beginning of a love affair, it was all so good.

twenty-eight

LAHAINA

It was Mattie who noticed the time and got everyone back on schedule. "If we're going to Lahaina, we probably should go up and change."

"Let's leave our suits on and just slip on cover-ups or pareus. Grab extra beach towels for the car and a few things for later." Chloe successfully hustled everyone along, and within twenty minutes they were waiting curbside while she fumbled in her purse for a tip for the bellhop.

Jill slid into the driver's seat and put the top down first thing. "I need you as co-pilot," she said to Chloe. "Pull out your iPhone. And why don't you choose the music?" She handed Mattie a CD case.

Cee-Lo was forgetting you by the time they stopped at the scenic lookout, well-sunned, blown and carefree, bopping along to some old classics, mixed with Lady Antebellum, Lady Gaga, and a bit of reggae, Mattie playing a random selection. They scanned the sea for about ten minutes, spotting eight whales breaching and spouting, frolicking in their waterworld. The colors of the water gradated from soft aqua near the shoreline, deepening to post office blue, cobalt, and indigo, finally darkening even deeper at the horizon.

"Did you ever see water so many shades of blue?" Chloe asked, feeling her heart lunge towards the sea.

Back on the road, steep spires rose up on the right as they headed around the point. A dazzling sea spread out to their left, wrapping around from Ma'alaea Harbor to Lanai, with

Molokini and Kahoolawe in the distance.

"One of the tours goes to that tiny island," said Mattie. "The bellboy said it has awesome snorkeling. The guide book says that despite cries of outrage from native Hawaiians, Kahoolawe was used by the US Navy for years as a bombing target."

Whale-watching boats dotted the horizon as they sailed along, sweet sounds of James Taylor coming on as everyone sang along.

"Word game!!" shouted Chloe, turning down the stereo. "Last letter...next word. You start, Mattie."

"Mike."

Jill was next. "Elephant."

"Tush," said Chloe.

"Hana."

"Aloha."

"Allspice." It was back to Chloe. "This is too easy. Let's do places. Maui."

"Internet," said Mattie. "It's a place."

"Texas," said Jill with a deep drawl.

"Singapore."

"East L.A. Oh yea, my favorite place."

"Antigua."

"You can't end a word with the letter it started with," Chloe reprimanded Jill.

"Andes then."

"San Francisco." They all let out little hoots and cheers.

"Oakland."

"Deer Park."

"Oh yea, where's that?" Mattie asked.

"Michigan if you have to know. Your turn, Chloe."

"The K town...Kuhuhula."

"It's Kahului," corrected Mattie. "So mine is Ireland."

"Denver."

"Whoa, baby. Back off." Chloe was back seat driving from the front seat. The traffic had slowed as they entered the fringe of Lahaina, and Jill was tailgating. "Well, will you look at this sweet little settlement?" Chloe's head was buried in her GPS. "Take a left up here, and we'll travel down Front Street. It runs along the sea." Jill turned up the music. Jackson Browne was *Running on Empty*, and the three babes entered town, amped up. "Says here this was the old capitol of Hawaii, whaling center of the world in its heyday. Then a little fishing village before it was the tourist mecca of Maui."

They cruised Front Street looking for a parking spot and found one directly in front of an unbelievable Banyan Tree that canopied the entire town square. It reminded Chloe of the Father of the Forest, the kiwi tree that had taken her dad's breath away.

"This tree is famous," said Mattie. "Imagine a famous tree."

"Only in the islands," came Chloe's reply. *And New Zealand.*

They parked and walked under the tree and stood a few minutes, listening to the chatter of birds.

"It says here that twelve species of birds live in this tree. It was planted in 1873 when it was only eight feet tall."

"Thanks, Mattie. I'm sure glad we brought our tour guide." Jill teased her, but Chloe appreciated all Mattie's little anecdotes and secretly wondered how she could walk and read at the same time.

They wandered through the old historic courthouse near the shore then over to the famous Pioneer Inn where they watched boats come in and go out, filled with tourists or fishermen. Chloe picked up a few brochures to check prices for the boats. A young woman with shell necklaces approached Jill, who purchased a dozen and lei'd each of the girls with a few.

"See, you just gotta sell a little," Jill said, anointing each of her friends.

Another vendor with little anklets made in the Philippines approached, and Jill turned away without even speaking to her.

"Yea, but it gets old," said Chloe. "A clue to you, Jill. You don't always have to advertise. You're so gorgeous all by yourself, but guys think you come on too strong."

"I do not," Jill protested, knowing there was a glimmer of truth to the statement.

"Yea, I have to agree with Chloe here, honey. You don't even give them a chance to come on to you cause you're so busy figuring out how to get them. You have to let them discover you. It'll make them feel better."

"Oh, and I'm alive to make them feel better." Jill was back on the defensive.

"I didn't mean it that way. Just that if you held back a little, you could see how well your unique attraction works. Don't you want to feel attractive?"

"Well of course, Ms. Expert."

"You don't need to get snooty, sweets," Chloe calmed Jill. "Mattie has a point. It's like the street hawkers, always approaching til everyone just says 'no'. On the other hand, left to window shop, we'll always find things we love. Guys will too."

"Might be a strategy. Gawd knows I could use a new m.o."

twenty-nine

LONGHI'S

They continued along Front Street, peeking in little shops, stopping in some of the galleries to comment on the various art, deciding they definitely preferred the local artists with oils and watercolors of bright island scenes over the same dark and brooding art they see all over the Bay Area. Ducking into a small shop Jill purchased half a dozen large and extra large tee shirts for her brothers and a couple for her nieces and nephews. Chloe glanced over the postcards, deciding that eight for a dollar was really great value and buying three dollars worth. "For the fridge," she said. "You know I won't write that much before we leave."

"They don't have a time limit, Chloe. You can send them year round," said Mattie. "No worries."

"No, I couldn't possibly. Friends have to receive postcards before you arrive home, or what's the point?"

"Send e-cards. That's the point." Jill put the brakes to that debate, and before long they walked through a white picket fence and found themselves at the Baldwin House and inadvertently on 'Lahaina's Historical Walking Tour'. Easily they imagined the town filled with whalers and sea captains, missionaries and heathens.

It was a different crowd now. Tourists of all ages, nationalities and ethnicities crowded the streets and the shops, but most were middle-aged haole couples, probably from southern California or Chicago. They passed national franchises – Bubba Gumps, Hard Rock Café, an Outback Steakhouse,

Starbucks and McDonalds of course, but there were also little local shops and the big Hawaiian franchises – Hilo Hattie's, ABC Stores and the T Shirt Factory. Timeshare kiosks sprouted on every block, offering 'free breakfasts', 'whale-watching adventures', and cute little necklaces with a tiny pair of gold flip-flops. Mattie laughed remembering her three-month stint selling timeshares in the city. It had been an early foray into moonlighting, an attempt to pay off her college loans. She was good enough, but it just wasn't her. Still she smirked at her private joke with each one she passed.

Sauntering arm in arm for about an hour, poking in and out of galleries, shops, historical museums and a sandal store or two, they became suddenly aware of delicious scents coming from the sidewalk, greeting them on the street, calling their names.

"You don't have to advertise," said Chloe, "but I smell a gastronomic treat." Jill discovered the source to be a restaurant and lead the way upstairs where they were escorted to a table in a corner, overlooking the ocean, the island of Lanai, and all the people playing on and in the water right there on the shores of Lahaina.

First platters of freshly baked breads arrived with pesto butter and a roasted red pepper hummus, plates of olives and antipasto. It went down perfectly with the crisp, well-chilled pino grigio Jill ordered as soon as they were seated. They had ordered a number of dishes to share, asking that the waiter bring extra plates so they could eat Chinese style.

"Sure," he said. "Just save room for dessert."

Within minutes a large salad arrived. It was romaine with tomatoes, onions, green and white beans, topped with gorgonzola and tossed with blue cheese vinaigrette. They passed it around along with more bread, but before they could eat it, a platter of grilled asparagus arrived, smothered in wild mushrooms and finished with Parmigiano Reggiano.

Salmon Mediterranean arrived next – 'Wild King Salmon

cooked in a 500° brick oven with vine-ripened tomatoes, kalamata olives, fresh basil and lemon'.

Chloe was talking about heaven again. "I shouldn't have eaten all that bread."

"Pass the wine," Jill said, reaching across just as the waiter picked up the bottle and refilled each of their glasses.

The Lobster Cannelloni came last: a Maine lobster and ricotta stuffed into fresh pasta and topped with a bubbly béchamel sauce.

"As much as I love Salmon," Chloe uttered, "this is the pièce de résistance."

"No argument from me," said Jill, "but it does get the carb award."

"I think the dessert tray will get that one," said Chloe.

"You could eat dessert?" said Mattie.

"I can always eat dessert," Chloe replied. "I just should have checked first. My daddy was the king of sweets. Got it directly from his dad, my Oklahoma grandpa. My grandma was a heck of a cook if memory serves me. She died when I was still in school, but every memory I have of her centers around food – picking figs and peaches in her backyard to make jams and pies, chasing down a chicken for her world-famous chicken and dumplings, nectar-berry pancakes on Sunday morning, piled so high you couldn't see over them. Many of my recipes today are from Nana. Anyway gramps would never start to eat until they finished grace and he had asked, 'what's the nature of the come along after?' Just had to know what dessert was before he began." Then once Nana told him, he would decide how much of what to eat for his meal. My daddy learned that as a boy, and I can remember it my whole life – dad always asking mom, even before he started grace, 'what's the nature...'"

"So let me show you," the waiter was standing at the table with a tray of the most delectable desserts. "A lilikoi cheesecake – that's passion fruit, macadamia nut pie, topped with almond whipped cream, Bailey's crème brulé, and our chocolate decadence – a fudge layer cake with chocolate mousse in three layers topped with dark chocolate ganache, served on a fresh raspberry coulis. Comes with or without ice cream. All we serve is island-made Tahitian vanilla. We have our world-famous hunky chunky cookies with dark and white chocolate chunks and mac nuts."

"Whew," said Jill. "Are we really going to do this?"

"Let's get two and pass them," suggested Mattie. "And bring three espressos. We'll need them just to make it down the stairs."

"Wasn't I good?" asked Jill. "He was hunky, and I didn't say a word."

"He was also gay. So yes, you did really well."

thirty

IAO

If they hustled across the island, they'd have time to hike the Iao Needle and wear off lunch, possibly even making time for manicures. By the time they drove the pali, hiked the stream and the needle to the lookout it was four in the afternoon. A winter sun caressed the valley, throwing soft light onto the coral trees that dotted the valley and reflecting the sky in the river. It meandered below as they crossed the bridge and made their way up towards the natural rock pinnacle presiding over the Iao stream and surrounded by the walls of the Pu'u Kukui Crater. Once used as a natural altar, the twenty-two hundred foot stone pillar is a basaltic core, covered with aeons of vegetation.

Chloe stopped to take a photo at a sign pointing up to the needle. It read 'no wheel chair access'. *Heck it would take an eagle to make that peak*, she thought. The irony of it all amused her, and she pulled out her camera. Then she took shots of the girls climbing to the top. One with the valley behind. One of Jill and Mattie hanging over the bridge. One of Mattie next to a sign, which explained the historical site so she wouldn't need her guidebook. They perched on the lookout where Hawaiian warriors stood for generations, looking down the valley and across to the sea. Chloe tried to set up the camera to take a timed shot so they would all be in it. Below the needle. Looking out to the spectacular scenery beyond. Hugging. Doing a cancan. Making faces.

"It says here that this was their line of defense." Mattie

read from a plaque. "Still Kamehameha got through."

"You need to be more on the lookout, Mattie honey." Chloe said it gingerly as if giving sugar with the medicine. "You know – protect your vulnerability, be a bit more cautious."

"Not *my* style," Jill joined in, "but I agree with Chloe. You tend to get swept up rather quickly, falling for a guy before you even know what he's about."

"Oh you do too, Jill," Mattie said.

"Yea, but I'm after sex. You're after love. There's a difference."

"Take off my rose-colored glasses? Is that what you mean?" Do I now need to defend romance? Should I feel ganged up on? "

"Hardly, darlin'. But you know what we mean, and you *do* wear rose-colored glasses when it comes to men. At least take them off. Or better yet, wear bifocals so you can see 'em up close and at a distance." Chloe was getting nitty now.

"I've never been conned," Mattie started.

"You're one of those women who finds out her husband has three other wives and ten children before she realizes she just isn't that special," said Jill. "We just don't want you so hurt again, Mattie. It sucks for us too."

"Okay, I'll try if you two promise me. PROMISE ME. Promise to tell me everything, even if I don't want to hear it. Maybe if I'd known sooner about Tom, I could have been smarter."

"Honey, you were a goner from the start. That was the problem."

"Chloe's right, and you're doing it again."

"No, I don't think so," said Mattie. "I really like Michael, but we've only had two dates, and…"

"One and a half," said Jill, tilting her head for emphasis.

"One and three quarters. Ten if you count electrical storms and initial chemistry. Anyway I can like him til he shows me otherwise, can't I?"

"NO," Chloe and Jill said in unison. Chloe continued,

"that's the whole point. Slow down and be more critical upfront; don't give him the benefit of the doubt. Be more discerning."

"Not that I watch her or anything," said Jill, "but Oprah said something years ago I really heard. She said 'when people tell you who they are, believe them.' Isn't that the best?"

"I do," Mattie said, thinking about it.

"No, Mattie, you don't. You make excuses for them, believe the best in them. When Bob told you his sister thought he drank too much, your antennae should have gone up. That's a red flag if I ever heard one, but you just told us he drank a little but didn't have a problem. He didn't have a problem until six months later when you were wasting all your time going to al-anon meetings and trying to cajole him into taking that first step."

"Jill's right, honey. The first time we were all out together I said something about how many martinis he had, but you defended him, made excuses for him. You know that."

"I get it. Must be a hazard I inherited from mom. And Grammy too if I think about it. I just don't get the clues. I love and trust everyone til they prove me otherwise."

"Yep, and we're just asking you to be more careful. If a guy gets drunk once, think twice. If he pulls out pills or other drugs, run – don't walk. If he asks to borrow money, say 'no', and never answer his call again."

"You can do it. We know you can." Uncharacteristically cheerleading, Jill grabbed Mattie's hand. "We're here for you, but you have to do your part."

"I get it. I will. Now let me think if I've seen anything weird from Mike."

"Well, he gets extra points for being so cute," said Jill, joking now.

They were walking back downhill wondering if they could catch manicures before dinner. In the fading sunlight between the bridge and the parking lot, they ducked into the ladies room to freshen up, changing clothes for the evening. Jill slid into jeans that hung from her hip bones and went with everything, especially her new green and gold leather sandals with tiny two-inch heels. Her top pulled it all together. A stretchy green and brown, earthy-toned gauzy print that crossed low over her pushed-up breasts, tied on the side and hugged her slim hips. She had her brown leather jacket just in case the theatre was cold. And she looked amazing.

Mattie wore the beaded blue dress from The Enchantress, and she felt like one as it embraced her petite body to just above the knee. For a wrap she had a silk pareu of various blues like the Maui sea and the new studded turquoise sandals that announced her outfit as a statement. *I am ocean; merge with me.*

Chloe's hair was in full glory from the natural humidity in the afternoon air. She flounced her curls, letting them fall over the shoulders of her black turtleneck. It was sweater-soft to mid-calf with three-quarter sleeves. A matching pair to Mattie's black-strapped platforms added three inches to her already tall frame. She brought along a pomegranate sweater that was nubbly with large buttons made from the trochus of Rarotonga. *Armani*, she thought. *Once a year they lift the raui, the ban, and for about two weeks islanders wade hip-deep into turquoise lagoons for the trochus round-up. Armani buys them from the Cook Islanders in container loads and turns the creatures' shells into buttons. Couture buttons.* She'd read it somewhere.

"Well golly, we sure scrub up nice," said Jill, admiring the lot. "There was a coupon in the room for a place in the K town. Do we still have time for a manicure?"

"I think so, and I remember passing the shopping center." It was the co-pilot. "Let's go."

By the time they found the mall and made their way to the Nail Spa, they were turning heads — clearly mainland girls, maybe an actress or someone famous. They heard the comments and absorbed them, smiling. When the girls were together and on like this, they were truly formidable, and once their nails were done, they'd be a force to reckon with. Air

Force. Task Force. May-the-force-be-with-you force.

thirty-one

NAIL SPA

"I'm so glad we quit bombing the Vietnamese so they could come to America to open restaurants and nail salons." Mattie was speaking matter-of-factly, a vibrating roller rising and falling along her spine, feet massaged by jacuzzi jets.

"That sounds a little racist, Mattie. If I didn't know you better..."

"But you do." Jill cut Chloe off. "We checked manicures and pedicures, and they were over a hundred dollars at the hotel. They're twenty here. She's just grateful, that's all."

"You too, I'm sure. Any time you can save money..."

"I'm not Jewish, Chloe. I'm Dutch. There are differences. And who made you so prejudiced all of a sudden?"

What started as a tease turned into a serious conversation about races, religions and cultures. While a small middle-aged Laotian cleansed and soaked Chloe's feet, she remembered taking a trip to the Midwest. *Bloody red state.* Tilly's sister had died shortly after Chloe's dad passed, and she went to lend moral support to her mom.

"I remember being in a small protestant church in a suburb of somewhere in Iowa when the creepiest feeling came over me. It wasn't the funeral or the deceased. I'd only met her once. But a strange and eerie feeling settled on me and just wouldn't leave. I spent the next couple hours trying to figure it out. Then later, sitting with mom in a diner on the outskirts of town I realized what it was. Like some bad Hollywood movie where bodies were being snatched, there with a forkful of coleslaw, I got it. Everyone, EVERYONE was the same. White bread. They were all white-skinned with European features and blue eyes. There were no Asians or blacks, not a Mexican in sight. The people in the town were all the same. Growing up in San Francisco, I was naturally surrounded by an ethnic smorgasbord, people of every hue and persuasion. In grade school I spoke four languages. My two best friends were from Hong Kong and Paraguay.

"Weird," said Mattie. "I've never been anywhere like the Midwest. Thank god. No wonder they want to ban everything and legislate their weird beliefs."

"Fear and ignorance never did win the race, but they end up starting all the wars." Mattie was opinionated about everything, but war, killing and torture really gagged her swaggering soul.

"But Hawaii get ethnic mix." The Laotian man spoke, clearing his throat. "We went to Texas first. My cousin lived there, but we couldn't stay. Everyone stare at us, don't trust us, so nail shop flop. Here we big success, and no one ever notice us."

"They threw eggs at our store windows." It was Jill's manicurist now – a tiny, scarred woman with black hair to her waist. "We couldn't go anywhere for the stares. You ever get the stare of hate? One guy spit at my boy. Only seven, my boy. Dat grown man just spat on my son's perfect black head."

"We love it here." The small man spoke again. "A world away from Texas. Better than home. Maui no ka oi." The girls had read this saying 'no ka oi'. It meant incomparable, without exception, the best.

"Maui no ka oi," they sang in unison as Chloe discovered yet another reason to love the place.

148

thirty-two

MACC

Fortunately the shopping center was close to the MACC, since the girls had lingered in solidarity and laughter while they got manicures and pedicures, tipping generously. Jed was waiting for Chloe out front by the sculpted gates, and she spotted him easily. He was tall too, wearing faded jeans and a blue shirt with tiny purple stripes, sleeves rolled up to just below the elbow. He obviously didn't own an iron, but at least it looked clean. He wore cowboy boots, his signature hat, and a dark red cordovan belt with a large turquoise-studded silver buckle, partially buried below the first hint of beer belly.

"You look amazing." he said to Chloe, then included the rest, "all of you. My favorite harem."

Finding their way to the back of the huge complex was easier with an escort. The cinema café was outdoors with a stage at the outer end and food concessions along the back wall. Circular white-clothed tables dotted the courtyard below trees that wore tiny twinkling lights up from their trunks and spreading out through their branches, creating the effect of a Parisian café in springtime.

Mattie had connected earlier in the day with Michael, who stood now by a table he'd been saving. He wore a navy blue polo shirt and grey slacks, Cole Haan loafers on bare feet. Mattie noticed him immediately. *My guy* she thought with a sense of pride. It was a feeling she couldn't remember having with any other guy before, except maybe her Dad.

"Hi, gorgeous." He greeted her with a hug. "How was your

day?"

"It was the best." Mattie looked over her shoulder at Jill and Chloe, nodding and letting them know she was remembering their pact. She was now officially on the lookout. If he didn't live so close, just across the Bay in Sausalito, if she weren't so attracted, *if only*, she might not even care. But alas, she did. Michael was different, and she had feelings already. Deep ones. Ones too new for labels or naming, too new for any kind of understanding. Who can explain electricity or the uncertainty principle? Or feelings that should have sent up a red warning light, telling her to be aware? Be very aware.

She leaned in anyway, needing the press of body against body, then stood back and asked, "do you like my new sandals? The girls got them for me."

"They're perfect," he said, taking her all in. "Come with me." He took her hand, leading her away.

"This is a sweet spot," said Chloe, admiring the courtyard, open to the stars overhead, going off like sparklers on the fourth of July. A small jazz trio was on stage, playing Brubeck.

"It's *the place* on Maui. There's a gallery, two theatres (one with the biggest screen on the island), dance studios and conference rooms. For the big performances they set up out here." Jed gestured towards the open lawn beyond the band platform. "And it all runs on volunteer labor. There were six thousand here a few months back for the Eagles Tour. Bonnie Raitt pulls a sold-out crowd in the amphitheatre as well, and two weeks ago, friends were scalping Katy Perry tickets.

Chloe was surprised. "Maui pulls big name talent from the mainland?"

"From all over the world. All the time. If you were a performer on tour, wouldn't this be *the place* to finish…and stay for some R&R? In fact many have stayed altogether. Kris Kristofferson and Willie Nelson are always throwing charity concerts for the Women's shelter and Big Brothers ~ Big Sisters. Dave Brubeck lives here, plays on Front Street over in Lahaina. Marty Dread does all the reggae concerts and benefits.

Randy Travis has a Japanese-style retreat. I run into Woody Harrelson all the time. Lots of celebrities chose Maui as 'home'. Even Oprah bought land here a few years ago with her trainer Bob. Hey, if you had the money wouldn't you want a place on Maui?" *YES!* Chloe thought, emphatically.

Michael and Mattie returned with two bottles of wine, uncorked, a red and a white, along with six glasses.

"So where's your guy?" he asked Jill, knowing it was her date who had got them all here.

Jill looked around, scanning the crowd for Dan, wondering if she'd recognize him in clothes – or he, her. "I'm on the lookout, but maybe we'd better order or at least get in line so we're not late for the show. Why don't I stand in cue and you all can sit here and enjoy your wine. I'll call over when I get near the front." It was self-serve with bar, dinner and dessert kiosks along the rear wall.

"We'll hold places with you," Michael said, taking Mattie's hand, two glasses of red and joining Jill as she made her way over. Mattie took note.

"He had a big championship meet today. I'm not surprised he's late."

"Don't you have his cell number?" Mattie asked.

"Good idea." Jill fumbled in her shoulder bag for her phone and Dan's number, which she found in an inner pocket, sandwiched between two condoms. She handed Mattie her glass and called the number, waited a few moments, then shut the phone without leaving a message. Jill never left messages.

"He'll show up, Jill." Mattie handed her glass back and clinked hers against it.

"To a great day!"

"Great day," Jill replied, beaming back at her friend but still hanging on to her concern.

"So tell me what you babes were up to today." Michael was interested, interesting, charming, not to mention – beautiful tonight. Mattie noticed.

Dan never did show.

The fivesome enjoyed fresh fish in a lemon-caper sauce and penne pasta with roasted vegetables, smothered in pesto, finishing with espressos. Jed had a sweet tooth and insisted on a couple desserts against female protest ('but we already had dessert today'), and they shared a chocolate mousse cake and lilikoi meringue pie, passing both with extra forks. Jazz, starlight, and good company – what could be better?

Jill tried calling Dan again, but to no avail. Still she wondered why he didn't make it…or at least call. Usually she welcomed uncertainties like spring rain, but this was different. She couldn't remember being stood up before, and it hurt in the place beneath her jovial surface, in the vulnerable little spot well hidden under her toughness.

The others took her under their collective wing, and she put on a happy face. Still she felt betrayed. She had cancelled Andy for Dan, and that made her feel even sillier. Before going into the theatre, Michael jogged up to the ticket booth and purchased a pass for Jill. Mattie gripped Michael's hand then turned to smile even more broadly at Jill, tilting her head in a clear *I-told-you-so* posture. Jill also took note.

It was the kind of movie that engendered post-film conversation. After a brief debate, they left cars in the lot and went in Michael's rented Explorer to a nearby nightclub Jed had suggested, where they found a booth near the back and shared a couple of hours in reaction to the film and each other, live blues, and heady liqueurs.

Dan never called. Never showed. Jill put on a brave face and joined in the fun. She was not one to be left out of a party. But inside she seethed.

By nearly one o'clock Michael announced that he really had to go. He had an early meeting with the County Council and needed to get back. The others were ready too, so they hugged goodbye back in the MACC parking lot, and Mattie and Michael left together. An awkward moment ensued as Chloe realized she wanted to go with Jed but needed to go with Jill who naturally protested.

"I'm a big girl, Chloe. I can find my own way home."

But Chloe insisted, saying, "I'll drive."

She turned and kissed Jed lightly. "It was fun. Thanks."

It left him wondering whether she was into him or not. He'd read the book and wanted to make sure she knew that he was, so before she could climb into the driver's seat he pushed the door shut with one hand and wrapped the other around her waist and in deep, intentional tones said, "it *was* fun. Let's play again before you leave." Then he met her eyes straight on and looked deeply into her lagoon-blues. Their lips melted into each other's like landing in a down blanket, sinking deeper and deeper, parting just enough to catch a breath then melding for more.

Chloe was speechless, closing the car door and looking up at Jed, grinning now, eyes twinkling.

"Whew," she uttered to Jill as she turned the key in the ignition. Jill patted her thigh. "Nice guy," she said, and she meant it.

thirty-three

MUTINY

The moment Jill entered the suite she checked the message light and picked up. There were five calls. She turned the speaker up and listened.

"Chloe, it's your mother. Just wondering how you are, honey. Isn't it lovely? I still remember all the golf vacations your Dad and I took on Maui. It was our favorite of all the islands. Especially the blue and gold courses at Wailea. Anyway, you don't need to call back. I know you're probably busy running around. But do play some golf if you get a chance. Well, too-de-loo, or as the natives say, Alooooha." Beep.

"Jill, it's Andy. I couldn't remember if you were busy tonight, but I was hoping if you got back before dinner you'd let me feed you. I'm a pretty good cook. I do remember you're all going to Hana tomorrow, so I'll just confirm our date Friday evening in case we play tag tonight. Or you get swept away by someone else. That would be easy with your looks. Anyway, call me if you get back, and when you get to Hana, don't forget Hamoa Beach. Aloha. God bless." It made the sting of being stood up even nastier.

"Hi girls. This is Lori at the office. Chloe, I tried to reach you all day on your cell. There's a bit of a crisis here." Chloe perked up again. "Mark Keller left and took four agents, and who knows how many clients, with him. They're apparently opening their own shop down by the wharf somewhere. Pretty chicken shit to wait til you leave if you ask me. Anyway call

155

me." Beep.

Chloe took a deep breath as her face pinched. She didn't want to think about the ramifications, but couldn't help herself. *Bummer.* She breathed again, a slow, collective breath. *Good riddance.*

"Aloha, this is Michael calling for Mattie. I guess you girls are out and about. Anyway I'm out with the frogs but looking forward to tonight. Hey I might just turn into a prince. Just wanted to make sure you had my cell number in case you wanted to reach me. It's 415-288-8415." Jill pressed 'save' and went on, hoping it was Dan.

"Jill, it's Eli again. Sorry to bother you, but someone at your office called asking about some program you recently installed for them. I walked him through some tech stuff, so he probably won't need to ring you. I'm still having trouble with the number one server. In fact I've spent all week with that g-d hardware. Anyway, I made an executive decision since you didn't call back and purchased a new one. State of the art. Quadruples our storage space. You'll love it. If we ever get the bad one working again, we'll have a spare for back-ups and all. I got a great price online, and I'll be setting it all up tomorrow. Seamless, babe. Don't worry. Everything here is just fine. Have fun, and be careful out there. Bye now."

Nothing from Dan. Jill's eyes grew dewy then she got angry, picked up the phone, punching in nine then the number.

"Hello," Dan answered his cell. She could hear music and loud background noises.

"Is this some sort of game you play with the tourists?" She was yelling into the phone.

"Who's this?" he asked.

"It's Jill, your date. Remember?"

"Oh, hi Jill. Did you go then?"

"Of course I went. We had a date at the MACC. Did you get hit on the head with a surfboard and get amnesia?"

"No, I just, well, um…when you didn't show up at the meet, I guess I figured you weren't interested. I mean, well, I

156

did place and all. In fact we're having a totally awesome victory celebration. Wanna join us?"

"Dan, you stood me up. You didn't score any points with me. You could have called at least."

"I tried, really I did. I couldn't find your cell number, and when I rang your hotel I couldn't remember your last name. Even though I knew the concierge on duty, she didn't know the three haole babes from San Francisco. How 'bout tomorrow night, doll?"

"How 'bout never," Jill said, hanging up the phone.

Chloe came out of the bathroom. "You over him?" she asked, squeezing Jill's arm.

"Yep. Over and out. Next!"

Chloe grabbed a couple of Baileys from the mini bar and took Jill out on the lanai. They were both feeling a little jilted by men they obviously didn't know well enough.

"We could use some of Mattie's medicine," Chloe said.

"The guy or the advice?" Jill realized she had been seduced again by a body and made an inner determination to meet some real men from now on. Like Andy. She could take lemons – she imagined herself squeezing Dan's balls – and make lemonade.

Chloe drank half of the bottle and realized that for the last couple of months, production had been off a bit in the sector that usually excelled at keeping the pipeline full. They had obviously been planning the mutiny for months. She knew exactly who the four were. They'd been more secretive of late, and they used to hang out together. In fact she remembered all of them in the conference room one afternoon a week or two before.

When she walked in, the room went quiet. She retrieved a video she was looking for and left, unsuspecting. As for Mark – she'd been waiting for a way to get rid of that prima donna for months. Now she wouldn't have to worry about lawsuits or problems. There would be a small dip in gross income to the company until her mid-range producers picked up the slack, but frankly at eighty percent agent splits the company was just making their overhead anyway. She may even do better with those five gone. *It's perfect being here...now. Gives me some perspective.* Chloe forced a smile, hugged Jill, and refilled their glasses. "I'm starting to like this place."

"I thought Michael had an early call," Jill said out of the blue. "So where's our girl?"

"Wait. I'm the den mom," said Chloe, poking at Jill.

As if on cue, the door opened and Mattie stood quietly, leaning against it.

"We know you're there for gawd's sake," Jill said.

"Oh, hi. I thought you'd be sleeping." She entered the suite then noticed the gals out on the lanai.

Jill was restless. "I'm about to head down to the pool bar. It's way too early to sleep."

Chloe spoke. "How was it, Mattie?"

"You both saw him in action. Now do you see why it's so hard to put the brakes on?"

"Honey," Chloe went on, "he's your first date since nearly two years of lousy ones with Tom. Anyone would look good after that rat. I mean Michael's adorable, but just take it slow."

"Naw. Get it on. He's a stud," Jill chimed in. "Just wear condoms and don't get emotionally attached."

"Well that's great advice." Mattie was getting sarcastic. "Just cause you never even give guys a chance to show their feelings, or when they do you drop them like radioactive waste, doesn't mean that's what we want from ours." She looked over at Chloe, hoping for agreement. "I want more. I want it all. God knows I've settled for less. And thanks for bringing me down. I had a wonderful time with Michael – who happens to be a wonderful man. But he's not my first, Chloe. I've had a couple sympathy dates since Tom."

"We're happy for you, Mattie, really we are," Chloe said.

"Sure, miss so-cautious-she'll-never-find-anyone and miss bang-'em-and-run. I'm in great company for learning the dating game."

"Yea," Jill joked now, "but maybe he's just not that into

you." Chloe and Jill broke out in simultaneous laughter.

"I'll have what she's having," said Mattie, joining them with a snort.

thirty-four

LANAI

Chloe went inside to the mini bar and set up the table on the lanai with ice, another glass and more little bottles. "We've got a better bar here than the pool bar. Stay, Jill. We'll solve all the world's problems."

"I'd just like to solve a few of our own. We are, after all, three fairly intelligent women. We should be able to fix what's wrong with us."

"Are you sure we want to go *there*?" said Mattie.

"Why not?" said Chloe. "I mean we just need to figure out what we really want..."

"And then a plan of attack," said Jill as if preparing a battle strategy.

"It's easy," said Mattie. "I want love. Lots of romance, great kissing of course."

"And great sex."

"Come on, Jill. It's Mattie's time."

"Caring and sharing, warmth and comfort...someone who wants me. Intimacy of course, emotional intimacy. What's on your list, Chloe?"

"Well, let's see. Poetry and laughter, good conversation. Great sex is nice, but not without great conversation (nodding to Jill). Intelligence. I have always been seduced by intelligence. Partnership. Passion. Compassion. Yea, I think two souls have to share a deeply spiritual life."

"Well, get ye to a monastery then. Join the Canterbury Tales," said Jill, spoofing and pouring another round. "My list is

161

easy: it starts with a gorgeous hunk of man, then excitement – you know the rush of chemicals, synapses firing. I mean what's love without a good deal of lust? That's what gets me to great sex. Not conversation. I need physical. I can take care of my own spirit. Rich would be nice and a good cook, since I can't, but the last two aren't necessarily qualifiers."

"Did anyone mention fun? I want a playmate too," said Chloe who had taken out a pad and pen and was making columns. "Okay so we're here:

Mattie	Jill	Chloe
Love & Romance	Great Sex, Lust	Poetry/Laughter
Caring/sharing	Hunk, physical	Conversation
Comfort	Chemistry	Intelligence
Intimacy	Rich	Partnership
Emotional	Good Cook	Passion/Compassion
Companionship	Lust	Spiritual & Fun!

"I'd say we have a working template," said Chloe, handing the list around. Add what you need."

"I need another drink," said Jill, emptying out another bottle, this time mixing some Cognac into her Baileys.

As stars twinkled overhead, three goddesses hung together on their lanai, sharing intimacies and trying to solve the age-old questions of what a woman really wants, finally agreeing it would be tough to find guys to fill the bill. "If we had, would we still be looking? Maybe it's mission impossible," said Jill.

"Maybe we don't recognize it cause we choose the wrong guys too soon or avoid the right ones cause we don't have our priorities straight." Mattie was philosophizing now. "Or maybe Michael's *the one* and I'm too busy being critical."

"Like you have even one tiny criticism of him," said Jill.

"Well," said Chloe. "Would you?" At that point Michael became *perfect man* for all of them. *Perfect fantasy man.*

Finally turning in, they snacked on chocolate covered mac nuts, left on their pillows.

162

"Good night, John Boy," Jill said, turning off the light.

And then there's the seduction of place, Chloe thought, rolling over to face out towards the moon, which looked like a freight train hurtling towards her. She became aware of a shaggy dog feeling that nuzzled in every time she thought of Maui – the island, the myth, the very real very present now of paradise. She was falling in love with an island. Who wouldn't? It was formidably beautiful yet interesting, sexy...and smelled great, was self-sufficient, active and adventuresome, had a sunny disposition and gave her all the stars. It was fun. It was poetry and promised more.

As if hypnotized by an unexpected heartsong, she got up and walked back out to the lanai. Date palms swayed in a gentle tradewind, reminding her of pyramids and camels, Ali Baba and palaces encrusted with jewels. *Open Simsim*, she whispered, wondering if Maui would reciprocate. Air carrying the scents and secrets of a tropical world caressed her skin, and she looked over her kingdom of torches and bedouin tents and a mandala of stars. *'God is good, Sabu'*.

thirty-five

TWIN FALLS

They were up by eight, only because Mattie had set the alarm, quickly falling into the chaos that inevitably comes before organization. The suite shrunk as the three tripped over each other, waited for shower time, booted up their laptops and iPads to make sure all urgent loose ends were handled, ordered up coffee and croissants and a plate of fresh papaya, mango, lychee, and other tropical fruits.

They dressed, packed and repacked. Jill checked in with Kimo to confirm catching Uncle Keoki mid day, and Mattie called to remind Michael she'd meet him later at the hotel. To avoid wasting precious time Chloe sent Lori a text message instead of calling: *thanks for handling the mess. I'm back Friday evening.*

By ten they were on the highway and barreling down the road, looking like the chicks from Thelma and Louise with Brad Pitt in the back seat, morphed into Mattie. They passed the subdivisions of Kihei and turned onto the cross-island road that led past wiliwilis and miles of sugar cane. Passing through Kahului, Chloe spoke up, "last chance for the trip. Anything we need?"

"Don't you dare stop," said Jill. "Especially at one of the marts. We'll never make it to Hana."

"I need film," said Mattie.

"Use my digital," Jill replied.

"Has someone got sugar free gum? Condoms?"

"You're covered, girl."

165

Chloe listened while the two squabbled, finally deciding that they didn't really need anything.

"Besides," Jill continued, "Kimo says there's a general store there that has everything. I brought four bottles of water, vodka, and bloody mary mix. Other than that we cleaned out the mini bar last night. We can make it a few hours."

Case settled. They swung past Baldwin Beach and moved slowly into Paia behind a traffic bottleneck, emerging on the other side and stopping for a few minutes to watch surfers at the Ho'okipa Lookout. Surf was up, and about sixty bodies rode waves at the east end and windsurfed at the west.

"It's absolutely glorious!" exclaimed Chloe. "I love this place!"

"Drive," said Mattie.

Within a few miles they passed a highway sign that said they were officially on the road to Hana. Then they saw it, a small hand-painted plaque that said 'Twin Falls'.

"Whoa, wait, stop. This is in our Lonely Planet." Mattie was insistent.

Chloe had already planned on stopping here, but hadn't realized it was so close out of town. She pulled the convertible over to the right, just adjacent to a small souvenir hut, parking under a giant mango tree. It took them about fifteen minutes to hike up to the falls, stopping on the way back at another pool which was much larger with various levels of rock encircling it and a rope swing on the far side. Naturally Jill dove in, giving the others permission to do the same. In no time they were on the far side, swinging out over the water and jumping in, shrieking and laughing and acting like kids again.

A group of locals, two moms and about six young children, picnicked on one of the big rocks, and before long the girls had competition for the rope swing. They gave up in no time. The boys were better and made much more noise. Chloe began swimming end to end, and Jill joined her, turning it into a race. Mattie edged back up the path where they'd left their things, spread a towel and laid out on the rock sunning and humming. She grabbed Jill's digital camera, shooting pictures and videos of her friends frolicking below. It was not rare for any of them to let out their inner child, but they were usually together when they did. Jill and Chloe got into a splash match then later fought each other off the rock near the shore's edge, so that it took them five minutes just to exit the water. Howls of laughter bounced off the rock walls, enclosing the pool. Mattie looked across at the moms who had to be about their age, maybe younger, excusing her nutty friends.

"You don't get out much, do you?" one said, shaking her head and smiling.

"Not nearly enough," Mattie acknowledged.

thirty-six

COCO LOCO

They bought three shave-ices at the little shack where they parked the car and then continued down the road, renewed. Their hair dried in the sun and wind, but their spirits remained wet and juicy.

"Word games," Jill said. "Favorite movies. Clockwise."

Mattie started. "Out of Africa. *My favorite.*"

Then Chloe. "Amadeus."

Then Jill. "Sideways."

"Sleepless in Seattle." It was Mattie again.

"English Patient."

"Oh, I loved that film," said Mattie.

"A 't' film." Jill was musing. "Oh, how about The Matrix?"

"Is Dr. Zhivago close enough? I can't think of an x movie," said Mattie in her most childish voice.

"If I can say Olmost Famous," Chloe chortled.

"Shindler's List," said Jill, back on track.

They went on for miles, passing switchbacks and waterfalls, gorges and one-lane bridges. A cascade of tropical indulgence infused their senses as mile after mile of fragrance flew past in a green blur. And always on their left the vast stretch of deep blue, far below and farther yet out.

"To Kill a Mockingbird."

"Dances with Wolves."

They traveled through a eucalyptus forest, energized by the acrid smell. It was even better than the sauna at the Bay Club.

"Chocolat," Mattie started up again.

169

"Turning Point."

"The Manchurian Candidate."

"Ēmerican Beauty." Mattie said, stumped again.

Chloe turned on the CD player and put on a Beatles anthology. '*The long and winding road...that leads to your door*'. "How appropriate," she said, making a mental note of how often things worked like this. *Synchronicity. Serendipity. Kismet. What's the right word?* She spent lots of time searching for right words.

For miles they saw signs advertising 'Bruddah Bob's Coco Loco Hut', 'One mile to Bruddah's Coco Hut', 'LAST CHANCE before the long and winding road to Hana', 'Only ½ Mile', 'Here come Da Hut'. They sprouted up like Burma Shave signs around each winding corner, so no one was surprised when Chloe pulled over at a little grass shack with about four sandwich signs on the road and more signs painted on the building and the block bathroom and hanging from the top of the shack itself: 'Fresh Tropical Smoothies', 'Dogs', 'Children Playing', 'Aloha means Coco Loco', and 'This is It ~ Bob's Place'.

Climbing out of the car, they approached another thatched shack. Jill spotted him first – must have been Bob. His two hundred pounds hung comfortably on a six-foot frame. He wore a graying black tee with 'HBO Sports' written on the left pocket and camouflage shorts that fell to just below his knees with pockets at the thighs and rear. Over his ponytail he wore a baseball cap, turned backwards. Purple-blue reflecting sunglasses hid his eyes, and a pencil was tucked behind his left ear.

No flip-flops here. Bob wore construction boots with his socks rolled down over the tops. A black Timex partially covered the tattoo that encircled his left wrist. Another tattoo of dragons and unicorns adorned his right forearm from the elbow to the wrist, and behind his left ear was a small yin/yang. He was tanned and beefy, about mid forties and at home in his body and his world. A beautifully trimmed beard met a thin mustache at the corners of his mouth. He looked up at the girls approaching with an easy smile and said, "Welcome. Aloha. What's your pleasure, ladies?"

He whacked the top off a coconut with a machete, inserted a straw and handed it to Jill, who reached the shack first. It was chilled and delicious.

"Oh, Mattie, try this." She handed it to Mattie who passed it on to Chloe.

"Yum. That's a little bit of bliss," Chloe said, nodding at Bob and sidling up to the bar. He was putting out coconut cups filled with toasted coconut chips. They were sweet and salty, crunchy and satisfying.

"Where you girls from?" he asked, offering them other fruits or smoothies.

"San Francisco," they said in unison then giggled in embarrassment.

"We're triplets," said Jill, explaining the obvious.

For the next half hour Bob entertained them with stories of his life in the islands while he made mango-papaya-banana smoothies and fish tacos with avocado, tomato, and fresh goat cheese.

He came over fifteen years before, following a bad divorce in Santa Rosa, falling helplessly in love with a Hawaiian princess. They began having babies, one then another and another, until they had seven. His wife's family owned the land, which ran along a small access road down towards the coast where they lived. They had chickens and goats, a fishpond and fruit orchards and a valley of wild trees – avocados, papayas, mangos, mountain apples, lychee, and seven varieties of bananas.

"Usually the kids help, but they're either in school or with mom in town today. Thursdays are slower, so I hold down the fort. We grow almost everything we serve, so the menu changes seasonally." He tried out a little pidgin on the girls but lost them. A few jokes went down okay, but the luscious food went down even better.

"How far are we from Hana?" Chloe asked when she could get a word in.

"Are you driving or flying?" he asked, laughing and slicing a fresh mango.

Jill got the joke. "Chloe's driving. I'm the co-pilot."

"Well then you ladies should make it in an hour and a half or two from here. Only about thirty-five single lane bridges and five hundred more hairpin turns."

"Word Games!!" they said in unison, leaving money on the counter for lunch and a bag of toasted coconut they took along for the car. As they drove off, blowing kisses, another rental car pulled in right behind them. *Popular spot,* thought Jill, sliding Carlos Santana in the CD slot. *Coco Loco.*

thirty-seven

HANA

Verdant cliffs, waterfalls that looked like ribbons of rainbows, and thousands of hairpin turns later, Chloe pulled into a gas station.

"Are we there yet?" asked Mattie, more troubled than the others by the long and winding road. She had asked Chloe to stop twice to pull herself back from the point of no return, each stop bringing her welcomed relief. Like a little cold treated with echinacea and herb tea, just stopping for ten minutes and walking around re-grounded her and calmed her inner ear. She remembered getting car sick as a child, when her family made cross-country treks each summer to visit their mountain cabin.

"Wanna drive?" Chloe asked, tired from the strenuous work of driving switchbacks but also thinking it might help. "The driver never gets sick." It turns out Mattie wasn't *that* sick, but she did switch seats with Jill who climbed in the back, stretched out and fell promptly to sleep.

It was Mattie who now read highway signs to Chloe. "I think we're here."

Chloe had seen a couple of Hana signs herself, but was looking for some sort of village or town center, and really had no idea where in the world they were. All she knew is that they were somewhere near the ocean in the country. Beautiful country. A few homes appeared by the road; they passed a sign for a State Park, rounded a few more corners, and finally spied a gas station. When she stopped all three emerged, eager to stretch their legs.

"Terre firma," Mattie said, opening the door and kneeling down to kiss the ground.

"Yikes!" said Chloe. "We're not in Kansas anymore. Check this out. Four eighty-nine a gallon. I'm taking up a collection."

Mattie followed Jill towards a small general store. It was single wall constructed on a concrete slab, at least a hundred years old. The front was plastered with handwritten notices for bands and babysitters, earthmoving and equipment rentals, adult ballet, web design, and lost dogs. After falling in love with one of the dogs pictured on the bulletin board, Mattie entered the shop. She found the chips and candy bars first then a display of smoked marlin and a basket of homemade chocolate chip cookies. She picked out a couple of large water bottles from a cooler shelf where Jill was deciding on beer.

"St. Pauli Girl or Steinlager?" she asked Mattie.

"Coors Light is fine with me, but then I'm not really a beer drinker. How about a bottle of vino?"

Jill spotted a bottle of Pilsner Urquel, a Czech beer her old lover, Zach, had introduced her to several years ago. Memories flooded over her as she reached in for a bottle.

Zach had been the closest Jill ever got to marriage. They met her sophomore year at Berkeley in the chess club but didn't date until midway through her senior year when she ran into him, literally, at the University library. After a few moments of conversation, he awkwardly asked if she wanted to go to the Roxie to see a foreign film, and even though she hated movies with sub-titles, she agreed. That weekend she went to his lacrosse game against Stanford, and by Monday they had practiced such athletics she could hardly walk.

Overnight they were an item, a couple, and although she kept her room with Chloe that spring, she virtually moved in with Zach. They had so much in common, much of which had to do with a love of sex – wild, athletic, unedited animal coupling – lots of it. As the school year concluded they talked about the future, their future, his in architecture, hers in finance, theirs – well they never could quite pin that down. On graduation weekend he proposed, even bought a ring, but Jill suspected it was more for show since both their parents were there, and what's a red-blooded, all-american couple to do but face the future together?

She hadn't said 'yes', but she didn't say 'no'. Instead she just changed the subject whenever the topic came up, which was less and less until it didn't come up at all. By summer he'd moved from his apartment in Kensington across to the city and into a remodeled warehouse on the upside of the Tenderloin district. To avoid a housing decision, Jill had taken a sudden trip to Europe, and Zach finally returned the ring for a refund before the ninety days ran out.

While Jill was in Florence, Zach met Molly, an architect from Stanford, also doing a summer apprenticeship at Newton-Bing, and when Jill returned in early September her things had been boxed and taken to Chloe's house on the hill.

Jill pulled out two six-packs of assorted imported beers and a 24-pack of Coors for their hosts. Tears welled up in her eyes as she tried to remember the last time she cried. *How silly* she thought, wiping them away and reaching back in to grab two Pilsners.

"Sixty-five dollars. Can you believe it?" Chloe was in shock. "I've never spent so much on gas." They met at the checkout counter. Mattie had a basket full of cheeses, crackers, chips and chocolate, cookies, tins of mac nuts, a newspaper and a can of dolmas. "I love these," she said, holding the can to her heart. "I'll get the food," she said. "But I feel your pain. Check out the price for a bag of chips."

"I'm on for the booze," said Jill, grabbing a bottle of red wine on display by the cashier, still ruminating about Zach and how he got away.

As the clerk loaded a box with the beers, two cowboys sauntered in, turning to hold the door for the girls.

"Let me get those," one of them said, taking the large box from Jill and morphing from cowboy to gentleman in an instant, carrying it out to the rental car.

"Do you know a guy named Uncle Keoki?" Jill said. "We're supposed to meet him here…or somewhere in Hana. We are in Hana, aren't we?"

"Sure and sure. We know Keoki. We know lots of Keokis. Is it the Keoki with the B & B, married to Emma Baldwin?" the tall one responded.

"That's him," Chloe said. *Is everyone on this island a Baldwin?* "Do you know his place?"

"Yes, ma'am, but you'll never find it. Why don't I call him for you? I'm Kepa, by the way, and this is Zach."

Jill turned, surprised by the name, the memories of her Zach, and the serendipity of all things.

"Goodness, we've forgotten our manners," Chloe said. "This is Jill, the cute blonde is Mattie, and I'm Chloe."

Zach tipped his cowboy hat. "Where you girls from?"

"We all live in the big city – San Francisco. Are you real cowboys?" Mattie was charmed.

"Work right here on the ranch," said Kepa.

Zach pulled a cell phone from his jeans pocket and dialed a number, handing the phone to Jill. "Just ask for Uncle."

By the time Keoki arrived twenty minutes later the five had gone through a six pack plus a few of the Coors and a bag of chips, and plans had been made to meet up later for a party at Zach's.

"We'll pick you up at Keoki's then. How's eight? My cousin's band is playing. You'll love 'em."

thirty-eight

B & B

Keoki was a bear of a guy – about six feet, coffee brown with reddish ecru hair in dreadlocks halfway down his back. Huge black eyes twinkled and creased in the corners; etched lines moved down and across his face, which beamed like a headlight. They felt immediately and warmly welcomed. It took fifteen minutes to get to his hideaway, with Keoki driving thirty miles per hour and waving to everyone they passed – pick-up trucks and scooters, school children along the road, friends manning roadside fruit stands.

He finally turned left down a little dirt road that was unmarked from the highway except for a tall lone palm with myriads of flowers at its base – impatiens in pinks and purples, orange birds of paradise and Christmas-red poinsettias. Kepa was right – they never would have found it.

The roadway wound down through a little grove of eucalyptus and ironwoods then opened onto a clearing with a cluster of thatched huts circling a main house, which was white with dark green trim and featured a large verandah filled with rockers, a woven swing, and green plastic chairs. Off to the side was a hammock, strung up between two giant bamboo.

Aunt Emma appeared on the front porch, waving. She was large, about five foot seven with black salt and pepper hair, braided then twisted round and round on her head, settling into a bun of sorts with little wispy curls framing her sweet Hawaiian face. Weathered and lined by life, she beamed as Keoki did. "Welcome, ladies. I'm Auntie Emma." Her voice was song.

They were offered a choice of two rooms in the main house, a cottage, or the tree house, which sat precipitously in a massive monkeypod.

"I'm not sure about all that climbing, late or maybe drunk," said Jill. "I think I need to be more grounded." She motioned over to the thatched bungalow nearest the house, and while she and Keoki unpacked the car, taking in bags and boxes, Mattie and Chloe disappeared, drawn by a little footpath beneath the tree house, which led down to a small black sand beach. Deep musky scents of rotting fruit and flowers decomposing filled their heads. It was a smell Chloe loved – the sweet fertile earth. They emerged onto a beach where salt air revitalized them. Sunlight shimmered across the cove and danced on the moving waters of the sea. *Dancing Water.* Chloe remembered her Nana's Cherokee name and understood for the first time what 'dancing water' meant.

Mattie looked at Chloe, and the challenge was on as they took off, sprinting to the other end of the beach and back, breathing hard and giggling like geckos, finally collapsing into a heap of hugs and yelps, wrestling and rolling around until every exposed inch was covered in black diamonds.

Arriving back at the clearing, they climbed up and peered into the branch house. It was built around an enormous tree, with different living areas poking out from the trunk's center – a sitting room, bedroom area, small table and two chairs next to a water jug and small mini fridge. Down a few steps was a split-level bedroom, suspended from a branch above. Both rooms were simple with Hawaiian print bedcovers and a standing hat rack with a few hangars for a closet and large woven baskets for clothes.

Their bungalow was even better and had a private bathroom they didn't have to climb down to. Gaily-colored print curtains danced in the afternoon breeze, and an umbrella stand by the door held hats, rain slickers and umbrellas, sunscreen and bug repellant. There was a queen bed centered on the far wall and a single, tucked in against the screened wall annex. Both were covered in hand-stitched Hawaiian quilts like the ones the girls had seen at the museum in Lahaina. Oblong lauhala mats covered the wood floors and crawled under an antique table, positioned between two chairs. A cobalt glass vase filled with tropical flowers sat at the center of the marble top, along with a few local Maui papers and some old magazines and books previous guests must have left behind.

Jill won the toss and chose the single bed, and they all settled in, hanging up a few things and sliding pairs of shoes under their beds.

"Uncle said to come on up to the house when we're ready. Emma has cookies and lemonade, and we're going sight-seeing.

"Bring hiking shoes," Jill added.

Chloe collapsed on the bed. "I don't want to go anywhere. Especially if we have to drive. But you can bring me some cookies and lemonade."

A ten-minute intervention ensued, and Chloe lost the battle. "Okay. Just give me half an hour of quiet then I'll join you on the verandah."

thirty-nine

CRAZY WISDOM

Despite growing up in a large extended family, or maybe because of it, Chloe needed alone time, quiet time. Had always needed it. Like air. It was the food she fed on, the source of her poetry and dreams, the still reflection that assures us we are real and true. Though tired, she was feeling virtuous and serene. She rolled over when Jill and Mattie left the cabin, retrieved her notebook, and began to write. She scribbled in the margins – little poems and haiku with sketches of Cymbidium orchids, plumeria, and tree ferns climbing up the page.

Back road blues and greens
Eureka, we're in Hana
Magic starts and builds

The wind talks through trees
Has a conversation with
Palm fronds and ironwoods

My ears listen in
Deep in conversation with
Restless wind and trees

Coffee and muffins
Jazz up my morning outlook
To be here now...grace

The wind is artist
Like Pollack, throwing colors
And angst on canvas

In my idleness
I watch a bird
Perched on a hibiscus

Double flamed flowers
Frame his home

I watch the springtime come again
And wonder if I will ever return

The view from the tree
Is so stunning it defies
A relentless fear

The sunlight plays tag,
Catches me and lifts me up,
Beyond the shadows

A perfect day
No work
All play

Crazy wisdom
Mango butter
Wet jeans

Chloe sat motionlessly on a paisley chaise in the corner of the room, her long legs tucked under, giraffe-like. She'd been in some sort of Zen induced trance – a place she loved and visited frequently – when she heard the soft sounds of music wafting in through the windows facing the main house. She delicately placed her pen inside her notebook as if to mark the page, and then put the notepad on the afghan at her feet and slowly untangled herself.

Pulling red Capri's on over her light blue thong, she checked herself in the mirror. *Not bad*, she thought checking out her little white tee with short, capped sleeves and big red hot lips. A slow smile appeared as she remembered the Stones concert in Golden Gate Park. She brushed her gleaming auburn curls, which were softer and curlier than she ever remembered.

forty

HASEGAWA

The music was Keoki, strumming his ukulele and singing in a sweet tenor voice while Emma danced a slow, undulating hula, graceful and weightless as though her large frame defied gravity. Her hands were birds and butterflies, rain and sun. Her hips spoke generations. Two dogs, a young rottweiler and a little reddish poi pup, sat at Keoki's feet, glancing up as Chloe arrived.

"Bravo. Mahalo." Jill and Mattie clapped and cheered to show appreciation for the impromptu show. "Hi, Chloe. How was your nap?"

"Thoughtful," she said. "I'm reborn."

"Have some refreshment, dear," Emma said, passing a plate of cookies to Chloe and tucking a gardenia behind her left ear. Chloe turned to thank her.

"They're the bomb," said Jill, reaching for another.

Mattie filled her in. "Keoki wants to take us to some ancient gardens – native plants and all. We knew you'd love that. There's a famous heiau there, an old Hawaiian temple and lookout that's like the largest one in all of Polynesia."

"And he promised to stop at a couple of beaches. There's a red sand one, a regular white sand one, a gravel one." Jill was jonesing for a beach stop, applying sunscreen and mosquito repellant on her uncovered skin.

"I'm ready when you are." Chloe took a cookie, thanking Emma with a hug for her gracious hospitality.

"I need to be back by six," Mattie added. "I'm meeting

Michael at the Hana Hotel at seven. If you and Jill are partying with the cowboys, I thought maybe I could use the car."

"Sure, honey, but make sure you get directions from Uncle. I think we passed it in town, but I'm not positive. It wasn't obvious." Chloe took the sunscreen from Jill and began spreading it on her face, neck and arms as they made their way to Keoki's Jeep.

"I've put beach towels and a cooler in the back," Emma explained. "Have fun."

Jill jogged over to the cabin to retrieve her backpack, a green bikini and a cold Pilsner while Mattie fumbled through her beach bag. "I think I left something."

They were back at exactly six pm, having hiked, swam and sunned all over Hana, stopping at last at the Hasegawa General Store for plate lunches and a frozen pizza. Other than Mattie, they'd be eating in. Besides after hiking at Kahanu and a good swim at the red sand beach, Jill and Chloe were starving. Mattie too, but she was more excited than hungry as she picked through her things, deciding on an outfit. She got plenty of coaching from the others.

"Not that. Makes your skin look dull. Oh, honey, you should throw that thing out. Or give it to Jill. It's perfect for her coloring. Green on a romantic date? Are you mad?"

She settled on a chocolate brown sleeveless dress that clung to her body and little gold espadrilles that wrapped around her tiny ankles. She blow-dried her hair, which hung long and straight and looked like ironed buttercups. The sun had highlighted it, and even Mattie thought it looked great. That was a first.

"Okay, right at the highway, six miles back to town..."

"You'll remember," Chloe reassured her. "Say hi to Michael."

"Don't do anything we wouldn't do," said Jill, leaving plenty of room for just about anything.

forty-one

PANIOLO BAR

Michael had called at about three, arranging to meet Mattie at the hotel bar, have dinner there in the dining room, then either stay for some dancing or call the girls, and – if the party was a smash – join them.

Mattie thought about being cautious with him when every fiber in her being said to throw caution to the wind.

"I have one question, Jill. At what point does one get to quit being so cautious, stop being on the lookout. I mean, do I ever get to stop being so focused and judgmental?" One would surmise that it simply wasn't Mattie's nature to do what she had promised the girls to do. She went on. "Can you stop once you're married? Or after your first child? Or your tenth anniversary?"

"Whoa, girl." Jill wrapped an arm around Mattie. "No need to be nervous. Just notice. Look, listen and learn. Just be with him instead of future-tripping some sweet little scenario of domestic bliss. That'll come soon enough if he's Mr. Right."

"Just have fun tonight," Chloe reiterated.

Mattie took a deep breath. "Okay, you two. I'll catch you later."

She relaxed a little as she got into the car. The keys were in the ignition. She checked the mirror, adjusted the seat, turned the music down from blaring, and curled around the circular drive and up the road. Yes, you could say she was nervous, but it was more like performance anxiety. Simply, she wanted to impress. She really liked Michael and had already fantasized

187

about seeing him once they returned home. *How do I put the brakes on my feelings? No one told me that.*

By the time she arrived at the Paniolo Bar, Mattie was filled with a glowing anticipation. After all, it had been twenty hours since she'd last seen him.

The bar was jammed. Tourists and locals, identified by their dress, hung on bar stools and gathered in groupings on upholstered chairs. Platters of pupus joined the collection of cocktail and wine glasses on table and bar tops. While a three-piece band played old Hawaiian favorites on guitar, ukulele and a washtub bass, a lithe young Polynesian with black hair to her waist danced hula. Barefoot.

Mattie scanned the room, unable to find him. She was, after all, a little early. Maybe fifteen minutes or so. Taking the empty stool at the end of a koa wood and brass bar, she leaned in to order a cosmopolitan. It looked like the kind of bar where the bartender could make anything, and that's what the girl wanted. Fidgeting, she dove into a bowl of mac nuts, washed it down with her cocktail then ordered another.

When the band took 'a quick break' the floor cleared a little, and swiveling around Mattie thought she saw Michael at the far side of the room. *No, that can't be him,* she said to herself, looking the other way. She looked back again, her eyes staring now at Michael, her Michael, with his arm wrapped around another woman. Two children, about six to eight, sat at a table with them. Boys, dark haired and polo-shirted just like Michael. It all looked so Norman Rockwell, except that it was *her* Michael. There with another woman. Playing family. They were all laughing as if over some great joke. Just then he leaned his head against hers and turned to tenderly kiss her cheek. As he did this, he brushed some flyaway hair out of her face as he had with Mattie just the night before.

Her heart gripped her chest as she looked away. *Why? Why had he not mentioned his family? A wife? He seemed so perfect. How could I not notice something? Am I that naïve?* As she shifted the blame to herself, a blush rose through her body, her face flushed, and tears began to collect behind her eyelids. She gulped down her drink and put twenty dollars on the bar.

"Are you okay," the bartender asked gently, noticing her flush, and her welling tears.

"I have to go," she said, stumbling off her stool and racing for the door. She bumped into a couple arriving arm in arm as she ran into the parking lot, where she stood, fumbling for her keys, raging inside and recognizing the old feelings of betrayal and self-scorn. Feelings she recognized all too easily.

Locking the doors she sat in the car, finally letting her tears fall, crying for the years she wasted with Tom, the emotions wasted on Michael. No wonder her friends were coaching her. She was helpless. Had they sensed something she was incapable of sensing? Like radar or a DNA mis-coding that happened sometime between ape and now, making her stupid at love.

Once her tears dried she drove down the road a couple of blocks to the old general store, walked in and purchased a bottle of whiskey. She didn't even like whiskey, but it seemed the appropriate medicine for whatever she had. Maybe it would drown her sense of betrayal, her feeling sorry for herself. Plus she couldn't possibly go home yet. The girls might still be there, and she simply couldn't face them now. At the counter she found some Kodak film then saw a little rice thing, wrapped in cellophane. It said 'spam musubi' on its hand-written label. She took it and a bag of Cheetos. *Maybe I need mix,* she thought, grabbing a guava-orange soda.

When Mattie got back to the car she heard the cell phone that she had left on the front seat. Reaching in, she checked the number, noted it was Michael's and shut the phone off. She headed south along the road, deciding she would find the beach they visited earlier and park there for a bit or at least until the girls would have left for the party. At Red Sand Beach she parked for a good hour, drinking whiskey, chased with guava soda. She actually liked the spam and rice, wrapped in seaweed, figuring out the caloric and carbohydrate content before she finished it. It was actually part of the plan. If she really wanted to get drunk, she could hardly do it on an empty stomach. That would be too easy.

The phone started vibrating on the passenger seat. She looked at it again and put it down. A few minutes later she listened to the message.

"Hey, Mattie, where are you?" He sounded concerned and as adorable as ever. "I'm here at the bar, and it's about twenty after. I'll wait. Call me."

Slime, she thought, taking another swig of whiskey then taking the phone and burying it under a towel in the back seat.

Eventually she decided to head home. Despite donning the light shawl she had brought, it was getting cold, and she thought she'd be a much more comfortable drunk curled up under the blanket of her nice queen-sized bed. She headed south again, watching for the turn off. Instead every dirt road had palm trees and flowers, and they all looked the same, but upon following them, she ended up in another place altogether. Dogs barked, lights flicked on, people came out on their porches with flashlights. She just backed up, turned around and went back to the highway. And did it again.

After about four attempts she decided to drive all the way back to town to return with the mileage counter on. She put the bottle under her seat, checked her tear-stained face in the mirror, and headed back to Hasegawa's. A pick-up truck nearly ran her off the road about a mile out of town. Shaken, she swerved over to the side, then realizing this wouldn't look good if a cop came by, she pulled back onto the highway and drove slowly on.

But despite counting the miles, Mattie still couldn't find the turn off to Keoki's place, so she opened her phone to call him. She had no last name, so that wouldn't work. She dialed Chloe's cell, but there was no answer. Jill's was next. Both were off or left back in the room. She made a clear, well actually sort of fuzzy, decision to return to the parking lot at the store, rather than park alone on a dark road, where she sat, contemplating her life through the fog of whiskey. Much of it looked like road kill – dead, twisted relationships strewn all over her past. It wasn't nearly that bad, but in Mattie's present frame of mind, well let's just say it was not at all pretty. She pulled the bottle back out and tilted back a few more. She opened the Cheetos and began crunching them, smearing orange gunk from her fingers all over the steering wheel, her face and shawl. The self-flagellations turned into self-pity, and what a pity party it was.

Dozing off for a while, she woke to the sound of boom boxes in a truck across the parking lot. Loud local boys about high school age were drinking and tailgating. She had no idea what time it was until she looked at the digital clock on the dashboard. 2:15. It was two fifteen! She sat upright, fastened her seatbelt and pulled out onto the road, determined to find her way home now that she'd slept it off.

But still she couldn't. Lost again she pulled in a gated road, turned around, and parked facing the highway. She locked the doors and curled up under the towel in the back seat. She was convinced she would find her way back once first light arrived.

forty-two

PARTY

Meanwhile Jill and Chloe were the life of the party just a few miles away, having a ridiculously fun time with their cowboys, an open bar, and stomping music. The band played J'awaiian and rockabilly, and the girls hardly left the dance floor. When Kepa or Zach went for more beer or weren't monopolizing them, their dance cards filled in quickly as plenty of other guys cut in. They even got to practice their pidgin, trying all the while just to understand local conversations. Fortunately they didn't have to do much conversing, dancing instead to rock and roll, grateful for a little aerobic exercise after being in the car all day. Jill took a break, swilling a dark beer. *Rehydrating,* she thought, reaching for another and taking a moment to fully appreciate Hana's hunky homeboys. *They don't make em like this back home.*

Things wound down a bit when the band closed up shop around two, and Jill and Chloe squared off with Zach and Kepa, respectively, finding their way to a little privacy and a lot of making out. It was nearly three when they left. Nearing their turnoff, Kepa spotted headlights on the side of the road. Pulling over he drove back into the turnaround.

"It's our car!" said Chloe as they pulled over and parked.

"Shhhh. It's probably M and M, doing it in the back seat, " Jill said. "Do you have a flashlight?" Kepa turned off his headlights then reached over and handed her one from the glove compartment. "Anyone got a camera?" he asked.

Chloe and Jill opened the truck doors noiselessly, crept

over to the car, and shined the light into the rear seat. Something moved under a large striped beach towel. They noticed she was alone and called to her, "Mattie. Mattie! MATTIE WAKE UP!!!"

Their friend stirred finally, startled by the lights, realizing it was the girls calling her name. She unlocked the door and nearly fell out on the ground. "Whaaat?"

"Are you drunk?" Chloe asked incredulously, trying to remember if she'd ever seen Mattie drunk. "Are you okay?"

"Mattie staggered to her feet, holding Chloe. "Take me home," was all she could muster.

Chloe drove the rental car while Kepa led the way, and Jill took the opportunity to make out with Zach.

The cowboys couldn't believe they weren't getting invited in, but it was obvious that Jill and Chloe were determined to be with their friend in her hour of need.

"Well then, thanks ladies. It was a heck of a weeknight. Keep in touch, ya hear? Aloha oi."

Chloe hugged Kepa while Jill and Zach locked lips again. Then they hopped in the truck, and the girls watched as the tail lights disappeared into the night. They stood for long moments catching their collective breath and finding appreciation in the swelling buttery orb as it played hide and seek with clouds and peeked through the needles of the ironwoods. Hana moon. Hula moon.

"What happened?" Chloe asked, helping Mattie in, cleaning her up and tucking her motherly into bed. "Here, have some water. You're probably dehydrated. What were you drinking?"

"I can't even talk about it. You guys were absolutely right. He's a snake."

"What?" Jill was surprised. "I wasn't right. I thought he was a doll. And a gentleman. What happened?"

"I was such a fool." Mattie started. "I went to the bar and after a few minutes I saw him, except that he was with a girlfriend – or a wife if I can believe my eyes. Their young sons were with them."

"Wait a minute. Hold on." Jill interrupted. "Are you sure it was his wife? That would be a total surprise. I mean it's not that guys always tell you, in fact usually they don't, but my radar didn't pick up *married* at all with Michael."

"Yep. He was holding her and laughing. He kissed her and tousled one of the boys' heads. I couldn't even watch. I paid my tab and split. And I've been driving around ever since."

"Oh, damn. I left my cell phone," said Chloe, surveying the room.

"And I turned mine off when the music started. I'm sorry, honey."

"I tried and tried but I couldn't find my way back, so I parked near the field, thinking when dawn came things would look different."

"I still can't believe it," said Chloe. "Didn't he call?" *This will make a great screenplay*, she thought.

"Sure he called…about twenty minutes later, but I turned my phone off. I checked the message later and…"

"Let me hear," Jill demanded.

Mattie put the messages on speaker and they all listened.

"Hey, Mattie, where are you? I'm here at the bar, and it's about twenty after. I'll wait. Call me." The second one sounded a little more intense. "Hey, Sweetie, now I'm beginning to worry. Are you okay? It's eight, and I can't reach you, so we're going to go ahead and start dinner. I ran into my sister earlier and thought you'd love to meet each other. She lives here in Hana with her husband and two sons. Chuck is in Taiwan on business, so Carrie brought her boys. Since I so rarely get to hang out with my nephews, I invited them along. Hope you don't mind. I figured you were into the family thing. But I especially wanted my two best girls to meet each other."

Mattie gasped, feeling sheepish and sorry. She had betrayed herself. What kind of freak would he think she was now?

Jill and Chloe stood silently while Mattie took in what she

had done. It was not like her to jump to conclusions. It must have been all that being on the lookout stuff. At any rate, they could all feel his sincerity...and her shame.

"Call him," Chloe said.

"I just can't. Not now."

"Call him." She dialed the number and handed Mattie her phone. "Tell him the truth."

Mattie was tempted to hang up or make up a story. Or have Chloe report Mattie's sudden illness, her allergy to moonlight, being hit by a train. It was four in the morning; she couldn't possibly speak to him. Then she remembered and took heart. *That's our magical time.*

forty-three

VERANDAH

Buttermilk lumps clotted the winter-blue sky when Chloe went out for a morning walk. She took the wooded path through the grove and onto the little beach where she walked, danced and jogged, working her legs, heart and lungs. It was downright psychedelic to feel so alive. She sat meditating for twenty minutes in a bamboo grove near the sunny entrance to the path. She listened while they whispered and rattled. Walking back to the cottage she couldn't imagine a living being feeling any better.

The clouds magnetized together, darkening the sky. *Tut tut, it looks like rain,* sang Chloe, walking along the trail.

Jill was up, re-packing her backpack for the day ahead. "Does it look like rain?" she asked when Chloe arrived.

"Oh yea. It'll rain."

The others were up on the verandah by nine, enjoying a large, country breakfast of Portuguese sausage and eggs, banana pancakes with keawe honey and wild island mulberries. Emma served espresso made from their own coffee trees and passed a basket of breads – dark, chewy, seeded mini-loaves, croissants as light as air, and homemade coconut muffins, coming back later with a platter of fruit in season: starfruit, bananas, coconut, mangoes, lychee, oranges and limes.

"Where's Mattie?" she asked. "Getting her beauty rest?"

"Naw," said Jill. "Late date." She didn't want to go into details. Not really sure herself what they were.

Michael had picked Mattie up ten minutes after the call.

Chloe had cleaned her up and brushed her hair before he arrived, and the couple had driven off, clearly in need of some communication and togetherness.

"How could you have thought I would be in relationship with another? What did I possibly do to give you that impression?"

"It wasn't you. Truly. The girls and I had a discussion, and I was just being uncharacteristically cautious. And jealous when I saw her. She was so beautiful."

"Sweet girl, she is beautiful. She's also my sister. Yes, I will always love her, but I was not...why didn't you just come over?"

"I froze. In my hurt and anger I just ran. I didn't think about it. It was visceral, instinctive. Tom two-timed me for nearly two years."

"I don't want to be misunderstood because of Tom. I know you're just getting over him, but you need to clean that up." He was visibly shaken. "I don't want to be second guessing all the time or wondering or having to censure myself depending on your possible reactions. Transparency is as critical to a relationship as it is in government." He had been hurt in the way that being misunderstood or misconstrued hurts, especially when one's innocent. "You stood me up. Didn't even call." He was being tender yet exposing his hurt feelings.

"Michael, you have to know how sorry I am for my behavior...all of it. I was wrong. And I wouldn't be here if I didn't care for you. Tell me we can work this out."

They drove around talking for an hour or so, then went back to the cabin where Michael was staying at the back of his sister's property. They snuggled on a screened-in porch under a chenille blanket, held each other, and slept until eight.

"I have to go to work," Michael whispered, rolling off the punéé and tucking her in. I'll come back for you at noon.

"No, it's okay. If you can take me back now it'll be better." Mattie knew the girls had plans, and she didn't want to screw things up or worry them anymore.

Chloe and Jill were still having breakfast when she arrived. Michael waved and left quickly. Mattie walked slowly up the stairs, greeting the girls and Emma, who was busy refilling coffee cups. "I'm done listening to you two."

forty-four

HEAVENLY HANA

Feeling the satisfaction of a truly memorable breakfast, Chloe sat by a varnished railing in the grey-green morning, feeding croissant crumbs to a fat crimson cardinal, while two yellow finches flitted from branch to branch on a narcissistic hibiscus. Jill scanned four local papers searching for financial news or stock indexes, and Mattie helped Emma, gathering platters and baskets and taking them into the house. They shared a second cup, pouring over family history books, filled with photographs of generations. Then Emma's billfold came out along with introductions for each child and grandchild.

Keoki rounded the circular driveway, pulling up by the front stairs and hopping out of his silver jeep. "Good morning, ladies. I trust you had a good time last night with our local boys." He had already tapped the coconut wireless. They looked up and silently nodded in unison. "I know it looks like rain, but if it didn't would you like to see a working taro farm? The Seven Sacred Pools? Hamoa Beach?"

"I'm up for anything you recommend, Uncle." Chloe gave him a hug.

"Do you have a time when you have to leave?"

"Only so we get back to Kihei before sunset," said Jill. I'm driving, and I don't do well in the dark.

"Assuming you'll want to make a few stops, you should probably be on your way by two then. How's that sound? That'll give us plenty of time. I'll bring umbrellas and ponchos just in case."

"Give us half an hour," Jill said, folding up the papers and heading over to the cottage.

Back in the bungalow, it was a feeding frenzy as questions for Mattie came fast and furious. She just looked at them and smiled generously. "I'm back," she said, all dimples. There was instant understanding that whatever hurt or anger, confusion or loss of self-esteem from her fauxpas the night before was fixed and righted. She appeared to have found her balance again, a lack of which had lingered from the Tom thing. She appeared to be her old happy self. She was back.

Mission accomplished. They accepted her two-word answer. Anything more would be overkill.

Entrusting their morning to Uncle's care, they visited a friend's lohi (taro patch), where they worked knee deep in the mud, planting taro as the sky closed in, clouds darkened, and rain splattered on the ponds. Huddled under a tarp, they shared tea and taro cakes and 'talked story' with uncles Keoki and John, learning all about the Hawaiian Kingdom, indigenous plants, non-profit fundraising and the best banana bread recipe. Old time jokes made rounds, with the women barely understanding when the two older gentlemen broke into a thick local pidgin. But they understood the language of music, and soon enough John and Keoki pulled out a couple of ukuleles and entertained their lohi workers with Hawaiian legends and pleasant song.

By noon Keoki was taking them to Hamoa Beach according to plan, but at the top of the stairs leading down to the beach, they all had a confab and a change of heart. It was far too gloomy to beach. The sky had no color, just blah grey – no color, no reflection, no illusions. Trees turned grey, the sea the same. It's as if it suddenly turned into a black and white world, which blackened as they stood there.

"There's a storm coming," Keoki said as he drove them back to his place. They packed, loading the car for the return trip just in time. As storm clouds began to unleash their bounty, they circled out, waving and blowing kisses to Keoki and Emma, who ran to take shelter on the verandah. They left, missing their new friends already but feeling grounded in their love of Hawaii and her people. Hana lived up to its reputation. It really was heavenly.

forty-five

RAIN

By the time they got up to the highway it was pounding and pelting, coming in sheets. It pounced against the car windows, leaping like lightening and pooling into puddles as it slid off the car. It raced like a flood or a river, and a shudder of adrenaline coursed through Jill. *The whole ocean is coming at me*, she thought, taking a deep breath and clutching the wheel.

Edging along the lagoon, silver and pockmarked, the day grew black as berries, and Jill switched on the headlights. It slashed again in earnest and the squall kept coming, forcefully incessant, driving harder again and again against the car. Jill fought with the road and the rain, dodging puddles and falling rocks, watching for overflowing streams and intermittently trying to fix the balance of warm or cool air by fidgeting with the defrost. Wind blew the branches of trees, palms, bananas, and wiliwilis. The frantic world was alive with movement.

Chloe loved it. It was wild and surreal. She steamed the window with her face pressed up to it. *Through these mists*, she thought, *everything connects. Beautiful rain, essential rain – like a blood bank, giving life to forest ferns and coqui frogs, adding volume to the tresses of rivers, ignoring houses and bridges and things man made, yet infusing the tiniest orchid with articulate and essential elements. It was another part of the hydrolic cycle – birthing rainbows and moonbows, cumulous puffs along great horizons, morning dew in the Sahara, and a snow cover on the slopes of Kilimanjaro.*

"All over Hana tiny frogs are waking up and breeding, loving each other in puddles and bogs from Haiku to Kipahulu.

205

It's the wake-up call of amour."

It brought Mattie back from feeling gloomy and slightly apprehensive. "Into every life a little rain must fall," she said, calming herself.

Chloe spoke softly. "'*Let the rain kiss you. Let the rain beat upon your head with silver liquid drops. Let the rain sing you a lullaby.*' Langston Hughes of course."

"Here's my quote," said Jill. "It's sheer fuckin' pandemonium out there, so shut up and let me drive." She clutched at the wheel, gritting her square, white teeth – those teeth that grrrrd and purred and glistened when the hot brunette animated. Instead she sat frozen in attention to the minutiae. She was stressing. Big time. Even the Gypsy Kings, screaching out *Bamboleo*, did not diminish her mild panic.

"This does not bode well," Chloe whispered over the seat.

Mattie was white-knuckling when Jill hit a loose gravel patch and rocks flew over the embankment and plummeted a hundred feet down to the rocky coast. Jill slowed as they approached a large puddle – more like a pool or a river – deciding how to navigate it.

"Stay high on the wall," said Chloe.

"Don't start now," Jill snapped, "unless you want to drive. I'm doing all I can to keep us on the road and the road kill to a minimum." She had noticed all the frogs too.

Mattie and Chloe backed off, since Jill was clearly freaking. They were mid stream when the car stopped. Simply stalled out. Sputtered and rocked and made profane sounds while Jill cursed back, but the bottom line was a car full of young lovelies stalled in the middle of a one-lane road in the middle of a two-lane storm in the middle of nowhere.

"Oh, no," Mattie squeaked. "Do something, Jill."

"Keep your panties on, Mattie. If you have any other good ideas, bring 'em on."

Chloe rolled down her window to check whether or not she could open the door without a flood. Carefully opening it she waded forward through the inundation to solid ground and searched for a board or large branches she might wedge under the tires. In no time at all another car came up behind them, stayed well behind the flood, slowing then finally stopping. A small Hawaiian boy jumped out and ran forward towards Chloe, helping her lodge a tree branch under the back wheels while Jill rocked back and forth, and the boy and his father, now out and helping too, pushed the car, easing it forward.

Chloe thanked them profusely then jumped back into the rental car, soaked pretty much through to her skin.

"Can you hand me a towel?" she reached over towards Mattie.

"Our hero," said Mattie, clapping and handing her two. "And chocolate," she continued, handing Jill and Chloe each a snickers bar.

"Glad we got a convertible," said Chloe, attempting to dry her hair and clothes while rivulets of rain found their way through the roof seals. "Now where's that sun?"

Jill grunted, ripped off a bite, and slowed down, making her way gingerly around the next few miles of precipices and switchbacks, avoiding any low-lying pools and even though a non-believer, praying to whatever god or goddess might be listening.

forty-six

SOUTH COAST

The drive home continued east to west, clockwise past the national park and seven sacred pools, where they stopped by a bamboo forest as the storm eased. At Lindberg's final resting place at Kipahulu, Chloe was treading carefully around the gravesite thinking about Charles and Anne and their great love and huge tragedy. *That great explorer of the human spirit took off solo for Paris across the Atlantic, but chose the Pacific to land at last. Maybe Maui pulled him too.* She had read about his love of the island, living simply in the end, far away from the paparazzi, the glitz and glitter of a famous life, dealing with cancer and choosing the embrace of tranquility and seclusion on the Valley Isle.

"Who played him in *The Spirit of St. Louis?*" Chloe asked.

Jill was nearly back to normal and relieved to stop for a minute. "Jimmy Stuart. I love aviation films. Ask me another."

Mattie weighed in. "What was Anne's book? My mom gave me a copy one year for my birthday, and I loved it. Reading that book was the very first time I ever considered our environment as something we should protect and value. I think I still have it."

"Gift from the Sea." Jill was quick.

"What a tragic life they shared." Chloe was thinking about the kidnapping of their baby. "Tragic and heroic. A full life. And didn't Anne just pass a couple years ago? She must have been a hundred."

"Ninety-five. She was ninety-five." Jill impressed even herself with her vast fund of general information. "Charles became a passionate conservationist. Their foundation today supports a balance of nature and technology."

"It's all about balance," Chloe pontificated, heading back to the car to balance the salt from the chips with something sweet.

Unmanned roadside stands offering fruits, flowers and little handmade artifacts crawled by along with signs for bed and breakfast spots, but the girls stayed buckled up, praying for sun. Prayers were answered. The downpour stopped almost as quickly as it came, but they were still in a low cloud. In an hour they had left behind the waterfalls and streams, the fusion of fragrance and cornucopia of color, for wide swaths of blue-black lava and an ancient, brittle world.

At one point they could almost reach out and touch the Big Island. Mauna Kea (White Mountain) stood there across the channel with just its tip white with snow, a lei of clouds surrounding its emerald hillsides. Then, as if by magic or prayer or turn of the radio dial to *'here comes the sun...here comes the sun, little darlin'*, the sun came gloriously out, easing whatever was left of anyone's tension. The girls breathed deeper, noticed and felt more. They exhaled.

A small church embraced the rugged windswept hillside. It reminded Chloe of stories she'd read of missionary days, and they stopped so she could take some photos and peek in the windows at the fantastic stained glass. It reminded her of Paris and her short investigation of that incredible city, which had included visits to Notre Dame, churches and chateaus. Chloe had grown up in a house filled with beaded and colored glass, bevels and blenkos. But again she noticed a difference. *It's the light. They call Paris the City of Lights, but Maui is the Island of Light, birthplace of the sun's magic.*

Continuing on they bumped and jolted while the road suddenly went from sections of new black top to old cracks and potholes. Eventually they arrived at the Ulupalakua Ranch and a local winery. They had already eaten everything they packed up – cold pizza, cookies, chips and cheese, and at the last waterfall they opened a fresh pineapple Emma had given them and feasted on every last succulent morsel. Still they were hungry as they pulled over to the little general store with a large verandah and boxes of scarlet rosebud geraniums. They poked through the shop and ordered lunch, sitting on the porch, looking over a hillside of lavender jacaranda trees. Elk burgers were cooked to order over an open grill and served on freshly-baked taro buns. Mattie had a grilled Jarlsburg sandwich and slaw.

"When did a simple burger get so gourmet good?" Chloe asked rhetorically, making a mental note to find elk meat back home. She had sourced buffalo, lamb, and others not so common for her culinary forays and raised with more humane methods. *I vote with my pocketbook,* she thought, wrapping her mouth around a juicy burger, letting every morsel satiate. At one point in high school Chloe had thought she had a weight problem, but when she began to consume only foods she loved, coupled with appreciation for all the folks that brought them to her table, the pounds shed and never returned. It was about then she began writing a diet book based on her success, but it lingered on some hard drive until years later when she found a book that already said it. It was the secret to *Why French Women Don't Get Fat* – they enjoyed their food.

The wine tasting afterwards was a letdown. Napa and Hunter Valleys, like the Bordeaux region proved the importance of geography and tradition in the production of fine wine. Island wines probably lacked a little of both. Besides, by then they just wanted to get home.

forty-seven

BI-COASTAL

As they curved around the slopes of Haleakala, they looked over Wailea and the south coast, then across the isthmus to the West Maui Mountains. Chloe first noticed the bi-coastal views. They made her heart heat, her mouth water, and took her breath away.

"Stop the car," she demanded.

Jill pulled over at a scenic lookout. "What's up, babe?"

"Nothing. I just have to stop to take all this in." Inexplicably Maui had touched Chloe deeper than the others. It was beyond the fun and beauty; it was something spiritual. Some great synchronicity grabbed her heart, and she listened as winds spoke, as rain chattered, as the outlook sweetened her afternoon.

Sitting on the hood of the car, passing a bag of corn chips, they took in the view. It swept from the south coast across the isthmus and the sweet, sugar cane heart of the island to Kahului harbor and the north coast beaches. They could see Lanai off the coast on the left and Molokai peeking out from behind the northwest cliffs on the right. Timeless mountains created a dramatic backdrop for the sea-to-sea scene.

"It makes me want to be an artist," Chloe said, gesturing across the immediate flora of the Kula slopes and the spectacular scene below.

"I took a watercolor class once. Now I know what for. At the time it was to lighten an otherwise heavy class load that semester." Mattie reminisced. "But I could paint this."

"I bet cowboys live on this side too." Jill joined the conversation, dipping into the cooler and handing Chloe a diet Coke, all the while thinking about seeing Andy again.

"Jill, darling, can you ever appreciate something for what it is without wishing it wore tight jeans hugging a great butt?" Mattie retorted.

"Are you still thinking of Zach?" Chloe continued.

"No, girls, actually I'm on to Andy. Remember the rancher-politician I met at the ag party? I've been saying no to him all week, put him off while waiting for surfer Dan to ravage my bones. Instead that board bloke just twisted my brain and stood me up. STOOD ME UP for christ's sake! Andy's the one. I can feel it. My Maui guy. He may be just what the doctor ordered. We have a date tonight. Dinner and."

"I remember him. Sort of cute if you're into older guys." Mattie was reaching.

"Yea, hunky-cute in that born-on-a-farm, tough guy way. Still he's refined from being a business owner and political wonk. I mean all those Chamber of Commerce meetings must have tamed him."

Chloe joked with Jill. "And you're going to put the call of the wild back into his life?"

"He's called me every day. Persistence is a virtue...unless he's just being bullheaded."

"Wow," said Mattie. "I was so into my own mellow drama I didn't even realize you had a new squeeze. Well, other than the hunk du jour."

"It's tricky, isn't it?" Chloe started. "Who we choose – who chooses us. And why. Places are like that too, grabbing your heart and romancing the shit out of you or beating you up and throwing you away. I wonder. Can we fall in love with a place?"

Mattie began singing. "I left my heart...in San Francisco..."

"I like Moby Dick's Ishmael," said Jill. "*I am tormented with an everlasting itch for things remote. I love to sail forbidden seas and land on barbarous coasts.*"

214

"You would," Chloe said, "but I think I'm falling. Wasn't it Mark Twain who said Hawaii was *'the loveliest fleet of islands that lies anchored in any ocean'*? Well this fleet is my new heartthrob."

"Didn't Jed call?" Mattie asked Chloe, a little concerned.

"Sure. He wants to see me again. We were sort of kisses-interruptus the other night at the MACC, and I wouldn't mind more. I sense Jed shares my sense of fierce independence, my need for wide-open spaces. All of us artists need space. And solitude."

"And just when did you become an artist?" Jill asked. "I thought you were my friend, the real estate mogul."

"It's the island. Makes me want to write and paint and dream in Technicolor or Kodachrome. Brilliant full-spectrum color! I wish I could paint this." She gestured again, sweeping her arms across the expanse of view. "But baring actual brushes and pigment, I can try with my pen. Or in my case, my keyboard."

"Go crazy, Chloe." Mattie signaled her approval with a little cheerleading, then noticed a vibration in her pocket and pulled out her cell phone.

"Hi Michael." Pause. "Well, let's see. We're at some sort of lookout that shows both coasts. It's awesome. Kula I think. Jill's jonesing for a new guy and Chloe's falling in love with the whole island. Sure, tonight's great, but did you get any sleep. Yea, that's what Jill always says – you can sleep plenty when you're dead. OK, eight then. Bye."

She turned to Chloe. "I need my beauty rest" and climbed into the back seat, squishing a beach towel under her head.

"That's my cue," Jill nodded to Chloe, finishing her soda and getting back into the driver's seat. Chloe stood for another few moments, letting the magic of Maui sink deeper into her bones and make its way clear to her heart.

forty-eight

1210

The pace picked up to a mad scramble once the girls got back to the room. Four faxes had been slipped under the door. The message light blinked with twelve messages. Chloe's iPhone once again had reception, and she dove right in, responding to critical e-mails. She figured all hell would break loose before the weekend, and she was right.

Jill punched '7' for messages and put the room phone on speaker.

Beep. "Hello. This is Andy, calling for Jill. I just remembered you're off to Hana, so I'll try your cell. Godspeed and have a great time."

Beep. "Hi, girls. It's Tilly. Chloe, it's your mother. I know I said not to bother calling, but I can't believe you didn't. Are you okay? I came over to the office twice this week to check up on things. Other than the mutiny by that arrogant Mark Keller and his gang, everything's going smoothly. Lori deserves a raise. And just to prove a point – that those who don't need it get more – we landed a new project, the glitzy new one at the marina. Eighty condos with commercial on the bottom three floors. We're all celebrating Friday night. Wish you were here, honey. No, not really. I'm glad you're there. You really needed a vacation. I just hope it's perfectly peachy. Don't you just love Maui?" *Just.*

Beep. "Is this Mattie Wilson? Aloha, it's Coco Bob from the fruit stand. I found a book with your name in it, and I remembered you girls said you were staying at the Fairmont, so

I thought I'd give it a try. Anyway I'm not coming to town until Saturday, so hopefully you have other fish to fry. I can bring it by. Call me: 872-COCO. Nice meeting you all."

Beep. "Mattie, it's Michael. It's Thursday night about 8:30. I have no idea where you are. I tried your cell, but it's not working. Anyway I hope you're okay. I know you said you were forgetful, but I hope you didn't forget me. Call me when you can."

Beep. "I forgot to leave my number. It's 415-288-8415."

Beep. "This is Eli. Hey, Jill, that finance company in Seattle called and wants a bid to handle the re-development and re-positioning of their entire Internet presence. Call George Shilling at 360-242-2000. The new server's awesome. I added four new accounts already. Little ones, but hey, it's all money. My brother's coming in to help out until you get back. Call me before the weekend, okay?"

Beep. "Chloe. Chloe Beech, is that you? Hi, it's Bill Grove. You handled the sale of my commercial complex in North Beach a couple years back. Anyway I called your office – glad to see Lori's still there – looking for some paperwork for a tax audit. Can you believe that bs? Anyway they said you were on Maui. I am too. In fact that's why I was selling out – to relocate to Maui. Anyway I'd love to buy you a drink. Call my cell. 260-2468."

Chloe stopped typing on her iPhone and listened, then punched in the number and hit 'talk'. Within seconds she had agreed to meet Bill in the lobby bar at seven-thirty.

Beep. "Chloe, it's Lori. I've been trying to call your cell, but you must be out of range down at the end of the world. Just wanted you to know everything's peachy. *She sounds like Tilly, who's been hanging around the office all week.* The five have disappeared. I locked the file cabinets, so we have some degree of control, though I think they set up their new office from our supplies closet, which is nearly empty. I assigned their closings to Molly, who is thrilled to pick up the slack. And the spare change. I'm off to Tahoe this weekend with my honey. Snow dumped yesterday, and you know how I love powder skiing. I'll see you Monday morning. Over and out."

How come my PA knows how to relax, and I don't. Wait, I'm here on Maui.

Beep. "This call is for Chloe Beech. We pulled your business card from the drawing, and you won the grand prize. Please call Derek at 877-4242 to arrange everything."

Mattie became excited. "Remember, Chloe...the hat you put your business card into at the club Wednesday night? You wrote 'Fairmont Hotel' on the back."

"Yea, but what was the grand prize?"

Silence. Neither could help her out. She keyed in the number and called. It was a helicopter tour for four, and they began collectively arguing over when and who the fourth would be.

"My card — my pick," Chloe said. "I'll let you know." Meanwhile I'll call for the voucher and book the flight. Other than Chloe, no one had ever been up in a chopper, and their excitement was palpable.

"I did a balloon once," Jill said. "Does that count?" She hit the pause button again, and it continued.

Beep. "Chloe, it's Jed. I couldn't reach your cell. How about a poetry slam Saturday night? We could catch dinner first. Let me know."

Beep. "This call is for Jill. Hi, Jill. It's Zachary — a flash from your past." For a moment she zoned in on her college love, then realized it was her Hana cowboy. "Well, past is prologue, and I'm in town for the weekend. Wanna dance? Call me. 287-2345."

Beep. "This is the front desk. One of our bellman found a wallet belonging to Mathilda Wilson. Kindly call or come down to the front desk if this is yours, and identify your things."

"Well, that had to be recent," said Chloe. "Like in the last ten minutes."

"I must have dropped it trucking all my stuff up to the room." Mattie looked guilty and thought to herself, *for being such*

a babe, how can I be such a klutz? This is not a blonde thing. THIS IS
NOT A BLONDE THING.

They settled into a rhythm sprinkled with good-natured chatter, as close friends will, returning calls, sorting laundry, and filling a large white logo'd bag for housekeeping. They unpacked clothes and shoes and put make-up and toiletry bags back in the bathroom, moving around the suite as if choreographed, occasionally coming up with some mojo or dog-eared joke.

Jill opened a nice chardonnay she had left in the fridge and poured three glasses.

"To Hana," she said offering a toast and shaking off the last of her driving jitters.

"Hana banana," Mattie smiled.

"To Keoki and Emma, Charles and Anne and all places wild and beautiful." Chloe clinked glasses, and they went about their sorting and shifting. Mattie took her wine into the bathroom for a long hot soak.

"I need a swim," said Chloe, stripping off her shorts and pulling on a bikini.

"I think I'll hit the weight room," said Jill. "Catch you all later."

"Meet me back here at seven." Mattie called from her inner sanctum. "I have a surprise."

forty-nine

FLOTATION

While Jill and Chloe indulged their egos and challenged their muscles, Mattie floated merrily merrily in a tub with so many bath salts, it was like a sensory deprivation tank, and it had the same effect. She remembered the professor in her esoteric communications class at college who introduced her to floating, meditating, hypnotherapy and other methods of deep contact. At one point she got up and turned out the lights, closing both bathroom doors. Now it was dark, quiet and warm. Perfect. Within minutes she was without thought, somewhere in a warm timeless dimension, and what followed was twenty minutes of the deepest meditation she'd had in months.

Suddenly a thought occurred. *Maybe I need to be more rather than less invested in my career.* She lay weightless, wondering how to go about that, then come up with a plan. Many plans. Her aunt wanted to retire. She hadn't come right out and said it, but she'd dropped some hints to her niece and a couple of other employees, who immediately became insecure about their jobs. Mattie could offer a buy-out. Structure it whereby she'd purchase shares over time, eventually taking her out altogether. Aunt Jo could retire, and Mattie would run the company, providing for Jo's future.

There were so many things she wanted to do. Floating, she came up with a myriad of ideas for modernizing, digitizing, and upgrading the agency. She could hire Jill to revamp their meager Internet presence and crack into Facebook and some social media. She could expand their lines and tours, hire college kids and young professionals to create eco tours and other products for a changing traveler. She could promote online memberships with prizes and discounts to generate some PR and sizzle...and more members. Presently half of the office space was an empty warehouse. She could enlarge and remodel the agency or do something else with the space to produce additional income. A duplex there would bring in six to seven thousand a month in rental income alone.

It was just what Mattie needed – something to get her excited again, to jumpstart her involvement, her dedication, give her a platform for her creativity and her diligence. She was so excited she turned on the jets and let the tub bubbles match her interior ones. *How nice to not be obsessing about Tom...or Michael or men in general. Yep, I need a project and a career move. I've played the dumb blonde for far too long. Time to step up.*

After another fifteen minutes, she rose, showered, washed her hair, and began the process by which she would transform from wet noodle to hot date. All it took was a little make-up and the right clothes, shoes, accessories.

After she got dressed, Mattie retrieved her wallet at the front desk and stopped in the jewelry store on the main level to pick up some items that she had left Thursday morning to be gift-wrapped. By the time Jill and Mattie got back to the room they had one thing in mind. "What's the surprise?" they asked in unison.

"Here," she said. "Trinkets and trip mementos." She handed each of them a small box, wrapped in a tapa print and tied with raffia. Inside each was a gold bracelet with one charm: a tiny gold pair of slippers, tropical footwear otherwise known as thongs or flip-flops. They had a small diamond where the toe strap met the top of the foot. On the back of each was an inscription: *Maui 2011.*

"Mattie, it's precious. Thank you so much." Jill joined Chloe in appreciation high-fiving her and breaking into a Paul Simon imitation of *Diamonds on the Soles of her Shoes.* "Cool, doll.

So cool."

"I figured it would be the first of many trips we'd be taking, so I wanted this to be the first charm. You both did this...for me. Thank you."

"Wait. We have something for you." Jill dug into a drawer in the armoire and brought out a gold-ribboned box. In it was the crystal angel on the lotus, which she and Chloe had found in the Paia shop. Chloe explained. "It's Mattie finding her wings again."

"Oh, you guys." Mattie embraced them both, feeling the glow of friendship. Their sweet interlude was interrupted when the phone started ringing. Housekeeping stopped by with an iron and more hangers and picked up the laundry. Chloe and Jill did junk and a po for the bathroom, and Mattie went out onto the lanai to do sunset, taking the chardonnay with her, along with a mood that was unusually triumphant.

fifty

BILL

Bill was the first to call up. "I'm here. Shall we meet at the Lobby Bar?"

"Sure. I'll be right down." Chloe was off with one final toss of her bright head. Curls cascaded like Julia Roberts' in *Pretty Woman*. Exercise and late afternoon sun agreed with her; she was glowing with good health.

"Aloha," he greeted her with a hug as she walked down the stairs from the arched lobby and into the luxurious lounge that faced out over a twinkling world. "You look fabulous! Maui agrees with you."

"I love everything about it. Everything." Chloe purred. "What is it about this place?" She had spent months working with Bill, having lunches and meetings and holding his hand during the final days of escrow when he was still hurting from the unhinging of his marriage.

"It has a very special pull for some people. I saw it on my first trip too, but it took me four years to relocate. First I had to go through the split." Bill didn't wear any trace of the dreaded look, particularly among men, of the recently divorced. Instead he looked tanned and whole. Wedgwood eyes gleamed from a calm and open face. His hair was graying and sun-streaked, and his physique attested to regular beach running, biking and surfing.

A young woman with blue-black hair, braided nearly to her waist took their order and set a bowl of macadamias on the small round table between their upholstered chairs. Chloe

225

fidgeted. Even her long legs didn't allow her to sit comfortably in the depths of the chair, so she took off her sandals and tucked her legs underneath, shrugging as if to say it was the best conclusion she could draw.

Bill sat to the front of the chair, legs open, arms resting on them, leaning in. "So how's business?" As he spoke he looked absent from his conversation as if searching for a memory.

"It's good," said Chloe. "Could be better, with the lingering recession and all, but I can't complain. I just lost my top producers, five of them, but we'll pick up the pieces in a month or two."

"Probably your prima donnas. You won't miss them." Bill had been in insurance, worked the agency with his dad for twenty years since high school, so he knew.

"Have you re-married?" It came out of her mouth like a buzzing little insect, and she immediately felt strange for asking so bluntly.

"No, not yet. Nothing but babes on Maui, throwing themselves at me. His eyes crinkled in the corners and he let loose a stifled little snort. "But I'm saving myself." He took a long draft of his Guinness and continued, a creamy ledge of foam still on his upper lip. "Seriously, I had enough good fortune to be able to actually take some time off, so when I came back to Maui I did just that. I bought a home in Wailea, modest by my old standards, but perfect for my two dogs and the kids, whenever they could visit. It's a block to the most perfect beach imaginable."

Chloe sipped her wine quietly, observing Bill's implacable boyish good looks. She didn't remember him being this attractive, and now she was absorbed in his aura, which extended a few inches from his face and body. Some part of her was listening, but her concentration was impelled as if by some gravitational force to his body.

"I still do a little business long distance with my best old clients, and of course I have residuals. One of the good things about my profession is that we have the best products available, so I find myself nearing fifty with a very secure future, financially at least. On the other hand I have become much more intuitive than I ever dreamed possible, especially for this ole man's man. Don't tell my volleyball buddies, but I've learned to meditate, and I've taken up painting."

"How wonderful. I think Maui has that kind of pull. There are all sorts of artists and healers here. I, myself, have written more here than in the last few months, and we've had a busy schedule."

"I bet you came to write," he said, winking and enjoying another drink of the black liquid.

"I did come prepared – pen, writing pads, iPad…all that. Just being away from work allows me to re-focus my energies. It's about the only time I can these days."

"As I recall you always had that creative spark. In fact you seemed just a little bit out of place at your agency. Not that you weren't successful and a total pro, but whatever you're up to now totally agrees with you. You'll know when you're on your soul path."

She was surprised to hear her old client talk this way, and it intrigued her.

"How long are you here?"

"We leave Sunday night."

"We'd better do dinner then," he said. "If you're free. Is Nick's okay? It's one of my favorites, right downstairs on the terrace. There's a swollen moon just poking up, so it should be perfect."

Chloe thought for about three seconds, wondering when Bill became such a romantic. She realized she had no other plans for the evening, nodded and finished her wine.

"Only if we solve all the world's problems," she replied, taking his hand.

"No problems, girl. Only opportunities."

That's right. He used to be a motivational speaker.

fifty-one

ANDY

Back in the room, Mattie had managed to tease Jill about Andy, telling cowboy and political jokes in an attempt to loosen her up while fussing over Jill's appearance. (What are friends for?) Even though Jill had the most amazing body – she should for her constant workouts – she was not a fashion freak and frankly needed help getting herself together. It wasn't her fault; she grew up with brothers. Even today she was more comfortable in jeans than anything else except bare skin. Still she decided that making an effort tonight was rational.

"Try the moss green skirt," said Mattie. "I know it will fit you. Naw, not with that top. Put the little blue dress back on."

"I'm going crazy, Mattie. He's a rancher, for gawd's sake. Can't I just wear jeans?"

"Jill, you're in a five star resort about to be wined and dined by Maui's next mayor or governor or something. He's probably taking you to the top restaurant on the island, and well, jeans will simply not do. Here, put this on." She handed Jill a flouncy print dress with a deep V top and bias cut skirt that existed to show off legs. Especially Jill's. It looked fabulous on the girl with the emerald eyes.

"Now that's sassy and classy. Wear this too." Mattie handed Jill a shimmery silk shawl with mirrored beads and a choker of bright little pearls and beads that lit up her eyes, finally turning Jill towards the mirror.

She felt the choke of something around her neck.

229

"Oh my gawd. I look like Paris Hilton meets Annie Hall."

"You do not. It's perfect. Now, the right shoes and a little more blush and..."

The telephone rang. "Hi, yes, sure. This is Mattie. She's almost ready. Come on up. Top floor, all the way down the hallway to the right. Room at the end. See ya."

She hung up the phone and turned to Jill. "He's coming," she said, mimicking Jack Nicholson in *The Shining*.

Jill took a deep breath and reached for her glass of wine. "I can't remember being so nervous." She picked up the clothes and shoes strewn around the suite and tossed them in the closet and shoved them under the bed. "Are we presentable?"

"More lip-gloss," Mattie said, handing her a tube.

The doorbell rang twice, and Jill looked up at Mattie apprehensively.

"Go on," Mattie encouraged her. "It'll be fine."

Maybe it was the age difference. Jill rarely went out with older guys – which of course was part of his appeal. Something new. With her normal stud boys she could be in absolute control, and if she didn't get what she expected, she just turned everything to her advantage and handled it. But Andy was a big unknown. *How big,* she was wondering, as she crossed the room and opened the door.

He stood there, taller than she remembered, dark in that perpetually tanned look of islanders and others who live near beaches or work outdoors. His eyes were kahlua or dark chocolate. She couldn't decide which. He wore a deep mauve silk shirt, tieless and open two buttons at the front. His left ear was pierced with a small diamond stud. Something else she hadn't noticed. *Was I drunk that night? Or do I just lack observational skills?*

"Hi, gorgeous. It's been a long week."

She moved towards him to give him her standard left cheek peck, realizing he wasn't opening to her. She looked down. He was carrying something; both hands were clutched around – a bible!

Jill stopped in her tracks. *Whaaaat?!&%o$&*!!* She looked back at Mattie who was standing quietly near the open lanai slider. *A bible??!!!* They mouthed in unison. Then Mattie began to make funny little guttural sounds.

He continued without missing a beat. "I prayed all week for the safety and success of your trip. I trust my prayers were heard."

"Oh, yea," said Jill, thinking of Kimo, Zach and Coco Bob, even the missing, stood-her-up surfer-Dan and all the other normal hunks she had met in her short stay. "We had a great time."

"Well I can't wait to hear all about it over dinner."

"And you're taking your bible?" she was incredulous.

"I'm working on my sermon for Sunday, and I thought you might like to give some input. You are Christian, aren't you? Besides, I take the Lord's word with me whither I go."

Jill turned towards Mattie, rolled her eyes, mouthing *'whither?',* and then she began to panic, trying to figure out how she could feign being sick right now. Or die even. *Help me* she implored with a helpless look at her friend.

Mattie just chuckled. "Y'all have a nice time."

fifty-two

M & M

She was still giggling when Michael knocked about fifteen minutes later.

"Well, you're all happy tonight. What's up?" He wore pressed jeans and an English blue VanHeusen with rolled sleeves. Though tired, his eyes gleamed, meeting hers, then he gave her a bear hug and handed her a bottle of red, a Haut Médoc from central France.

"Oh, Bordeaux, my favorite!" Mattie gave him a warm kiss. "I am having the best day. Must be because I started it with you. Then there was my bath." She waxed on about the tub and sensory deprivation while taking two wine glasses and a corkscrew off the bar in the entrance and leading Michael out onto the lanai.

"But all the giggles are from Jill's date. Remember the tall guy at the party Monday? The rancher dude running for office? Well, Jill's been putting him off all week, but after Dan's no-show and all our conversations about trying new things, she finally said 'yes', and guess what he showed up with? A bible!" She began laughing all over again. "He's a preacher."

"Did she slam the door on him or what?"

"Naw, she went. I mean we'd spent an hour getting her ready. She was gritting her teeth, but she was hungry so she went. At least she'll get a good meal out of him."

The moonlight on the lanai turned Mattie's hair to spun gold and leant an extraordinary ambience to the hour. "Check out the moonbow," Michael said, pointed over her shoulder. A rainbow of muted colors circled the full moon. "The moon is full at two am." *He is so detailed. Is that a red flag?* She never meant to go back to careful noting, but new habits are reluctant to die. *But romantic. Only a romantic would notice the full moon. A moon that could shower orchids over every continent in only twenty-four hours.*

"It's yummy, isn't it?" He licked his finger and ran it around the glass rim, making it sing. *Yes, a total romantic, like myself. Is that his love song?*

When she did not appear to respond, he changed the subject, pulling his chair closer and leaning in. "My work's going well, and I still have a few loose ends to tie up between now and next week. The report can be finished once I get home, but all the samples are in and supporting documents have been turned over to the committee. The mayor seems pleased with the report, if not the results. As you can imagine in this ecosystem, things are fragile at best. Rampant growth has given Maui lots of environmental headaches. Nothing that can't be remedied if acted upon quickly, but overall things are deteriorating."

Bathed in moonglow, Mattie pondered its creamy whiteness, falling under some mad moon spell. She could hear his voice, but her thoughts rambled independently. *Why is the moon, though reflective of the sun, thought of as dark, exotic and erotic, occult even, while the sun is light and energy, clarity, the obvious, the hot fire of day against the mood of moon. It's two hundred and forty thousand miles away, yet responsible for tides and cycles that influence all earthlings. The sun is reason. The mystery is as biomorphic as the moon.*

"Honey?" The deep caress of his voice brought her back from the edge of the moon.

She didn't skip a beat. "But it all looks so pristine to us. I mean have you ever seen such clear water? And the beaches aren't all full of silt and kelp and pampers like back home."

"Oh, it's still ahead of the degradation curve, but the changes have been shocking. Anything from your Aunt? Things okay at work?" He was acutely aware of her remoteness.

Slowly and hesitantly Mattie opened up, sharing her insights and plans from her late afternoon float. "I got so excited, Michael. You can't imagine. And I can see it working. I'm sure I'll have my auntie's support."

"And mine. It's fabulous. Why don't we do a trek in Belize? I have a project down there in a couple of months, and we could organize a group to go and help with the work. I can see good things coming from this." Michael's excitement was palpable and confirmed Mattie's deep feeling that she was on the right track, rather than indulging some half-soaked idea.

Wait. She stopped. *He's suggesting a future relationship ...seeing me beyond Maui.*

She took a sip of wine and let it ignite her body and her imagination. "You really think we could work together?"

"Mattie, despite my workload this week, I've thought of nothing but you." He leaned in, taking her hands. "I hate to sound trite, but I knew when I bumped into you at Borders that I'd be a goner. I was so worried for you last night I was nearly frantic – not my style. My sister was concerned too. Anyway I can't imagine a better time to just spit it out, so..."

Stop. Don't say it. Not this way. What happened to Michael, the romantic?

"So I want you to meet my family. At least those that are here. Chuck's flying back from Malaysia tomorrow so Carrie and the boys are coming to town to meet his plane. I thought maybe we could all get together for a picnic or lunch somewhere. Tell me you haven't already made plans."

"No, sweetie. And even if I had, I'd change them." She was still feeling guilty for the misunderstanding and her outlandish behavior the night before.

"You just called me sweetie. Am I your sweetie?"

"You're not the only goner." She grinned, then got up and moved over onto his lap, taking his wine glass and placing it on the table. She kissed him ever so tenderly, and his response picked up the pace.

"I never think of the future. It comes soon enough." It was

another Einstein quote, which arrived in her brain just when she needed it.

"Our friend, Albert?" He raised his eyebrows.

Be bold, she remembered. *Ballsy I know, but Jill would approve. Chloe too. Hey, it's the new me!*

"My roomies are out for the evening. Shall we order room service and lock the door?"

"I thought you'd never ask."

fifty-three

1210

The dawn sprawled across the room, coloring in the lines from the soft grey world Chloe observed for an hour while she scribbled furiously in her notebook. Dinner with Bill turned into a fun food frolic. The cuisine was superb and her favorite – Mediterranean. By the time the tiramisu arrived they were feeding each other little bites of bliss. Shared food always felt like family to Chloe, but it was the conversation, which deepened throughout the evening, until she was confessing her private needs and desires, that touched her. One can only confess interior worlds to friends.

Sunlight finally pierced the lanai, and Chloe closed her eyes to feel its warmth. She longed for a crystal palace. All prism and rainbow, light bending through gemstones and diamonds and splitting, like atoms, to catch the sun.

The others were stirring. "It's our last day," said Chloe. "What's the plan?"

"It's our second to the last day." Jill corrected her. "And I want to go up to the mountain top."

"Preacher got to you then," said Mattie, giggling again.

"Is this a private joke?" Chloe felt left out and couldn't for the life of her figure out what was going on.

"Come on, you have to tell Chloe," Mattie insisted.

"Well, the hunky rancher-politician dude turned out to be a preacher. Arrived bible in hand." Jill made a scrunchy little face, turning her lips into monkey lips.

"I don't believe it," said Chloe. "He actually showed up

with a bible?"

"Yep, we didn't either," Mattie jumped in. "I think it's a first in the annals of dating. I mean I've never even heard of such a thing. Not only that – he was obviously hot for her."

"Maybe it was hiding his anxious member." Giggles.

"Okay, you want the story? The truth and nothing but the truth?" Jill went on. "All the way down to the lobby I was racking my brain trying to come up with some excuse or feign an illness or fall down the stairs or something, but when I saw his Aston Martin parked dead center at the porte cochère I figured well, a little ride wouldn't hurt. Besides I was starving, and he mentioned some fancy sounding place, so I figured I'd let him read scripture while I gorged on foie gras and a thirty year old red."

"You can't be serious. You actually went out with a preacher?" Chloe was still stuck on the picture of him at the door, holding his bible. *Probably a leather-bound family bible from his missionary kin.*

"I actually did. And other than a simple question, which came near the end of the evening, we had a pretty good time. I mean the food was awesome, and he's a great conversationalist with lots of interests."

Mattie squeaked again. "What was the question?"

"Have you been born again?" said Chloe, totally deadpan.

"Nope. He leaned over, got real quiet, then asked if I'd ever considered sex on a first date?"

They howled in unison.

"Have you ever not?" said Chloe. "Seriously, he wanted sex before marriage? Maybe he thought it would be anonymous. I mean someone not known to his church or state. Knew you'd be leaving soon. Maybe he's got his own tourist m.o. and needed someone off island for christ's sake."

"Well, by the time he was asking it, we were parked along some beach making out and he had such an enormous hard on I could hardly refuse. I mean I didn't know if it was Viagra or not, but it occurred to me I could actually chalk up a new notch

– 'preacher man'. So we went back to his place, passed the Virgin Mary in the foyer and leapt up the circular staircase two at a time. The house was huge, right on a beach, but you should have seen the master bedroom. Bigger than this whole suite with gadgets that dimmed the lights and found just the right music. He put on Marvin Gaye's *Let's Get it On*. So predictable."

"Now I have a few ideas about how good I am in bed, but I'm a tough critic on men, and I have to say he was the most into pleasuring me as any guy I've ever had. He had a drawer full of little toys and vibrators, a little red riding crop I really got into, and a sort of harness hammock thingy we tried for about two minutes. Not my cup of tea. Oh, and a special lube that made me instantly hot."

Chloe and Jill sat frozen in space, eyes widening as the story unfolded. Despite hearing Jill's prowess tales for years, they were still nonplussed.

"Did he handcuff you?" asked Mattie.

"No, he fell from grace." Laughter. "I cuffed him and played whipped cream games. I was lost, but now I'm found. Hallelujah!"

"So are you meeting him for church Sunday morning?"

"Naw, I've already been baptized." This resulted in rounds of hoots and shrieks of laughter. "If sacred cows make the best burger, make mine a black and blue burger." She was on a roll.

"No wonder you have to get thee to the mountain top," said Chloe. "So let's go."

"Wait," said Mattie. "I'm meeting Michael and his sister's family for lunch. Can we go later?"

"I'm open. I think I have a date with Jed tonight. Probably ought to call him. Plus I have an hour or two of business details."

"I have to work on the proposal for Seattle," said Jill. "Could be a big deal for my little company."

"Jill, I got a brainchild. Or maybe it was a bodychild. I don't know. Oh, god, you guys won't believe it." Mattie continued filling the girls in on the great ideas she got in the jacuzzi/flotation tank. This time the thoughts came out even better. *By the time I propose this to Aunt Jo, I'll have it down.* The girls were impressed and totally got it. "But the best thing is that by re-invigorating our lackluster website, we can do more tours, more memberships, take on new clients and new directions."

"Sounds awesome," said Chloe. "I always knew you had it in you."

"And the best is that I can hire Jill to re-do and re-position our online image."

"Well, is my business on Viagra or what?" Jill said. "Eli said he got some new accounts this week too. Maybe I can give up my day job." As soon as she said it, she thought twice.

No one suggested she couldn't or that she might want to go slowly. Au contraire, it was an obvious next step for Jill. Obvious to everyone in the room.

Maybe I could give up mine, Chloe thought quietly to herself.

fifty-four

COCO BOB

Chloe was poolside and Mattie out with Michael when the phone rang in the room. Jill was there, knee deep in a proposal for the Seattle company, clicking away on her laptop, hypothesizing financials then dragging and dropping figures and graphs into a PowerPoint presentation.

She hesitated. She was on a roll, but picked up the phone by the third ring. "Hi. I mean, aloha."

"Aloha, is Mattie there?"

"Not now, can I take a message?"

"Not really. It's Bob from the fruit stand. I have her book. Should I bring it up?"

"Sure, Bob. It's Jill here. Come on up. 1210."

When he arrived he handed Jill a hardback, *The DaVinci Code.* "I read it of course. Interesting. Say, aren't you the one who does websites?"

"Among other things, why?"

"Well, driving to town today I was thinking about how I could expand my little fruit business beyond cracking coconuts and making smoothies."

"There are endless possibilities," Jill responded, immediately groking where he could go with a strong brand and managed Internet presence.

"I was thinking maybe our whole little co-op could start selling stuff online…"

Jill was quick. "Get a few more ideas like that, couple with a great Coco Bob logo, and we'll take you national. Heck, international. Fruits and flowers, tee shirts and juicers, managed Hawaii tours." *I could tie it in with Mattie's new tour business.* Jill had a way of thinking in big pictures. Big, connected, empowering pictures. It was one of her strengths. Plus she could do financial logarithms in her head. She took a deep breath and looked Bob right in the eye. "I'm not talking website. I'm talking half a million your first year. Take you public in four."

"Well that would be the best year I ever had times ten," he said, a gleam in his eyes. He imagined a new truck, paid help, a vacation with the family...or just his wife. A day off. "If you think you really can, we should definitely talk."

"We're talking. How about you buy me lunch down at Caffé Ciao while we brainstorm? I'm famished." *Set the precedent. Not a penny of my own money on this one. He's got equity. And relatives.*

"Great. Let me move back my twelve-thirty," he said, taking out his cell phone. *I could get Josh and Angel into Seabury Hall. Then Stanford. Fix the roof. Remodel the kitchen.*

Putty, she thought. *I can make this guy a star, take a piece of the action, get a retainer upfront...I can quit my day job!*

As they entered the café on the lower level, their senses filled with aromas from the deli and coffees. Jill walked up to the counter and ordered a roast squab sandwich with bamboo and hearts of palm salad with spicy red peppers and olives. "Have you got a nice oaked chardonnay?" she asked. Seated on the terrace, Jill and Bob clinked glasses, handshaking their deal. Then Jill flipped open her legal pad, and they went to work.

fifty-five

KEA LANI POOL

Chloe was sunning poolside with a stack of books purchased at Borders and the hotel gift shop: *The Maui CEO,* another Hawaiian anthology titled *Island Fire, Hidden Maui, Maui 101 ~ Your Guide to Island Life, Hotel Honolulu,* and *The Hawaii's Kitchen Cookbook - Chef's Edition.* Books were Chloe's compulsion; she liked them better than shopping, better than skiing, better than shoes. She lay out now, slathered in Uncle Bob's Coco Tan, trying to decide which to start with.

The Maui CEO was on top, so she began there, reading the subtitle: *Import from China, Sell on eBay, and Live Wherever You Want.*

Yea, but can a writer make it here? Can I make it as a writer period? Can I run my business from a distance? I guess I could always get a real estate license here, but that would defeat the whole point. She was in thinking mind, trying to figure out how to spend more time on Maui. She wasn't yet to a Ben Franklin, weighing the pros and cons of a possible relocation, but throughout the week the island had definitely grown on her, changed her coding in some inexplicable way. The way a friend morphs into a lover – a little seduction here, more fun there, until there's a tipping point and the relationship shifts like a fault line.

Maybe it was as simple as meeting other transplants like Bill and Jed and seeing how easy it had seemed for them. Neither had wilted from the tearing of roots. Au contraire. Maybe it was her restlessness with the business scene back home. Maybe it was the fact that she really could afford to

243

make changes, even failing, and return to a going concern. Maybe it was a wild love of words and stories shoving her over a cliff. But Jill as usual was right; Chloe had safety nets.

She picked up *Island Fire* and read from the foreword:

"The islands are here, both in body and in spirit, with their many layers of settlement and terrain, the cities, the plantation towns, the rain forests, and rural valleys, the waterways, the caves and craters of volcano country. Hawai'i has always been a place where nature and culture continually intertwine. This book contains a world where an island itself can have a voice and sing, where a sacred rock has the power to draw fish toward shore, where sharks are ancestors, and the dead often speak to the living."

Then for just a moment she felt her dad's presence, hovering over her left shoulder. *At least I'll never be alone,* she thought, her lips curving up at the ends while her eyes closed.

"Whatcha grinning about?" Jill whispered in her ear. It shocked Chloe, who shot up, grabbing her towel. "I'm the one should be grinning. Just got two new accounts. Big ones."

"I was thinking about Dad. And Maui." Chloe was off in some other world.

"I said I just closed two new accounts. Coco Bob – remember the guy with the fruit stand? I'm on for upfront fees to cover costs and a large piece of the empire I'll be building. And Eli text-messaged my IPhone. We're waiting for the green light, but the Seattle thing's most likely in the bag. Huge advance and at least two year's worth of work."

"Don't forget Mattie's new website," Chloe said.

"Honey, I've got it all figured out. I'm giving notice the minute I get back Monday morning. I had a long talk with Eli, and he's excited and on board. He wants to quit his day job too, handling tech support for that DVD drive company. E also might bring in a friend who designs apps. We're working on a formula by which he can buy in with new accounts he brings or years aboard, or some combo of both."

"Eli's a great partner. Plus he's wild about you."

"Me? Eli and me? I don't think so. He's been a really good buddy and friend..."

"Exactly. A man friend. Not a sexual conquest, a friend. Imagine the possibilities."

"Eli's like a brother, Chloe. You know that. It's probably why I trust him. He's never pushed for anything further, and he keeps up his end of our little business."

"Well then it should be perfect. And god knows you have enough cushion to handle any loss of income while you expand JVV Net."

"We'll need a new name right off. When I started the biz it was just me and a handful of friends who needed websites or marketing advice. If we're expanding, I'll need a makeover myself."

"How about Jeli or Ejil or some acronym of your names?" Chloe was reaching.

"Nope. Needs to be a big bold statement. With all the thinking about taking Bob to the top and eventually public, I think we need a name that can go the distance as well. Something suitable in every language. Something that sells itself. Something that will look just fine on a stock ticker." Jill grinned just thinking about it.

Chloe couldn't remember Jill being this excited about anything recently. Oh she always had a surface enthusiasm about every new beau, every generation of digital gadgets, new investments, but this was different.

"Go for it, Jill. This is just what you need. Now."

"Yea, I get that. I can't cruise away the rest of my life doing guys – guys – guys. Or as my older brother says, 'you have a brain for god's sake. Use it.' I think I just might. And so what, you reading the rest of your vacation away?" Jill pointed to the pile of books.

"I just thought I'd see what kind of books are published about Maui, so I got a little taste."

"Looks like the whole enchilada to me," said Jill. "But if the cookbook works, I'll be coming over more often. Bob mentioned doing a cookbook too, all about coconuts – coconut recipes like haupia and rukau, iki mata – you know the raw fish in coconut cream. He mentioned a pumpkin soup with coconut milk. Yum. And salads, fried coco chips, coconut cake, coconut cream pie. Plus there are apparently huge health benefits. Oils for tanning or massage. He knows the entire history of coconut palms in Polynesia and the tropical world. That guy has endless ideas for expanding his business. He just has no idea how to get from here to there. Good thing that's my forté."

"It is definitely your thing. Now can you expand me back to Maui?"

"What do you mean, Chloe? Are you serious?"

"I think I want to spend more time here. I was thinking maybe a couple months' sabbatical later in the year to write and see if I can handle being away from work. Mom thinks that if I'd simply get serious about golf I could cure my workaholism, but it just isn't my thing. But a writing retreat – now that might work. Hey, at least I can imagine it. It's a start."

"Well, I'm not telling Tilly. She would have a fit. As would everyone on your staff, your friends, family. What are you smoking, girl?"

"I'm serious, Jill. I've wanted a change for a long time. Even though I'm suited for the business I'm in…"

"Suited? You're a natural. It's your niche."

"Even still, I'd like to see if I could lean into what really pulls me. Taking a leave I can try it out. See for myself one way or the other. Try it on."

"Yea, and have the other blood suckers drain you dry while you're gone. You trust your team too much. Look what happened just this week." Jill had seen Chloe go through lots of ups and downs, not all market driven.

"Jill, good friend and buddy, like you I have a cushion. Do you understand how lucky we are in this? Under the worst case scenario, I could always be a sales agent or manage a real estate office…anywhere. I have a few property investments, and they're all going up. I could take out equity loans or re-fi. I have

246

enough projects right now to keep my agents busy for two years, raking in profits with or without me. I think Mom quite loved going back into the office. She'd keep an eye on things. And I could promote Lori to Manager or hire a top one from the competition."

"Well, say all that was covered. You would actually leave us and move a million miles across the sea?"

"It's not so far, and besides we have phones and e-mail..."

"And Skype. Gawd, we'd have to grow headsets. Darlin', can you do my back?" Jill handed Chloe some sunscreen just as Kimo showed up.

"Here, let me."

"Kimo, where've you been hiding?" Chloe asked, realizing she hadn't seen him in a couple of days.

"Even da beach boys get days off," he replied, carefully pushing Jill's straps aside to get to her neck and shoulders. "How you girls gettin' on?"

"Your aunt and uncle are utterly charming, Chloe replied. "We had an awesome time in Hana."

"You too, Jill? Keoki said you had da cowboys all over yous."

"Well, well, isn't the coconut wireless working overtime these days? If you must know, we had a ball. Party, beach, sightseeing, but the best part was just hanging out on the verandah with Keoki and Emma. Seriously. The very best part of Hana." Suddenly she thought of Zach. *Yikes. I forgot to call him back. I got so wrapped up in my expansion plans, I forgot to call a guy.*

"So, you girls busy tonight? Dis your last night, no? We should party. Da guys been on me all week fo one repeat performance. I sure we can find live music somewhere. I stay pau at eight. How 'bout it?"

"Thanks, Kimo. That was perfect." Jill took the sunscreen back and rolled up on her elbows. "I think we have plans. Sunset on the mountain and all that."

"Absolutely." Chloe took her cue. "We have to do

247

Haleakala…now that we can pronounce it. We're just waiting for Mattie before we leave."

"So you get plans fo latah too?" Kimo was insistent.

"We're sort of all over the map right now. Let me find out when we all get together. I'll call your cell later, ok?"

"Das fine, but I en tell da guys fo shower and spit shine just in case." He winked at Jill. "Call me." He walked off, and Jill carefully observed his backside, his thighs, wide shoulders and smoldering milk chocolate skin. *Mmmm.* She looked over at Chloe. "Zach's in town. I forgot to call him back. Just got too involved with the proposal and then Bob's re-structuring."

"You – too involved with business to chase the boys? This is a good sign, Jill. Didn't the preacher call?"

"He's probably still sleeping it off, poor baby. Plus he has a sermon to prepare for tomorrow. He'll probably raise the congregational roof about sin and hellfire. Or maybe a little redemption story. He has quite a range." She rolled her eyes and hooted. "He invited us to…"

Chloe cut her off. "I'm doing church of the beach tomorrow. We're all doing church of the beach. Big Beach. Little Beach. We're doing Church of the Beach tomorrow."

"I believe. I believe." said Jill, bowing her head submissively. "But should I do tonight?"

From around the corner of a cabaña Mattie joined them, virtually dancing. "I never think of the future. It comes soon enough."

fifty-six

HALEAKALA AHA

At exactly six thirty-five Mattie, Chloe and Jill stood at the summit of Haleakala, hugging the railing of the observatory, peering out over the crater across the sea to the top of Mauna Kea on the Big Island, rising above a cloud shroud. The flash colors of the west Maui sunset gathered on the horizon, and as the sun settled in for the night, a ribbon of rainbows line-danced where water met sky.

"Oh, my gawd. Did you see that?" Even Jill was surprised.

"A ten," said Chloe, "like the green flash."

"Yea, except it was green, blue, red, and orange." Mattie weighed in. "And purple at the end."

They stood for minutes, watching the afterglow, still dazzled by the display and catching their breath from the high-altitude climb up to their vantage point.

"It's all so magical here," said Chloe. "The dawn, the beach, sunsets, moonbows. Now this. I suppose dinner dates will be a come down from the magnificence of this day."

"Speak for yourself," said Mattie, eager to get rolling downhill.

"Come on," Jill took their arms. "I'll drive."

"Can I sit up front?" Mattie asked, realizing there would be just as many turns and switchbacks going downhill.

Jill had put off confirming anything with Kimo, but did not particularly want to be alone on their last night on the island. Chloe offered to take her out with them to dinner and the poetry slam, but Jill was 'not into poetry' or Jed, and she said she'd probably call Kimo later and hook up on the dance floor. After all she'd been too busy today to exercise. She'd missed her workout, so dancing made perfect sense.

Michael and Jed were waiting in the lobby when the girls finally got back to the hotel. They had met on Wednesday, so they greeted each other through the Saturday night crowd – mostly guests cueing up for their cars – and waited together over cocktails at the Lobby Bar. A trio of Hawaiian musicians played well-known ballads while a young woman undulated gracefully, mimicking the words with her hula hands.

Mattie spotted Michael the moment she entered the hotel through its open archway, steering the others across the expanse and out onto the lounge.

"Hi, girls." Michael got up, looked briefly into Mattie's eyes then kissed her and wrapped an arm around her shoulder thinking. *Can I let her know how completely crazy I am about her? Is it safe?*

"Hey," said Jill. "Sorry we're late. I did a downhill slalom like the proverbial bat out of, but alas we just *had* to do sunset at the top."

Jed reached for Chloe. "I'm so glad. Isn't it amazing? Did you get a green flash?"

"No, we got the rainbow flash," said Chloe, taking Jed's outstretched hand. "Good call on that one. Thanks." She flashed her very own rainbow smile at Jed, squeezing his fingers.

Jill moved in towards one of the chairs. "Why don't I keep your chair warm and your drinks company while you two go freshen up?" She settled in between Jed and Michael.

"Call Kimo," Chloe barked. "We'll only be a few minutes." Then she hesitated. They were a bit under dressed for a Saturday night, but neither wanted to leave. "Jeans are ok?" She looked at Jed.

"I thought so," he replied, admiring his outfit which was sort of retro Hawaiian cowboy – jeans and aloha shirt, cowboys boots and his hat, which tonight sported fancy bird feathers

around its brim. "You look fine, and if you want to eat before –
and everything will be closed afterwards – we'd better go." He
put a ten-dollar bill on the table and took Chloe's arm.

"Catch you all later," she called over her shoulder. "Have
fun, kids."

Jill flagged a cocktail waitress and sat down between Mattie
and Michael.

"Go ahead," Mattie encouraged. "Call him. You'll have a
great time."

"You kids run along. I'll be fine." Jill finished another
cosmo and the entire bowl of nuts then made her way up to the
room, tossing herself on the bed and sprawling corner to
corner. *I miss my bed*, she thought. *I miss my work.*

The telephone rang, and she listened to Kimo leave a
cheery message about some hot band at the Marriott, pleading
with her to come on over and dance. "Bring da uddah chicks
too."

Jill rolled off the bed and crossed the room, pushing the
message button. There were only four.

Beep. "Chloe, it's your mom. I got your e-mail and
pictures. Thanks so much. I almost forgot how well you write.
I'm so glad you're loving Maui. It reminded me of why I do
too, aside from the golf. It's gray and cold here. Thanks for the
sunshine. Sorry I missed you. Catch an extra sunset for me, ok?
And I'll see you soon, honey."

Beep. "Mattie, it's Susan from the office. I hate to bother
you, but your aunt Jo is in the hospital. Nothing serious. She
took a fall, and they're keeping her overnight for observation.
She wants you to call her at St. Francis: 415-924-4000. I'm sure
she'll be fine, but she wants to hear from you. Everything here
is good. We miss you though. Have a mai tai for me, and call
your aunt. Bye then. Aloha."

Beep. "Jill, it's Eli. Way to go on the Coconut guy and
Seattle George. I'm in one hundred percent on the venture. I
think I'll wait to give notice til after we negotiate and structure
our future. Wow, that sounds great – our future. Well kiss a

frog, why don't you?"

She didn't know quite what to make of it. Of course she knew he'd be on board, but there was another layer, an undertone in his message that was neither all business nor all friendship. She replayed it, and for a moment, for one timeless moment, she thought of Eli as something other than her geeky friend.

He wasn't her type, exactly. He was okay looking, but clearly had never pumped iron. He did ride a bicycle – all over the city and out to the redwoods and the wine country, so she knew he was in shape, but he was only about five foot nine, just four inches taller than she was, and she liked tall men. Still she had always loved his clear, blue tile-roof eyes and silky dark brown hair, and he had a brilliant mind – the kind that saw the world in abstractions and solutions.

All of a sudden a rare anxiety bubbled through her like champagne. She saw Eli in a totally new light – a green flashy kind of light. Beyond servers and software, accounts and binary code. More like a partner and a possibility.

Beep. "Hey gorgeous. It's Kimo, da Hawaiian boyfriend, remember me? Last chance fo get crazy wid you big brown chocolate hunk. Tonight. Club Marriott. I stay waiting." She erased the last message. *That boy has mad cow disease.*

I think I'll stay in. I have some companies to develop. Now where's that room service menu.

fifty-seven

BISTRO

Michael had wanted their last evening to be special, so he took Mattie to Roy's Bistro, where he had reserved a quiet little table tucked in the far back corner. They wined and dined, feeding each other and sandwiching in little kisses and long, loving stares. Mattie realized that she wouldn't recognize a red flag if she saw one now, being colorblind whenever she was in his presence, so she consciously threw out her clue radar and leaned into the man and the mystery.

"I won't be back until next Friday," he said, "but I'll call you every day."

"I have so much to do. If Auntie agrees, I'll be taking on a new business, so I'll fill the time. Heck, it will take me until Friday to unpack. Will you come see me when you get off the plane?"

"On my way home. I have to go to Belize in a couple weeks. Can you come with me? We can plan the tour and the environmental campaign. And be together."

"I'm assuming when we're tired of being joined at the hip we'll actually get things done. It won't work at all for me to run the business into the ground."

"I'll help you," he said. It was the sweetest offer she'd ever had, and she'd had offers. There was her first lover who promised her the shirt off his back. If only he'd had one. And Tom, who promised to be faithful – over and over again.

"You can help me. Just don't promise me anything."

"There's a story to that one, but I think I'll pass. Let's write a new chapter. Let's just for a moment imagine a life together. A good life. A happy life. I really think it can be that simple." He wasn't sure of course, but he felt in his heart that with Mattie the odds shot way up.

"Oh, honey, you're such a romantic." She smiled, her eyes glittered, and there in the darkened corner of a dark little restaurant, on a dark street in the dark of night, the sun came out.

fifty-eight

STREAMS OF CONSCIOUSNESS

Jed was on stage, performing a long, stream-of-consciousness poem about blue highways and road trips. Chloe took a sip of her Perrier and lost his performance, heading out on her own, tendrils like streams of feelings enveloped her. They sparked her life, sustaining and driving her. She had spent the week paying attention, and Maui and its whole zeitgeist cast of characters spoke and whispered and cajoled. Doing a Ben Franklin earlier, she had seen it herself in black and white. Still it seemed a totally irrational step, which might put her on a crash course. Or was it? Was it a calling? Her calling? Was she prescient? And would the gods be with her? She looked at all the reasons, deciding to give herself a month to make some sort of rational evaluation. Two weeks would be better so as to not lose momentum. It might take a month, maybe two, but Chloe was nothing if not patient.

"He landed back where he began, starring up at the little red house in his little red state, and headed back to the coast."

The applause brought Chloe back. *How self-absorbed I've been*, she thought, standing up to greet Jed, returning to their table. *Or maybe it's time for self-absorption.*

Back in the suite, Jill was finishing up the draft of a mini-business plan for Coco Bob. Plates of lasagna and salad, burgers and fries, and three bottles of beer from room service were strewn around the suite. Her both her laptop and the iPad had migrated to the lanai, where she finished up some

255

marketing notes. Venus hung near the horizon, whispering *you go girl!* Moonlight rained down, covering the work with a kind of unsung blessing. Even Jill noticed. Every breathtaking detail. She felt like howling at the full moon – which floated in a cloudless sky, illumined with magic, hanging over paradise.

fifty-nine

SUNDAY MORNING

Chloe sat at a little wrought iron table at Caffé Ciao on the ground floor. She had already walked the beach for nearly an hour as another glorious dawn joined her, dancing along the horizon and the water's edge, splaying its fingers in colors and shadows until the sun finally rose enough to warm the beach.

She stopped at the café to pick up a local paper, but the aroma of freshly brewed coffee reached out and grabbed her, so she settled in for a cappuccino and a banana muffin, still warm from the oven. Turning to 'Classifieds', she found rentals easily enough, but then it got tough. Apt/Condo rentals – Home rentals – West, South, North, East, Upcountry – Room for Rent, Roommate Wanted, Vacation Rental, Wanted to Rent, House Sit, House Exchange, Rent or Lease – the list seemed endless. It occurred to her she was not the only one wanting a place on Maui.

She began scanning the ads when one reached out and grabbed her, practically jumped off the page –

BIG Bi-Coastal Views from
charming 2 br cottage.
fully furn., chef's kit.,
jacuzzi on deck.
Avail. March 10th.

She noticed immediately that it became available on her birthday, pulled her iPhone from her sweatshirt pocket, and punched in the number. It wasn't eight yet, but she called anyway.

"Aloha. Good morning," a cheery voice answered.

"Hi, I hope it's not too early, but I'm sort of the early bird, and...well, I'm calling about your ad."

"Oh, I guess it broke today. What can I tell you?"

"I'm visiting from the Bay Area and looking for a place for awhile. Just for myself. A kind of personal writer's retreat."

"You're a writer?" she sounded excited.

"Well, not exactly. Not professionally...yet, but it's my dream."

"I happen to be a writer myself. I work with the Maui Writer's Conference. You'd love it. Anyway, I'm off to southern France until next winter to research a book set all over Europe.

"How fabulous! You're published then..."

They spoke for about ten minutes, and by the time Chloe hit 'end', she had made a new friend and an appointment in an hour to see Mango Cottage and meet Elizabeth.

She ordered two cappuccinos to go and filled a bag with assorted muffins, signing the room number. Then she flew up the stairs, two at a time, clear to the top floor.

"I was wondering where you'd gone," said Jill, fresh from a shower. Chloe entered the room, breathless as Jill went on. "Shhh, Mattie's sleeping."

"No she's not." Mattie poked her head out from under its traditional morning burial. "Wow, that smells great."

"Brought you cappuccinos."

"And food!!" Jill said. "Thanks, I'm hungry as a bear in spring thaw." She took the bag and pulled out two muffins, eating one while handing the bag over to Mattie.

"I think I found it," said Chloe, clearly excited.

"Oh, god, did you lose something too?" Mattie asked.

"No, little girl. A place. A home. My little Maui retreat."

"What *are* you talking about?" Jill asked, her face full of banana mac-nut muffin.

"I'm going up to see it, but I'm sure it's perfect," Chloe

said, reading them the ad.

Silence followed.

"You're serious. You'd actually leave your business, dessert your mother, your friends, your responsibilities..."

"Yes, Jill. I'd actually do something for myself for a change. Something I really want to do. I have to. And I didn't imagine for a moment that the people I love would begrudge me that...family, friends, or associates." Chloe was indignant.

"Oh, they won't, honey," said Mattie. "We'll all support you. If it's what you really want, I'll be there for you."

"It's all I think about. I can't remember wanting anything so much, except that my Daddy not be dead. All the more reason I have to live. Now."

"You've been under some sort of Maui spell since you got off that plane," said Jill. "Me, I can't wait to get back to work. I was brainstorming company names last night. Do you like this? Tech Island ~ marketing, design and support for your financial survival. I was up til one, working on a proforma for Coco Bob. I'm so excited. And listen to this." Jill walked across to the desk and replayed Eli's message. "What does that mean?"

Chloe responded in a measured tone. "Oh, hard-hearted one, it means that he's as excited as you are about the company's direction and working more closely with you. Something you said must have made him think there might be more."

"But I didn't..." Jill protested.

"You probably just effused. Anyway you could do worse."

"Yea, the preacher called thanking me for the inspiration for his sermon. Invited us again to his church. I told him we were doing Chloe's church. The beach, right?"

"When did you get back, Mattie?' Chloe asked.

"We had the *best* night. Romantic dinner, some live blues at a little club just down the way, then back to Michael's. He brought me home just an hour ago. He's working today but will meet us at the airport later or for dinner." Mattie sipped her coffee, rolling her eyes. "You're looking at a lady in love."

Oh, no…not again thought Jill and Chloe. But somehow they both knew this would be different, better. Maybe it wouldn't last forever. Nothing did. But their friend was happy, truly happy for the first time in months.

"Well, I thought we should have a special last day, so although I did mention church of the beach, I need to see a gal about a house. I need the car. I can drop you there and meet you later or…"

"Or nothing. We're going," said Jill most emphatically.

"You might fall in love yourself," said Mattie, "and I, for one, wouldn't miss that."

sixty

MANGO COTTAGE

It was good for Mattie and Jill to see the place, making it real for all of them. Chloe drove effortlessly upcountry to Lower Kula, guided by the GPS she had set to the exact address. She spotted the mailbox painted with mangos and pulled down into a little driveway, hedged in with rosemary and lavender on one side and a wall of hibiscus and gardenia on the other. It was the road by the lookout where they had stopped on Friday, coming back from Hana.

"It's déjà vu," Chloe said as if in a trance, a strange look coming over her.

"I don't get that, but it is cute. A bit rustic," Jill said, motioning towards the home, "but wow, check out that view!" Maggie was rubbernecking over the front seat, taking in the scene and a view over the whole wondrous world. "I could live here," she said, patting Chloe's arm and thinking about how bright her own future looked. "Well, I could if I weren't into mergers and acquisitions back home."

Elizabeth ambled out the front door and through a screened porch to greet them. She was older, tall like Chloe, maybe forty-five with an animated face and amazing eyes. They were butterflies and heat-seeking missles all at once. A salt and pepper braid hung over one shoulder *Does no one in the islands know about hair color?* Mattie flashed.

"Aloha," she said, extending an unusually large hand. Chloe clasped it. "Hi, I'm Chloe, and these are my friends, Mattie and Jill."

261

A golden retriever came out from behind the owner, tail wagging, heading straight for Chloe.

"Excuse Rufus. She loves people. My friends all over upcountry have offered to take her while I'm gone."

"Oh please," Chloe interrupted. "I love dogs!" She squatted down to massage and commune with Rufus.

"Welcome to Mango Cottage. It's a little humble, I know, but it's home," Elizabeth turned, showing them through an arbor of lilikoi vines and morning glories and onto a small porch. Chloe plucked a plumeria, placing it behind her left ear. "I must have built the last little house on the hill. Everything now is monstrous – six or seven bedrooms, with guest houses (we call them Ohana) bigger than this."

Clay pots filled the porch with flowers and herbs. Fuchsias hung in baskets from corner beams. Elizabeth opened the front door and sunlight flowed through the prism of beveled windows in the entrance hallway, sending rainbows of light waves around a room too adorable for words. *Perfect feng shui*, thought Chloe.

Open beams lifted the center to cathedral heights, sloping towards the right to an open and spacious kitchen with an island and dining nook. "If you like to cook, you'll love my kitchen." Chloe nodded approvingly, checking the details of the layout, noticing a wine cooler, dishwasher, granite countertops and a sub-zero fridge. There was a greenhouse window over the sink, loaded with pots of thyme, savory, basil and chives.

A small wood stove shared the left wall of the dining area with tapa cloth, masks and carvings that looked Pacific Islander in origin, though not necessarily Hawaiian.

"Does it get cold enough for a fire?" Chloe was truly curious.

"Not really, but I find it comforting on winter nights. And for ambience it's the best."

Looking straight out through floor to ceiling windows they saw it – the view that made all the difference. Chloe stood speechless, taking it all in – the rainbows, the start date, the view which had stopped her before. Then just below on the lower edge of the property she spied a fenceload of blackberry bushes and two lemon trees, loaded with yellow fruit. Goosebumps covered Chloe, head to foot, and she heard her dad whisper clearly into her left ear: '*perfect*'. It startled her – both the voice and the meaning. It occurred to her that he had always wanted her highest happiness, not necessarily her commitment to his business. He was the one, after all, who encouraged her writing, who framed her grade school poems and read her stories as if they were the latest best sellers. Come to think of it, Tilly was that kind of support as well.

Who can explain the cosmic mysteries? An explosion of passion rocked her to some essential core. It came like an epiphany with an exclamation point! Like finding the holy grail – remembering her dream, vivid now in every lucid detail. It was her aha moment. Her tipping point.

She saw an agent, a book deal. A two-book deal.

Chloe caught her breath then caught up with the others in a passageway that led off to the left and to an open hallway, filled floor to ceiling with art – paintings in every pigment, framed and unframed, carvings and wall hangings, little objects des arts. "As you can imagine, I have many artist friends," Elizabeth explained as she led them to a back room. It housed a double bed with a lovely Hawaiian quilt, *for guests*. It was obviously a writer's office, a haven that held and juggled worlds of words. Chloe recognized it immediately. There was a large desk with a fairly new computer and bookshelves that took over the room. It opened onto a small patio with cracks where little ferns and tuffs of monkey grass grew through, an orchid garden with tree ferns and fig trees. Sunlight drenched the space, making it warm and inviting. *I could write here*, she thought. *I could live here.*

A bathroom separated the office from the master bedroom – with its queen-sized bed, large koa wood armoire, and chenille chaise, which faced west. A wide deck ran the length of the view, wrapping around the master bedroom and all along the front of the house, past the living room and dining nook. It was screened and covered, with large cane furniture and the proverbial hammock at the bedroom end.

Taking a few steps down below a hefty plank table at the far end of the porch, they arrived at the Jacuzzi, surrounded by jasmine and impatiens, pink day lilies, crocus, iris, and lavender roses. *Lavender roses!* An outdoor shower hid in a fern grotto off to the side of the hot tub.

Elizabeth pointed to a woven chaise. "I sunbathe here. Nude." The girls giggled. It's totally private, and I never wear a suit in the Jacuzzi."

"Awesome!" Mattie opened her arms to the scene below, coast to coast across the expansive plains of paradise. "This is the bomb. I'll come visit."

Chloe's heart had been opening since she first opened the paper, since pulling into the driveway, since meeting Rufus and seeing the orchids, as if lifted from her page. And then there was the cymbals' crash, the recognition of the bliss dream and berries and lemons. "It's perfect," she finally said, turning to hug Elizabeth.

"If you want, I can leave you my beamer. It's a couple years old, but drives like new. Sometimes I think it smells new still. It will need driving though, while I'm gone. If you'd rather not I can…"

"No. I own a BMW myself. It will be perfect." *perfect…Perfect…PERFECT!*

Jill was restless. "Okay, sign the lease, ladies. It's beach day."

"It's our last day." Chloe spoke to Elizabeth, making excuses for her friend's rudeness.

"We'll talk more later," Elizabeth said, handing Chloe some papers while showing them out. "Here's a rental application. You probably know the drill, being in real estate."

"No, actually I've never rented a place. Other than my dorm on campus, I've always lived in our family home. Say if you need a drop-in place in San Francisco on your way to

Europe, just call Mattie. She'll be holding down the fort, and we have a few guest rooms."

"How generous of you." She went on, "recycle pick-up is on Friday, but sometimes they're here before dawn, so I always put the bins out Thursday night. There are some tricks with the solar panels, but. Oh, I'll just e-mail you a detailed list of idiosyncrasies along with names of a few local contacts."

Chloe wished she could spend the whole day. She and Elizabeth could have lavender tea and get to know each other better. She was certain they'd be friends. *Maybe a mentor.* "I have a million questions about your writing," she said. "Maybe I can come a couple of days before you leave to go over everything and help you transit."

"What a grand idea. Wait. I'll be right back." Elizabeth turned and went back into the house. Chloe waited in the morning fragrance while Jill and Mattie wandered off through the gardens on the south side and back to the car. She read the words, calligraphied over the lintel:

"Do not believe anything because it is said by an authority or it is said to come from angels or from gods or from an inspired source. Believe it only if you have experienced it in your own heart and mind and body and found it to be true. Work out your own path through this world with diligence. The Buddha."

Elizabeth emerged in moments. "Here. I want you to have this. Mé alofa. That's Samoan for a little offering. I signed it." Chloe took the book and read the cover. *The Choice.* "I came here on holiday once too." There was warmth in her smooth voice as she smiled at Chloe, nodding. "It's always been a safe haven here for me. May it be for you as well." It was said like a blessing.

"Thank you," Chloe responded, turning with a grateful heart and saying a little Buddhist prayer.

"Looks like good luck for you too," said Jill, climbing in the driver's seat. Little did she know.

sixty-one

BIG BEACH ~ LITTLE BEACH

As fast as possible and just nine miles over the speed limit – everyone knows that cops set their radar for ten miles over the limit – they drove back down the mountain and out to Makena, also known as Big Beach. They had checked out of the hotel when they left earlier, Jill spending ten minutes separating and itemizing phone and food bills, finally deciding to split everything evenly on three credit cards. Jill had filled a styrofoam cooler with beer, which now shared the back seat with Mattie and the beach bags, while their luggage stuffed the trunk.

Michael had given them directions, and they were on the lookout for a roadside stand that said 'Fresh Fish Tacos' directly across from the parking lot. Jill spotted it and pulled over on the shoulder, hopping out. "How many?" was all she asked.

Moments later they were parked and making their way through a narrow keawe and ironwood arbor along a needle-strewn pathway. They arrived at a wide expanse of glistening white sand that stretched as far as they could see, and Mattie led them to a perfect spot – like an animal Mattie could always find her spot – between the trees and the shoreline, the dead center of the beach. Chloe immediately set up the picnic, removing her sarong and using it as a tablecloth, then laying out the fish tacos while Jill opened three ice cold Coronas. "Bon appetite," she said, taking a mouthful and sending a shower of blessings in the four directions.

They chatted while they ate, soaking up the sun and rehashing their Maui week. Then they quieted, snoozing, reading, and watching purple bird auras circling overhead in a cloudless and endless blue. Jill looked down at her tanned toes with red paint and breaking the silence, she reached in the cooler for another beer.

"Kimo says we can't miss Little Beach. Anyone else for a hike?" Mattie and Chloe followed Jill to the west end of the beach and up a trail in the rocks that led to a smaller beach across the promontory. There families of nude sun worshippers swam, ate, threw frisbee and played a full assortment of instruments. It was a whole tribe of happy, naked souls, oblivious to the world beyond, to traffic and politics and Maui prices.

A man, mid-twenties, with rasta dreads and an accent approached them. "I can read your future," he said, greeting them.

"How much," Mattie asked.

"I work only for donations. If it resonates, you can give me something. Anything."

"Me first then," she said.

He took a long drag off a joint, which he then passed around. "It's sacrament." Then he took Mattie's hands. "You are stepping up, stepping into more responsibility. I see you managing people, and the company will thrive in unimaginable directions. I see much travel – for work and pleasure – and a man, a lovely man. You will have two homes and a commute...I see a bridge, yes, you will drive across a bridge and be very busy and very happy."

Mattie melted and the others jumped to attention.

He took Jill's palms next, looked into them then into her indigo eyes and began. "You will leave your job soon. There is another that calls you. Move towards it. It will unleash your creative potential and your business acumen, bringing wild success. Big, international success. I see a partner. A dark stranger you will come to appreciate in unique ways."

Jill looked embarrassed and busted at the same time, handed the fellow a $20, stripped off her bikini and ran out into the water.

"Chloe. Chloe." He spoke her name softly as he consulted the astral. "You are about to embark on a bold new adventure. The muses are calling you from across the Pleiades where you once lived. You must learn to trust your gut and lean into your left-brain. It will give you direction and answers. Do not fear. You have multiple safety nets and an older man who is always near you, watching over you. I can see him now, there, near your left shoulder."

Chloe knew it was her Dad and blinked away the tears that began welling up. "Did Jill fix this?" she asked, not really believing the funky-smelling beach bum. It was too obvious.

"It's a gift," he said. "Ever since I came to Maui four years ago I have this gift. Before I was a carpenter and a tile setter in Sydney. Now if I even pick up a hammer, I lose my gift. Spirit tells us. All we have to do is listen and act. Life is so easy, no?"

"No, it's not that easy," Chloe quipped.

He looked deeply into her eyes. "On Maui it is."

"Yes," said Mattie. "Life is good."

"You will be first to marry," he looked directly at Mattie, as if entering her soul through her aquamarine eyes. "I see a wedding next year – here on the island." Mattie glowed. "He is your soul mate."

"Thank you. Mahalo." she hugged him, reaching in her bag for bills, a lifetime of romantic notions validated.

When he wandered off Chloe and Mattie sat under a hou tree talking about intimacies and psychic predictions while Mattie relaxed a little into taking off her clothes. "I don't think I've ever been nude in public," she said.

"This isn't public. This is family," Chloe said, taking her hand. "And there's always a first time." They ran down to the water's edge then waded in, swimming over to Jill who was already surrounded by guys.

"That blonde one looks a bit like Tom," Chloe said,

pointing to the guy on the left.

Mattie grinned her biggest grin, dimples animating her lovely face. "Tom who?"

sixty-two

ALOHA

The afternoon passed in beach bliss as bodies tanned, minds loosened, and the sweet young lovelies wrung the last drop of nourishment from the island. By four Chloe gathered her little tribe to head back to the car, and they drove back to the hotel where they'd arranged to use the showers in the spa. Chloe had attempted a late check out, but their suite was booked, plus the spa option seemed just fine. In fact they hadn't used the facility nearly enough during the week, except for Jill who somehow had squeezed in daily workouts.

Soaking in the huge hot tub, playing with the jet sprays and taking a long last shower, they erased the salt and coconut oil sandpapered on with the fine grains of Little Beach. Flat ironing Mattie's hair, Chloe noticed sizzly highlighted streaks. "The sun did you good," she said, combing.

"Well, " Mattie crooked her perky little mouth at Chloe, "not exactly. I sneaked down to the salon yesterday. Doesn't it look natural?"

"What other little sneaky tricks are you up to?" Jill asked, flossing then applying lip-gloss.

"Well, if you must know Michael's taking us to the airport then to dinner. I know how you love airplane food."

"I think it's you who orders special meals. I can eat anything."

"And do," Chloe chimed in.

"When you two are done primping, I'll be at the pool bar. Gotta tease Kimo one last time." Jill flashed her teeth, patted

271

kisses on each of their heads, and jogged out, leaving a cloud of Byzance behind her.

"Sorry you stay go and dat we nevah fine nuf time together." Kimo grabbed Jill and swung her around behind the towel shack for a long, deep, most satisfying kiss. He had waited all week hungering for more. "But tanks fo da fantasies. Dey was great. Come back any time en torture me." He flashed his gold tooth through a monster smile.

"The pleasure was all mine," Jill took the bait, grabbing his buns and pulling him closer.

Mattie and Chloe were at the Gecko Bar, coiffed and sparkling.

"Oh damn, you girls stay hot!" Kimo bear-hugged each one, flashing that smile again. "Mai tais?" he asked, rounding the bar.

Chloe picked up a tattered paperback from the book recycle rack alongside the bar. She opened it randomly and read, smiling in utter and complete understanding.

"Usually a person seeking an island craves simplicity and glories in a world that is still incomplete and therefore full of possibilities.'

Mattie held up her glass. "To Chloe, my dear, darling ex-roomie. Here's to your Maui sabbatical. And thanks for the trip. I'm reborn."

"Here here!!" Jill clinked her glass, thinking about a new investment – a location for her new company.

The soft late afternoon sun slathered each of them in a glow, and Chloe reached in her shoulder bag for a camera. She handed it to Kimo, who must have done this before. He shot them clinking at the bar, with the beach sparkling behind them, Jill and Chloe, Mattie and Jill, Mattie and Chloe, Chloe with her book, Jill with pineapple teeth and an umbrella in her left ear, all three showing off their matching bracelets. When the towel boy walked by, Kimo handed him the camera and jumped into the shot, taking over the frame like a big Hawaiian god, and they all looked gorgeous and golden.

"Well, didn't we find our smiles?!" Mattie said rhetorically.

"I'd almost forgotten you lost yours," Jill teased. "Mine's grown so broad it hurts, but it hurts so good."

A slow knowing smile spread across Chloe's face, sweet as the taste of a ripe upcountry mango.

Michael suddenly appeared and wrapped his arms around Mattie, nibbling seductively on her neck. "Yum. Bar snacks," he said, hugging her tightly now and greeting the others. Chloe glanced at her watch.

"Oh my god, we have to go." She took a black silk scarf out of her bag and tied it around Jill's eyes.

"What," Jill protested. "You getting kinky, girl?"

"Just close your eyes and come with me," she said, blindfolding Jill. "We have a surprise." They led her away, around the side of the pool and through a little garden stinking of white ginger and plumeria.

"Voilà!" Chloe ceremoniously removed the scarf. A new ECO-star helicopter sat on its pad with a glass shield that offered 180-degree views of paradise and earphones that would feed them dramatic music along with the captain's voice-over, as they skimmed over the island. Lifting off, Jill reached over and grabbed Chloe's hand. "Isn't this the cat's meow? I thought they were booked and you couldn't..." The rotors drowned her out. M&M sat behind, adjusting their earphones and planting kisses, and as they swung up, circling around towards the pool, they floated up along the beach to Little then Big Beach and on along the south shore, cruising counter clockwise around the island, back to Hana, over the ranch. They passed perky sun tipped peaks and waterfalls all shiny in the sun's last glow. Haleakala was bathed in a honey-colored sunset, and for a moment Chloe thought she could see her little house below, nestled just there in the berry patch on the slopes of the sun's house. Miles of emotions flooded over her as she remembered all the sites she'd inspected by helicopter before – none more precious than this. Her new home.

They flew for fifty minutes as the sun lowered and joy filled hearts bursting with a week of fond memories.

When they landed at the Kahului Airport, Jed was there with Michael's Cherokee. Chloe had arranged for a hotel drop off of their rental, and the Jeep was loaded with suitcases. "Come on, we're taking you gals to dinner." Michael helped haul the luggage through the ag check, then waited with them in a short Hawaiian Air line, while Jed circled a few times until he spied them curbside.

Within minutes they were stuffed into a corner booth at Marco Polo's, ordering plates of pasta and anti-pasta and a veal piccata and osso buco for the meat eaters. A classic Barolo turned into two as they neared flight time, goodbye hugs and 'aloha's.

Settled on the night flight they toasted again. "Here's to new names," said Chloe.

"Yea, I'm born again." She laughed and they all giggled, thinking about the preacher politician. "Call me Tech Gal from Tech Island." Jill snorted, thinking of Eli and what he'd look like after six months at the gym. *We could make membership a company perk.*

"I'm in love," sighed Mattie. "even though I missed Valentine's Day."

"We missed Super Bowl too," said Jill., "And Glee," said Chloe. "But what's your new name?"

"Cruisin' and Trekkin'. How's that for the agency name?" She didn't usually drink this much. "Seriously, I called my Aunt Jo, and it's a fait accompli. She took a bad fall, but she's fine. Guess it got her thinking about her mortality. Mom's with her. They both approved heartily of the buy-out, so we're meeting with some lawyers tomorrow. She thought 'Hot Tickets' sounded like it had appeal to the older cruisers and younger trekkers." Mattie reached for her green sweater and then saw it in her mind's eye, hugging the back of her chair at Marco Polo's. Shaking her head she made a mental note to call Michael as soon as she got home. He could bring it with him.

"Yea, you're one pretty hot ticket," Jill said, raising her glass again.

"And wasn't Maui's magic the perfect Rx?" remarked Chloe. She thought of her future hideaway on the slopes of Haleakala. *I miss Maui already.*

"Forget Bali. In September we're doing Greece. The three of us," Jill said. "We can sail around in search of the perfect man."

"Or churches and bell towers," said Mattie, thinking of wedding bells peeling out over vineyards and whitewashed houses with their red tile roofs.

"Or tomatoes," Chloe added, *for the perfect Greek salad.*

THE END

About the Author, Publisher

An island girl, Karen was born on an island and has been in love with islands ever since. As a passionate entrepreneur, she established and managed eight companies in the US mainland, Hawaii, and the South Pacific – living and working on over eighty islands, among island characters and the magical fusion of sea and sky.

It was out in the islands, waiting for boats, sea planes, helicopters, and other island hops, that she wrote fiction, non-fiction, and articles for magazine publications...and shot thousands of photographs.

Other works by the author:
Neosomaniac (Mad about Islands) 2011
Island portraits: 20 years/80 islands

The publisher, **Resource Unlimited** is a consulting firm, specializing in:
Professional Writing & Editing ~ Business and Creative for non-profits, corporations, and publications
Brochures, newsletters, web content, resumés.
Book Publishing ~ editing, layout, design, photography
Publicity and Media Relations ~ marketing, advertising, social media, blogging, political & media campaigns
Project Management ~ strategic counsel, analysis, organization, planning, rebranding, repositioning, fundraising, rainmaking
Digital Photography ~ books, projects, websites, archives

http://www.mauiwriter.com
http://www.mauiwriter.com/resource.html

Contact the author: neosomaniac@gmail.com